THE LOST RELIC

ENIGMA FILES
BOOK 1

JOSHUA JAMES

PROLOGUE

The E.N.I.G.M.A. Vault, Eastern U.S. Branch

———

RONNIE PULLED the cap of his security uniform over his dark hair and reached for his rifle. "Dunno why they bother giving us all of this equipment," he grumbled. "It's not like anyone's getting as far as the vault, and this stuff weighs a freaking ton."

Marcus snorted. "You think? Because all that tells me is that you never went through basic. This is a cakewalk compared to that. You know, this one time, we had to carry eighty pounds of gear through a sand pit..."

With his face still turned toward his locker, Ronnie rolled his eyes. He didn't know why he bothered. Marcus pulled this crap all the time, just like his brothers. Everything was a game of one-upmanship, a perpetual flex. They'd both gone through the same training to get here, signed the same waivers, faced the same exams. So what if Ronnie had never been active duty? Marcus had bitched about their ENIGMA training regimen just like everybody else. God forbid he try to bond.

"... so compared to that," Marcus finished, having regaled him with his meandering tale of physical prowess, "this is nothing."

"Congratulations." Ronnie slammed his locker. "That's, like, the fifth time you've told me that story, and I still don't care."

Marcus' laughter followed him through the hall. He was still chuckling when he caught up with Ronnie. "Man, don't be like that. You know it's hard out here for a short king."

Ronnie didn't break his stride. "You know what your problem is, Marcus? You've got Chihuahua energy. You bounce all over the place, yapping your head off. People don't care that you're short. They care that you have a complex about it." He let his eyes slide sideways toward Marcus' face. "Maybe if you weren't so insecure, you wouldn't need to brag about stupid shit you did in basic back when you were eighteen."

Marcus let out a wheeze and clapped his hand to his chest. "Brutal, Ronnie. Don't hold back."

Ronnie was about to respond when a slim figure dressed in a black peacoat and dark suit exited one of the doors lining the hall and strode toward them. He touched the brim of his hat as he passed.

"Good afternoon, sir," Ronnie barked.

"Good afternoon, Mr. Herrera. Mr. Michaels."

Marcus gave him a crisp salute. When the man had passed them, Marcus craned his neck over his shoulder to get a look at him.

Ronnie elbowed his partner. "Stop it."

"But isn't that... you know..." Marcus dropped his voice to a whisper. "*Him?*"

"Yes, and you're better off ignoring him," Ronnie replied.

He had only met Porter a handful of times. Once during his

interview; once when he signed on for training; once when his training was complete and his employment at the Vault officially began; and twice since, at his annual performance reviews. Porter was never the only man in the room, and he barely spoke. All the same, his presence left Ronnie unsettled and anxious. He wasn't entirely clear what Porter's role in the Enforcement Network was, but he was pretty sure he wasn't an HR type.

For once, Marcus didn't argue. Maybe Porter gave him the same vibes.

At the far end of the hall, Ronnie and Marcus stopped to scan their badges to get through the first set of mechanical sliding doors. This brought them to another hall, at the end of which stood a second pair of doors. Each of them scanned their thumbprints, prompting the doors to open into a freight elevator. They entered in silence and began their long ride down to the Vault.

Marcus shuffled from foot to foot. Something was clearly on his mind, but Ronnie was in no hurry to ask questions, just in case he ended up listening to another long-winded story about his past exploits.

The third time he sighed, however, Ronnie turned to him. "What?"

"Nothing," he said.

"Cool."

He shuffled his feet. Sighed again.

"Seriously, what?" Ronnie demanded.

"It's just... does it seem weird that he was here? The whole place is usually empty by now, except for security."

"So he had to stay late. Do some overtime." Ronnie shrugged one shoulder. "I don't ask what these people do, and all they ask of me is to do my job." There had been a time when he was more curious, but given what he'd learned in training, he wasn't in a huge rush to get more involved with the organization than he had to. Being a security guard meant putting his life on the line for them while he was on the job.

He was pretty sure that the more he knew, the more trouble he could get into off the job, and Ronnie had no intention of drawing his family into all this. The less he knew, the better.

The elevator stopped at last, and the rear door's control panel hummed to life. Ronnie lowered his eye to the retinal scanner. Marcus had to stand up straight to reach it.

Only when their triple confirmation was complete did the doors to the elevator open. If they'd failed their retinal checks, it would have gone into shutdown mode until someone could come and collect them. In the years he'd worked for ENIGMA, Ronnie had only ever gotten stuck during planned training sessions. The only time he'd ever had to retrieve anyone from lockdown was about a year back, when one of the new enforcers panicked. The poor guy had been terrified when he was finally retrieved, and the sedative cocktail that the system piped through the air supply had only helped a little. He'd spent two days in the infirmary after that, and Ronnie and the guys had laughed about it for weeks.

All that security was why he doubted he'd ever need his weapons and gear. When the two of them stepped out of the elevator into the high-ceilinged room beyond, the vault door lay before them on the far side of the room, and good luck getting through that. It looked like one of those old bank vault doors, reinforced and set into concrete more than a meter thick, all of it thirty stories underground.

If someone wanted to stroll in there, his weapons would be the least of their problems.

"There you are." Parker rose from her chair to meet them. She bumped knuckles with Ronnie, then with Marcus. "I thought you'd decided to skip out on us for the night."

Ronnie checked his watch. Phones didn't work down here, and

even beyond the lack of cell service, anything digital that wasn't provided by ENIGMA tended to get a little wonky. He'd had to resort to an analog watch on shift.

"According to this, we're right on time," he remarked.

Carson laughed and hooked his thumb at Parker. "And according to this one, we've been abandoned. She's champing at the bit."

"I am not."

Carson lowered his voice, ignoring Parker. "She's got a date tonight."

Ronnie laughed as the color rose in Parker's cheeks. "Guess you'd better get going," he said.

"With pleasure." Carson saluted them. "Have a good night, folks." He rose from his chair and lumbered toward the door. He was the biggest of them by a long ways, and he could probably bench-press Marcus without breaking a sweat, but Ronnie had noticed in training that he was slower than the others. Probably a result of hauling all that muscle mass around with him.

When the other pair scanned their retinas, the door hummed but didn't open right away.

"Weird." Parker tilted her head. "You think we need to try again?"

Carson frowned up at the ceiling. "I don't think that's the problem. I think it's making another trip."

Ronnie's hand involuntarily tightened on his rifle. Things didn't change in the vault. One day was much like the next.

"Were we expecting a drop-off tonight?" Marcus asked.

Carson shook his head. "Nobody mentioned one to us."

"Maybe one of the janitors got lost," Parker said.

"It's not a janitor," Ronnie said. Only moments ago, he'd been convinced that the vault was impenetrable, but now... now, the hair on the back of his neck stood at attention, and his heart thrummed inside his chest like an engine turning over. "Something's off."

"A janitor wouldn't have a badge," Carson agreed.

"Watch it be some dipshit enforcer getting us all worked up." Parker snorted. "Do you believe how much those guys get paid? They should dock 'em a fee for not keeping us in the loop."

Ronnie hadn't realized that he was counting under his breath, much less why, until the elevator hummed again. He knew exactly how long it took to travel from the ground floor to the Vault.

For a single breath, there was silence as the four of them stared at the elevator door. The other three waited for something to happen, but Ronnie was the only one who lifted his rifle to his shoulder.

Which was why, when the hum started, he was the only one who was armed and ready.

It started low, like the distant buzzing of a handful of bees or the drone of flies around a garbage can. As the intensity built, so too did the volume, and the hum climbed to a whine. Parker yelped and clapped her hands to her ears.

Ronnie didn't blink.

On the reinforced elevator doors, a small patch of blue light pooled against the metal. In a fraction of a second, it grew to the size and shape of a man, until it formed the outline of an imposing figure in a metal suit.

Ronnie's eyes couldn't make sense of the shape, or why and how it was moving, ghostly, through the steel. The figure itself looked like a phantom, so thin he could see right through it into the elevator. He tightened his grip on the trigger, firing at the figure's legs, targeting its thighs. The bullets would do some damage, but the capsules inside contained a sedative strong enough to take out a horse; protocol demanded that he shoot to injure, not to kill. ENIGMA would want to question the intruder.

To Ronnie's dismay, however, the bullets passed straight through the figure and exploded against the far wall of the elevator, beyond its ghostly form. When it passed through the door entirely, his bullets ricocheted off of the near side of the doors instead.

Once it was through the door, the figure stopped shimmering, and the hum that had accompanied its arrival abruptly died. From blue and nearly translucent, it solidified into what seemed to be the very real, very solid figure of a man dressed in a metal suit. It was sleek and clearly high-tech, conforming to his body, a gold exosuit with some sort of black reinforcement at the joints.

The strangest part, the detail that made Ronnie fall back a pace, was the helmet. Unlike the rest of the suit, the helmet was decorative. Instead of showing the man's face, it was embellished to look like the head of a man with rays of golden hair framing his face, and oversized eyes that bored into him. It disturbed him, this juxtaposition between modern and archaic: not just because the elements were so at odds, but because he recognized them.

Ronnie retreated another pace and opened fire again. "Hand of the Sun!" he bellowed. "It's a Hand agent!"

Marcus was already fumbling with his gun, and Parker had rolled out of the way. Carson, however, was close enough to swipe at him with one huge hand.

The man in gold didn't hesitate. He barely turned his head to meet Carson's gaze. One minute, Carson was snarling at the interloper. Then there was a pop, so loud it left Ronnie's ears ringing, and a sizzle, and Carson was down.

Parker was screaming, but Ronnie didn't stop to look. The golden man was moving now, striding toward the door of the vault. Marcus finally had his gun, and he moved to block the agent's path.

The golden figure shimmered blue once more, and he walked right through Marcus.

Ronnie could see his coworker standing frozen in surprise for the few fractions of a second that they occupied the same space. Then the golden man was through, solid once more, and Marcus toppled to the floor. He heaved a few times, retching bile and the remains of his dinner against the tile.

The Hand agent strode toward the door of the vault, and Ronnie gathered himself to fire one last time. Surely the door would be enough to stop him. It wasn't just metal, after all, ENIGMA took precautions, surely they would have something in place to stop an attack liked this—

He fired at the man's back. Too late. He was already sinking through the steel and into the vault beyond.

Marcus choked out a curse as he pushed himself up to one knee. His usually copper skin had a greenish cast, and the whites of his eyes were scarlet with newly burst blood vessels. "What the hell?" he finally managed.

"I don't..." Ronnie began. Any other words he might have managed slipped away when he saw Carson.

There was a hole in Carson's forehead; he'd seen that much. He knew what bullets could do to a man's skull, but this—this was different. Worse. The skin around the bullet hole appeared to have melted like plastic.

Parker collapsed to her knees beside the big man's remains. Ronnie averted his eyes, but the vision of the damaged face danced behind his eyelids.

Somewhere above them, alarms were blaring. Good. Maybe backup was on the way, although what sort of backup would be required to deal with the Hand, he could only imagine.

"Are there more of them?" Marcus asked.

Ronnie shook his head. "Don't know."

"What do we do now?"

He made himself look at Carson again. He thought of his daughter and his wife, and how it would feel to tell them that he'd taken the coward's way out. That he'd let a bad man steal something that could do even worse things.

He pictured Alaina explaining to their daughter that daddy's funeral would be closed-casket.

Ronnie took a deep breath. "There's no point shooting him when he's blue. I don't know how he's doing that, but it looks like things can't hit him when he's... doing that. He didn't go for his gun until it stopped, so if we're going to hit him, we're going to need to aim for him when he's gold. Parker, get up."

The younger woman trembled and lifted her hands toward Carson's face, as if she couldn't believe what she was seeing.

Ronnie kicked her thigh, hard. "*Get up*. We're going to form a line. Cut him off."

Parker rose on shaking legs.

"Marcus, get left. See if your bolts are any more useful than the tranq ammo. Parker, get right. Use whatever the hell you've got. I'll take the middle." He hated to do it, hated to take the risk, but Marcus was still coughing up bile, and Parker was clearly losing her shit. If he couldn't hold the line himself, it wasn't fair to ask anyone else to do so.

Parker hadn't even drawn a weapon when the hum started up again, and blue light spilled out of the vault door. The intruder wasn't just walking now. He was running. He'd gotten whatever he came for, and he was ready to go.

Ronnie screamed as he opened fire.

To his dismay, the man never solidified. He stayed blue and ethereal, like a being made of light and water. Neither his tranq shells nor the modified bolts from Marcus' handgun hit him.

Instead, the bolts left a trail along the far wall, exploding in a shower of sparks and smoke.

Ronnie was blocking the agent's path, and he told himself that he wouldn't flinch. He would hold the line. But just before the ghostly man reached him, Ronnie dove aside. By the time he spun around, the man had passed through the elevator door, leaving only stunned stillness in his wake.

Ronnie let out a ragged breath.

One breach.

One breach, in the three years he'd been working for ENIGMA. But that was enough.

He looked at Carson's lifeless body. Not only had Ronnie not been able to slow the intruder down, he'd watched the enemy take one of his own in the process.

He clambered back to his feet. His eyes fell on the vault door.

What else did they take?

THE LOST RELIC

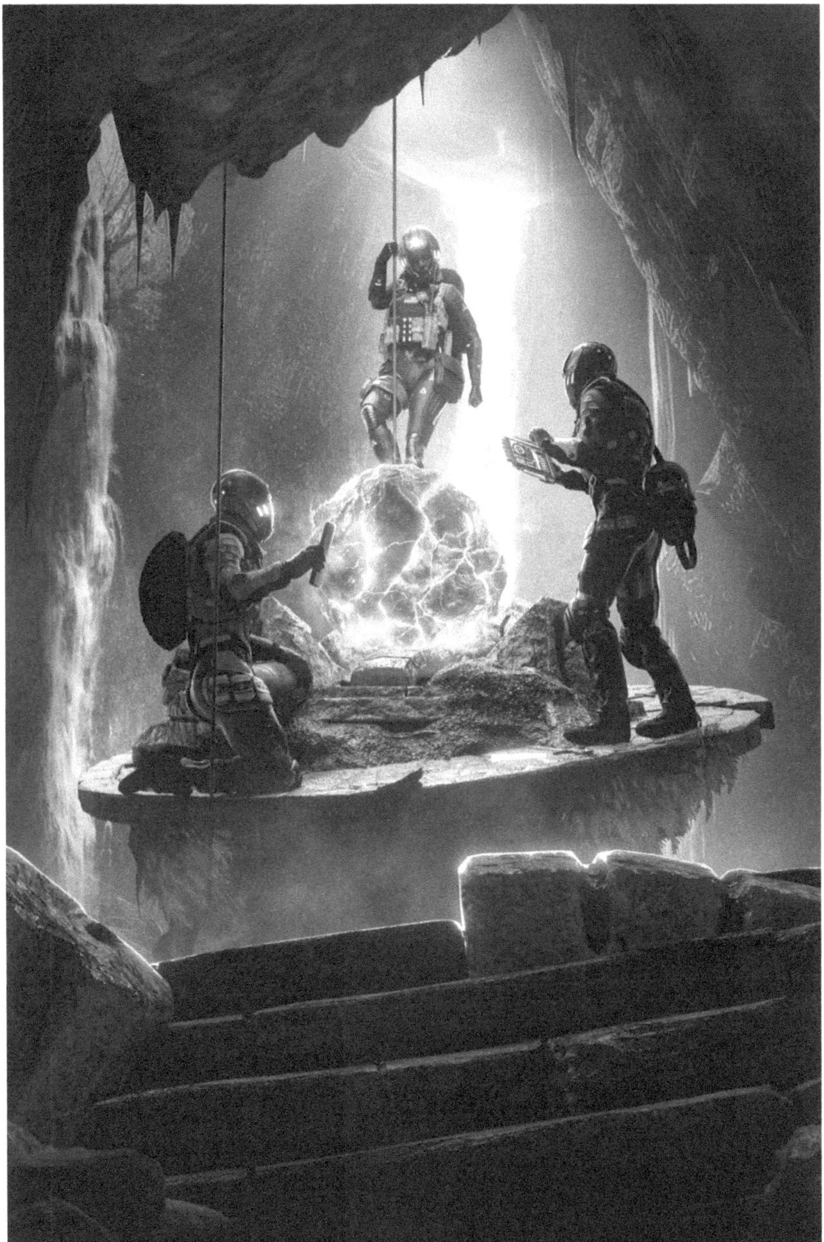

1

Palmdale, California

RHETT ZAPPOTIS CROUCHED behind the shrub and wished to God that his leg would give him five minutes of peace. He was in the middle of something, dammit. If he'd known this was how the day was going to go, he'd have taken a stronger painkiller at breakfast.

A few yards away, a twig snapped, and Rhett held his breath. His finger twitched on the trigger of his gun, but he stopped himself from firing just in time. That particular itchy trigger finger had gotten him in trouble more than once, but he'd gotten better at listening. Waiting.

Another twig. Something rustled in the undergrowth.

Rhett took a deep breath, braced his bad leg under him, and rocketed out of his hiding spot, squeezing the trigger for all he was worth. He was out in the open before he registered that he was aiming not at a person, but at the chubby bulk and gangly legs of an overweight yellow Lab. His finger was still on the trigger of the Supersoaker when a barrage of NERF bullets pelted him from two directions.

"No! McNugget!" Rhett stumbled to a halt. "You blew my cover!"

McNugget's pink tongue lolled from his mouth as he tried to lick the stream of water Rhett was still squirting in his direction. When he stopped, McNugget dropped to the grass on his belly and licked the water from his fur instead.

"Got you, Uncle Rhett!" Kosta held up a hand for a high five. His sister, six-year-old Anna, tapped her palm against his.

"You did." Rhett pressed a hand to his chest and forced a smile. "Using McNugget as a decoy was a dirty trick, though."

"He's a good boy," Anna said proudly. She jogged across the lawn to where the damp Lab was still rolling in the grass, and gave his plump belly a loving pat. He thumped his tail and licked her face.

"That he is. I admit defeat." Rhett ruffled his fingers through Kosta's hair and set out for the porch. If he'd planned ahead, he would have worn his brace, but his sister would have noticed if he wore loose pants to a picnic on a hot day, and the idea of having his brace on where Zoe and the kids could see was...

Not humiliating, but unthinkable. The reminder of everything that he'd been through would have hung over him like a pall all day. Civilians didn't want to think about veteran injuries on Memorial Day. Zoe wanted to celebrate the fact that her brother had made it home alive, rather than dwell on all the people who hadn't.

Rhett couldn't forget, but at least without the brace to remind him, he could forget how many of those deaths were his fault.

His brother-in-law, Cliff, met him at the porch steps with a beer in each hand. "Need a reload?" he asked.

Rhett dropped the Supersoaker in the grass before mounting the steps. He needed one hand for the railing if he was going to make it up without grimacing. "No, thanks. I don't handle firearms when I'm drinking."

Cliff laughed, but Zoe shot him a suspicious look. Rhett replied with a thin smile and lifted his fresh beer in a toast.

"Need any help?" he asked Cliff. "Believe it or not, I can be trusted to man a grill."

"Nah, I'm good." Cliff waved him away. "Make yourself a plate. Get comfortable. Today is your day."

This time, when Rhett winced, it had nothing to do with his leg.

He wandered over to where Zoe was laying out the rest of the food. "Tell me what to grab."

"Nothing," Zoe said. "Sit down. You must be tired, running around like that."

Rhett might not be willing to push back when Cliff dismissed him, but Zoe was another matter. "I can help. Should I get the napkins? The plates?"

"I've got it." Zoe stepped around him. "Sit."

Rhett bit his cheek and clutched his beer more tightly. He hated how weird things had gotten between them, ever since he was discharged. Their parents pretended that nothing had happened, that everything was fine. They made things easy on him.

Zoe had never made things easy. She was good at being a sister, but she sucked at letting things go.

"I'll be right back," Rhett said to no one, and followed Zoe into the house. Instead of going to the kitchen, he turned right and made his way down the hall to the bathroom. He didn't bother closing the door before he yanked open the medicine cabinet and started spinning bottles so that he could read the labels. When he finally found the Tylenol, he yanked it off the shelf and shook three pills into his palm. He swallowed them dry, then chased them with a mouthful of beer.

"Please tell me you're not popping pills in my bathroom," Zoe said from behind him.

Rhett forced himself not to jump. He took his time setting the bottle back in its place, then closed the medicine cabinet door. Zoe stood behind him, arms crossed, one shoulder resting on the doorframe. Rhett met her gaze in the reflection.

"I'm not popping pills," he said evenly. "I'm—"

"Mixing analgesics and alcohol." Zoe rolled her eyes. "At least close the bathroom door next time. I don't want my kids to start asking uncomfortable questions."

Rhett gritted his teeth and smothered his reply before it could burst free. He forced a smile instead, although in the mirror, it looked more like a grimace.

Zoe cleared her throat and turned away.

It was only three pills, Rhett wanted to say. *Just enough to get me through the day without hurting too much.*

But that would have been a lie, because even when the throbbing in his leg dulled, the *real* pain remained.

That night, Rhett dreamed of the mission. The last mission. The one that ended it all. He woke tangled in the sheets, sweating profusely, his skin somehow clammy and blistering hot all at once.

He reached for the glass of water on his nightstand before realizing that it wasn't the dream that had woken him. On his bedside table, the cell phone was buzzing, the screen lit up with an unknown number.

Rhett declined the call and drank the glass dry. His throat was still raw, either from thirst or from crying out in his sleep, and he swung his legs over the side of the bed, determined to get another. When he rose, his ankle rolled, and the resulting spiderweb of pain lit up every nerve in his bad leg at once. He dropped back to the bed with a gasp.

"Sonofa*bitch*." He ran his fingers through his short hair, which was still sticky with cooling sweat.

The phone lit up again.

He let it ring through this time, and focused all of his energy on making the muscles in his leg relax. Sometimes when he did something to aggravate it, the muscles locked up. Next time, he wouldn't be a baby about it. Next time, he'd wear the damn brace.

He tried to stand again and knocked sideways into the table, sending the water glass flying off. It hit the hardwood floor and shattered.

Rhett was still cursing his leg and his luck and his pride when the phone rang a third time. This time, he scooped it up and answered before dropping back to the bed.

"I don't know who this is," he growled, "but it's four in the morning and you've got the wrong goddamn number. Stop calling."

"My apologies, Agent Zappotis," said a smooth voice on the other end of the line. "My sources indicated that you're an early riser. Or does that not apply to family vacations?"

The hot coil of pain that had been making its way through his body cooled with all the suddenness of a plunge into an icy lake. Rhett swallowed hard and gripped the phone. His other hand clutched the sheets in a tight fist.

"Who is this?" he asked.

"I'm with the Enforcement Network for Intelligence, Global Monitoring, and Assessment," the stranger said. Rhett was pretty sure that it was a man speaking, but his voice gave nothing else away. His accent was subtle and difficult to place. Rhett was pretty sure he was American, and likely not from the South, but the lilt in his words wasn't strong enough to be from New England.

The name of the organization didn't tell him anything, either, which was its own kind of clue.

Rhett finally got up and made his way to the bathroom in shuffling little steps. "Who gave you my number?"

"It was in your files."

Rhett flicked on the bathroom light. It had been instinct, to get away from the windows, but he hadn't really thought until that moment that someone might be tracking him. "I'm retired," he said coldly. "Lose my number."

"If you insist. I'd like to make you an offer first, if you don't mind."

Rhett braced one arm against the sink. His pallid reflection stared back at him from the wall. "I do mind. I've got a pension. I'm done. Surely your records show that."

"I'm prepared to offer you more than money," the voice said. "Although there's also ten million dollars on the table, should you choose to accept my offer."

Rhett paused. Ten million. That was big kid money. Bounty money.

Trouble money.

"You said there's more?" he asked, in spite of himself.

He made his offer.

"No." Rhett straightened up. "No, that's impossible."

"Not for us."

Rhett rubbed his temple. "What do you want me to do?" Asking was a bad idea. Good people didn't call folks like him, in the dead of night, to offer ten million dollars and the impossible in exchange for a little favor. He was going to ask for something big.

"I'm afraid I'll have to tell you in person. If you're willing, we'll book your flights, reserve you a room, and of course pay you for your time. If either of us decides we're not interested in working together, we'll pay your way back to California as well. No harm done."

He didn't quite buy that, but still, how could he say no? He'd be a monster to say no.

"Fifteen million," he blurted.

The man laughed. "That's quite a bold counteroffer."

"Inflation," Rhett deadpanned, "and I have no idea who the hell you are. Fifteen million, and... and the other thing. Take it or leave it." That way, even if the man's promises were as BS as they sounded, he could still do some good.

He didn't haggle. "Very well. We'll conduct the interview and decide if you're worth the higher price. I'll have the details sent to you."

Rhett opened his mouth to ask how, but the line was already dead.

Cambridge, Massachusetts

"DO YOU SEE THE DIFFERENCE," Dinah asked, "between the traditional iconography and the images from el-Amarna?"

Her student—Jeffery or Jeffie or Geoffrey, Dinah couldn't remember exactly—stared down at the pages with a blank expression.

Dinah took a calming breath. *Lord save me from undergrads who don't even pretend to do the assigned readings.* Her own undergrad days weren't far behind her, but she'd been a good student. A great student, even. One might have gone so far as to suggest that she might have been gifted. Certainly her advisor had seemed to think so.

Not that it mattered these days, but it did make it awfully hard for her to sympathize with students who couldn't pass an intro-level course that was graded primarily on attendance.

With excruciating patience, Dinah pointed to the first picture. "Most of the dynasties allowed and even encouraged the worship of a number of regional gods. Each of them had their place in the pantheon, and each of them granted power to the pharaoh. For example, you have Osiris." She pointed to the god in question. "Lord of fertility and agriculture. The god who died and then returned to life, thanks to the work of Isis, his sister-wife…"

Jeffrey/Geoffrey snickered.

"… who was symbolically considered to be the mother of every pharaoh. Osiris' death and rebirth represents the ebb and flow of the Nile. Their son, Horus, was the god of the sky, and the pharaoh's protector. Each of the gods, major and minor, represented some aspect of the world, and reinforced the rule of the pharaoh in some way." She paused to let that sink in.

"Uh-huh," maybe-Jeffrey said.

"But during his reign, the pharaoh Akhenaten tried to eradicate the pantheon and replace it with a single god, Aten, of whom he was the living embodiment." Dinah tapped the other picture. "As you can see here, Aten is depicted in the hands of the sun—"

"Will this be on the final?" Jeffie interrupted.

The fraying threads of Dinah's patience snapped. "Yes." She sat back, smiling at Geoffrey. "And you can read all about it in Chapter 19 of the textbook, which I recommend you do by Wednesday, because I will *not* be allowing make-up exams."

The undergrad groaned and made a series of halfhearted attempts to get Dinah back on track, but they were fruitless. Helping students understand the material was one thing, and she was always happy to host extra office hours to do so, but the semester was almost over, and as usual, a swarm of students had descended upon her in the hopes of squeaking their low grades up to passing. She was tired of explaining the same things over and over to kids who couldn't care less.

When the door swung closed behind the still-grumbling freshman, Kesa McKean looked up from her desk with a grin.

"Depressing, innit?" she asked in her thick Aussie twang. "Wait 'til you've been doing this as long as I have. I swear, they're getting lazier by the year."

"Not all of them," Dinah said.

"Sure, but a lot of 'em. You do what you can an' hope a splinter of information sticks in their tiny brains." Dr. McKean tapped one temple and grinned. "I know you're still fresh meat, Bray, but you'll get used to it. And every once in a while, someone'll come along who actually gives a rip, and you'll remember why you went into this in the first place."

Every once in a while. That was a bleak thought. Dinah didn't have the heart to tell her officemate that she hadn't gotten into history for the love of teaching, but for the love of the subject itself. So many of her peers had looked at history as something written by and for their white counterparts, but Dinah had been drawn to the study of ancient history like a moth to flame. People were more than happy to let her teach about the pharaohs, and left her alone to putter around researching whatever more obscure areas of history caught her fancy.

Some days, it was enough.

Today was not one of those days.

Her afternoon freshman course dragged on for what seemed like an eternity. Half of the students stared down at their laps, flagrantly defying the university's texting policy. She didn't bother calling people out anymore; that had gotten old during the first semester.

The other half of the class had the decency to at least feign interest. Three of them even went so far as to get into a discussion about the Ptolemies. Even so, Dinah could feel the pull of summer vacation dragging on all of them. They were all ready to be done, including her.

With one last reminder that their finals would be proctored on Wednesday—which was, as always, met with a groan, as though this was somehow a surprise—Dinah set them free. They trickled off with their backpacks slung over their shoulders, their phones already out, their minds on the present day. Dinah lingered to collect her notes from the class.

When a shadow fell across her desk, she assumed it was a student, stopping by with yet another request to extend the deadline for the final. The no was already forming on her lips when Dinah lifted her head.

It was not a student. It was not, in fact, anyone Dinah had seen before in her life.

The person before her was tall and narrow, dressed in all black, with features that Dinah couldn't quite place. Both their features and their complexion were ambiguous enough to give her pause.

Regardless, they weren't a student, so Dinah fell back on politeness. "Can I help you?" she asked. "I'm guessing you're not here for Egyptian Studies 001."

The person's lips turned up in a smile that disappeared as quickly as it came. "Correct," they said. Their voice was low and smooth. "I'm here to speak to you. Dinah Bray, isn't it? Doctor Dinah Bray? I'm quite the fan of your work."

"That's me." Dinah held out a hand. "And you are..."

"Porter." The person's brief smile flashed across their face again as their cool palm met Dinah's. "And I'm here to make you an offer."

Cartagena, Colombia

FABIEN RESTED his elbows on the rooftop and watched the street below. It was his fourth visit to Colombia, and he was waiting for a man he'd only ever seen in photographs.

Not good photographs, either. Most of them had been blurry, taken from a distance, depicting a man in motion. Only two of them had been clear enough to make out the man's face in detail, but they were enough. Fabien was an expert when it came to faces.

Tomas Arturo Cabal. Father of two by his wife, and at least three others by different women. Churchgoer. Billionaire. Murderer, and worse. Not, to put it bluntly, a good man.

Fabien propped his chin on his elbow, leaned against the half wall of the abandoned building, and waited.

According to the docket, Cabal would be leaving his tailor's at approximately three forty-five. He had a meeting at four o'clock, and the route between the two stretched just below where Fabien stood. His wife and children were at home. If necessary, Fabien could return to the house in the evening, but he preferred to leave people's families out of things, if at all possible.

It was hot on the roof, and the sun was beating down on the top of Fabien's head. The bald cap trapped his sweat in, which meant that his scalp was being steamed like a Maine lobster beneath the layer of silicone. Fabien scratched it, but didn't take it off. Like his glued-on facial hair, it served a purpose. Someone would see him, it was almost inevitable, and when they did they'd identify a fat, bald man with a bushy mustache.

The door of the tailor's opened from within, and Fabien straightened up. A man in a Panama hat stepped through.

Dammit. Fabien spat on the floor at his feet. He was too high up. The brim of the man's hat shaded his face too much to be sure. He reached for his gun and held it low, out of sight of the pedestrians three stories below. If it was Cabal, he could get a clear shot. But if it wasn't...

No one had ever claimed that Fabien LeRoux was a man of morals. Which wasn't to say that he'd never met a moral in his life, just that his were... different. Slippery. They shifted to suit his needs.

All the same, Fabien wouldn't shoot unless he could be sure it was Cabal on the other end of the barrel. Partly because that would be wrong, yes, but also, it would blow his cover and make the whole job harder.

The man on the street greeted someone, and stopped to talk. To Fabien's great irritation, the other person stood directly in his line of sight. Which meant that he was facing the right way, but Fabien still couldn't see.

Perhaps it would be a wash. There was a single good stretch of visibility here, but if he failed now, Fabien would have to relocate. There was no good spot to set up at Cabal's next destination, and no telling where he would go from there. If Fabien pulled out now, it would mean waiting for Cabal at his house.

Where his kids were.

Where they might see.

Where the memory of their father's death would haunt their home forever.

It was a sure bet, but Fabien would give a great deal to avoid that eventuality.

Then, on the street, the two men shifted. The stranger moved aside. Tomas Arturo Cabal tipped his hat in farewell, revealing a clear view of his face.

Hello, Mr. Cabal.

Fabien's shots were clean: one in the forehead, one in the chest, one in the gut as insurance. They hit in a straight line, the third bullet leaving the rifle as the first struck home.

Cabal collapsed on the street as the people around him screamed in horror. Fabien waited long enough for someone to point up at the fat bald man on the roof, then ducked out of sight and disappeared.

His small hideaway for the evening was two towns away, and it took a few hours to make his way there along his chosen route. He waited until he was within sight of the door before pulling his burner phone out of the small bag strapped to his chest. The fat suit, mustache, and bald cap were long gone, revealing the muscular man with short-cropped hair beneath.

He dialed the only number, and the phone rang once before the line picked up. No one spoke, but Fabien could hear heavy breathing coming from down the line.

"Está feito," he said. He waited for a grunt of acknowledgment before ending the call. He'd ditch the phone later, crush the SIM card into dust. Tomorrow, he'd be on his way to South Africa with no one the wiser.

He yanked open the door of his hideaway—and froze. There was a man inside, dressed in black.

Fabien had left his rifle outside of town, hidden in the spot where he'd retrieve it tomorrow. His 3D-printed slim pistol, however, was still within reach. It was in his hands before he could think, held between him and the stranger.

"Putain qui es-tu?" he demanded.

The stranger's eyes glinted like flecks of mica in the dark room.

Fabien couldn't see his face, only the brightness of his eyes and the flash of white teeth when he spoke in English. "It would be short-sighted to kill me here, don't you think?"

Fabien sucked in a breath. "Sometimes short-sightedness keeps you alive." None of the other shadows within the room moved, and when he stepped back a pace, there was no sign of anyone flanking him. "Are you alone?"

"Yes, if you can believe that." There was amusement in the stranger's voice. "I take no issue with your line of work, Mr. LeRoux. In fact, I'm here to make you an offer."

The man's casual use of his name—his real name, not any of his innumerable aliases—made Fabien's blood run cold. He tried not to let his alarm show on his face as he stepped into the room, closed the door, and turned on the light. He didn't trust the man as far as he could shoot him, which with the right weapon would be pretty far indeed. Fabien was an excellent shot, and even a skinny man like this stranger presented a large enough target for his purposes. On the other hand, Fabien had a lot more to lose than to gain by shooting him. If the man knew who Fabien really was, then he might know other things. Whoever he worked for might know those things as well, and they might not take kindly to his disappearance.

"Very well," Fabien said, giving the stranger his best unflappable smile. "Let's hear what you have in mind."

2 RHETT

THE LAST FLIGHT brought Rhett not into New York or D.C. or any of the Eastern cities he'd first assumed, but to the airport in Cleveland, Ohio.

"This has to be a joke," he muttered. But evidently it wasn't, because there was a driver waiting by the gate holding a sheet of paper, with his name haphazardly scrawled in Sharpie.

"Do you need to collect your bags?" he asked.

Rhett shook his head. He had a backpack, his brace, and a cane for good measure. He'd seen no point in packing anything else. Either he'd be headed back to California tomorrow, or the man who'd offered him fifteen million could advance him enough for whatever expenses he might accrue in the meantime.

"Then let's get going." The young man waved him out to his car.

The man wasn't dressed like a special agent, and the Uber sticker in his window confirmed that he was either ignorant of the larger situation, or fully committed to the bit. Rhett folded himself into the back seat of the sedan and stared out the window as they navigated through the Ohio suburbs and out onto the highway.

"How far are we going?" Rhett asked him.

The driver gave him a funny look in the rearview. "You don't know?"

Rhett shook his head. "I'm hoping you do. Someone ordered a ride for me."

"Huh." The driver considered him, then shrugged. "According to the map, we're about fifteen minutes away."

Rhett let his forehead rest against the glass. They passed a billboard advertising a Christian hotline, followed by others supporting a slew of conflicting political pundits, then one promoting milk. Not a brand name, just milk.

It was possible, he reflected, that he'd made a terrible mistake.

They finally pulled into what appeared to be the parking lot of an abandoned mall.

"Maybe I've got the address wrong." The driver frowned and reached for his phone, but after a few moments of tapping his thumbs against the screen, he shook his head. "No, this is right, I guess." He twisted around in the seat and frowned. "You want me to let you off here?"

"It's fine," Rhett said. He fished a ten out of his wallet and handed it over. "Do you mind waiting a couple of minutes? Just in case I'm wrong?"

"No problem." The driver was still eyeing the mall with grave suspicion. "This seems kind of..."

"Unusual?" Rhett supplied.

"I was gonna say freakin' creepy, but sure." He tucked the ten into the cupholder and killed the engine. "See you soon, I guess."

Rhett offered him a weary smile and climbed out of the car, clutching the head of his cane as he went. His leg was feeling good at the moment, and the cane was good for more than walking. He couldn't very well stroll through airport security with a Glock in his pocket, after all.

The mall was silent when he stepped inside, and the stale air made it seem like it had been abandoned a long time. There was no AC running, no filters, no lights. He passed an empty jeweler's, and an old phone store with graffiti spray-painted across the window in an illegible tag.

"Dammit." He pulled his phone out of his pocket. The unknown number was still in his calls list from yesterday, but when he tapped his thumb on the entry, the call was declined. He couldn't tell if it was from the shitty rural service or a bad listing.

He was contemplating his next move when a reflection in the glass of the display window caught his eye.

He didn't think. He moved.

The driver must have taken a back entrance into the mall, because Rhett hadn't heard him come in. He slipped one arm out of the backpack straps and used the other to swing it with all his might, catching the man in the chest with its full weight. It was enough to throw him off-balance, and by then the handle of his cane was already on a collision course for his kneecap. The man landed hard on the floor of the mall's atrium, and the next instant, Rhett was on him. He dropped his bad knee onto the man's chest, knocking the wind out of him, and grabbed his head between his hands, pressing the pads of both thumbs against his eyelids, hard enough to make him scream.

"Not the eyes not the eyes *nottheeyes*!" The man lifted both hands above his head and let them drop to the ground where Rhett could see them.

"Tell me what's going on," Rhett snarled. Any pain he might have felt was washed away by the rush of his adrenaline. "Now. Or you're going to need an eyepatch."

The man whined, and a sharp noise cut through the empty

mall, like water dripping, or like heels on a concrete floor. Someone was walking toward them, clapping as he went, a condescending little golf clap that made Rhett's already riotous pulse spike further still.

"Impressive," the newcomer said. "I admit I had my doubts, given the extent of your injuries, Agent Zappotis."

Rhett released his grip on the driver's head. He didn't recognize the tall, slim man who stopped a few dozen paces away, but his voice was familiar enough.

"What is this?" Rhett asked as he pushed himself to his feet. He made sure to step right on the driver's gut as he did so, a little thank-you for his role in whatever was happening. "A trick?"

"On the contrary." The man dipped her chin in his direction. "A job interview."

It was tempting to tackle him, too, but Rhett tamped his annoyance down. He didn't owe these people anything, and he didn't like surprises. On the other hand, what if what he'd been promised was possible?

Instead of telling him just what he could stick where, Rhett gestured to the empty mall. "Nice place you've got here."

The man smiled. "It's private, and nobody thinks twice about an empty mall these days. We just had the place redone."

As the driver struggled to his feet, Rhett shuffled away so that he could keep both individuals in his line of sight. "What happens now?" he asked.

The man checked his watch. Analog, which was odd. Most people these days preferred digital, unless they were flaunting an expensive accessory, but his seemed quite plain. "I'll take you to the lower lobby, where you can enjoy some refreshment while we wait."

3 DINAH

DINAH WHEELED her suitcase into the mall, eyeing up the empty stores with mounting suspicion. She'd been all in on Porter's offer of employment, despite the fact that it seemed too good to be true. Still, on some level, there was a part of her that had always believed that she was destined for greater things, and when Porter had assured her that someone else would be on hand to proctor and grade the students' final exams, well, that was just the icing on the cake.

Except that now, she felt like someone was going to jump her. This wasn't the academic haven she'd imagined when she packed her bag the night before.

"H-hello?" she called. To her dismay, her voice cracked. *Get it together. You've been in creepier places.*

True, another inner voice replied, *but never at the invitation of a stranger who made unsubstantiated promises about future employment.*

The sound of footsteps inside the mall made Dinah jump. To

her great relief, it was Porter, strolling up with his hands clasped behind his back.

"Hey." Dinah's shoulders relaxed slightly. "This is, um…"

"Not what you expected, I suppose," Porter finished in that smooth, soothing voice. "I understand. I'll explain, but in the meantime, I want to ask you to translate something. Just to make sure that we're on the same page."

"Translate?" Dinah's voice quavered again, and she coughed into her fist. "We couldn't do this over a video chat or something?"

Porter smiled. "I'm afraid not. Please, come with me."

Dinah trotted after him down the long empty walkway, past the darkened food court. Above them, lights flickered on as they went, and darkened again after they had passed.

"If you don't mind me asking, why not move locations?" Dinah asked. "Doesn't seem like you're going to bring in a lot of business here. Unless you're remodeling?"

"Our enterprise isn't portable, I'm afraid," Porter explained. His stride was so long that Dinah had to struggle to keep up. "We were here before the mall was built, and for a time it served our purposes. For now, it's a suitable cover, but I expect that we will eventually have to look into renovating the first floor."

"Right." Dinah looked up at the glass-lined walkway of the second floor, which was just as empty as the first. *Seems like they'll need to remodel the whole thing, but I'm not sure it's my place to break the news.*

Porter turned sharply into one of the abandoned shops. Unlike the rest, with their desks and empty display cases and unlit dressing rooms, this one contained an assortment of items encased in glass.

Dinah's face lit up, and she dropped the handle of her suitcase as she hurried over to one case in delight. She might not know much about how to revive a dead mall, but this she could appreciate.

"Oh, wow." She pressed her nose to the glass and left a foggy imprint of her breath. "This is a great reproduction. It looks like something taken out of a fourth-dynasty tomb!"

Porter chuckled. "What else can you tell me?"

There was a note of condescension in his voice, but Dinah didn't care. "It's a funerary frieze. All those images of food and drink? They're meant to provide sustenance for the dead in the afterlife. And this bit here, it's a list of all the other things the occupant will need." She squinted at the text. "Hang on, Baefra? As in, the son of Khufu?"

"The very same," Porter said.

Dinah straightened up. "Why bring me here to translate something you already—ooh, red slipware!" She scurried over to another case, the question already forgotten. "Lovely, lovely. Quite a collection you've got. And—"

She spun in a slow circle, eyeing the treasures. There were scuff marks on the floor, as if the cases had recently been moved here from somewhere else. The slipware certainly wasn't a reproduction, which implied that everything else might be real, too. If so, she had some ethical qualms about authentic funerary items being stored in a shabby, dead mall in rural Ohio. She was debating whether or not to bring it up with Porter when her eye landed on the casket.

It was separated into two pieces, one in each case. The mummy had been removed, and the inscriptions inside were clearly visible. Over the years, Dinah had seen caskets from a number of dynasties, designed for everyone from pharaohs to commoners. Some were plated in gold; others were little more than painted wood and cloth. But this one…

Well, this one made King Tut's tomb look like a kid's arts and crafts project.

She loped toward it, her eyes soaking in the details of the face.

"What happened to the mummy?" Dinah asked.

"We didn't take it, if that's what you're asking," Porter replied. He followed Dinah as the latter circled the cases, watching her with the same intensity with which she was studying the casket.

That was a pity. Too many mummies had fallen prey to grave robbers and, during a surreal period in the Victorian era, to people who consumed powdered mummies or mixed them into paint to achieve the infamous 'mummy brown.' So much history, destroyed for no good reason at all.

Her concerns about historical integrity were dashed from her mind, however, when her eyes landed on the columns of inscription inside the casket. "What?" she asked, laughing softly to herself.

"You can read it?" Porter asked.

"Yes, but..." Dinah shook her head. "But this is impossible."

"Who did the casket belong to?"

"I don't know, because this can't be right—"

Porter's voice cut her off. "Who does it say that it belonged to?"

"Osiris." Dinah chuckled again. When she glanced at Porter, however, the other man wasn't laughing.

Silence fell between them for a moment. This time Porter was the one to break it. "You read hieroglyphs well," he said. "What about cuneiform?"

"Yes, but—"

"Akkadian?"

"A little, but—"

"Ancient Greek?"

"I do, although—"

"Latin?"

"Fluently, but—"

"Amharic?"

"Of course!" Dinah lifted her hands, hoping to stop Porter's tide of questions. "But are you going to tell me why you have an item that claims to be from the tomb of a literal god?"

Porter clasped his hands behind his back and tilted his head to one side. His dark eyes fixed on Dinah's face. She had the uncanny sensation of being read, as if Porter was looking for something inside her.

"Yes," he said, "I am. Shortly. But first, I need to collect one more of your colleagues." He turned away, and Dinah nearly collapsed with relief at having been read and found worthy.

Porter was almost to the door when he stopped. "Do you speak or read any Asiatic languages?" he asked.

Dinah shook her head. "Not yet."

"I like your optimism." Porter reached for the light switch.

Before the room went dark, Dinah stole one last glance at the casket that claimed to have held a god.

4 FABIEN

FABIEN EXPECTED the driver to follow him into the empty building, and so, when he heard footsteps on the floor behind him, he didn't wait to see what the woman would do. His hand flew to the slim pistol at his hip, drew it, cocked it, and fired in one smooth move.

The driver howled as she toppled, clutching her thigh. "What the hell?" she squealed. "Where did you get a gun? *You shot me!*"

"And I'll shoot you again," Fabien said amiably, "unless you stop squealing like a stuck pig and tell me who you work for."

"ENIGMA!" the woman howled. "I work for ENIGMA. Jesus Christ, you could have just asked."

A figure emerged from the hall, and Fabien trained his weapon on him. It was the man who'd called himself Porter. He strolled forward, visibly unimpressed with Fabien's threat.

"You sure got here quick," Fabien observed. "Looks like I should have taken your flight."

"You had business to finish," Porter noted. "And so did I. I strongly suggest that you consider your next move carefully."

Fabien's gaze bounced to the injured driver, then back to Porter. He couldn't see further into the darkness, but he suspected that unlike the first time they'd met, this time Porter wasn't alone. "How so?"

Porter bobbed his head from one side to the other as if weighing the options. "You could take a break from shooting people and follow me. Or you could leave now, and nobody would stop you. I suspect an industrious man like yourself could find a way out of rural Ohio without too much difficulty."

"How do I know you won't have someone shoot me in the back the moment I turn to leave?" Fabien asked.

Porter smiled again, just for a moment. His emotions passed over his face like quicksilver. Or like impressions of emotions, made by someone who was trying to mimic ordinary feelings. "The same way you know that I can deliver on my earlier offer—which is to say, you don't. But you've trusted your gut with me so far, so what does your gut tell you now?"

Truth be told, Fabien's gut hadn't been instrumental in his decision to come or not. He'd been thinking of the offer Porter had made him. It was probably bullshit, but...

But what if it wasn't?

He lowered his gun.

"Excellent." Porter waved, and a pair of armed figures dressed in Kevlar uniforms emerged from the dark hall. They ignored Fabien and swooped in to reclaim their injured associate, who was mewling as she clutched her leg. "I'm sure that we can all agree that we appreciate your restraint not only in aiming for the leg, but in missing any significant arteries. A calculation, I presume?"

Fabien nodded once.

"How chivalrous." Porter waved for Fabien to follow, then turned to the stairs. Ordinary steps ran alongside the silent, immobile escalator. Fabien followed him down.

He wasn't particularly surprised to learn that there was another structure beneath the mall, one that was much closer to the image he'd conjured in his mind when trying to picture where a person like Porter worked.

Fabien was also unsurprised to note the abundance of security cameras lining the walls. There had been a handful scattered throughout the mall itself, and not the cheap fakes that people used to deter petty criminals, either. These were well-hidden, and they actually worked.

Porter, and whoever he worked for, wanted people to underestimate them. Fabien wouldn't make that mistake. He was supposed to be untraceable, yet Porter had known who he was and still waited in his hideaway with an offer of employment. He was either an idiot who thought he was untouchable, or he ought to be taken seriously.

Fabien suspected the latter. It was safer that way.

They navigated a sleek, well-lit hall in the basement level, passing dozens of unmarked doors, all of which were locked. Porter chose one, seemingly at random, and waved Fabien inside.

There were two guards, one short and one tall, just inside that watched Fabien without a notable shift in their expressions as he entered.

At the far end of the room, a man in jeans and a t-shirt sat at ease in a chair. A cane rested against the backpack at his feet. He was eating an apple. Loudly. It seemed like a statement. His features were distinctly Mediterranean, and his black hair fell in short curls around his forehead. He looked like he hadn't slept well in at least a decade, but judging by the way he sized Fabien up, that wouldn't stop him from turning on him if he saw fit.

Beside him, a nervous-looking young black woman in white slacks and a formal blouse fiddled with her hair. Definitely the odd one out.

"Lovely." Porter waved Fabien to an empty chair. "We're all here. It is my immense pleasure to welcome you to ENIGMA."

5 RHETT

"THIS IS IT?" Rhett waved to the room. It was clean; he'd give it that. But so far, he hadn't seen a single thing to indicate to him that Porter's promises had been anything more than outright lies.

"This is our administrative floor," Porter corrected. "As I explained to Dr. Bray, we're somewhat... constrained by the location of our facility. The vault itself has been updated innumerable times over the years, but the location predates the founding of this nation."

The newcomer smirked. "Let me guess. This mall is built on an ancient Indian burial ground." Rhett sized him up, taking note of his lazy posture, his French accent, his lean build, the gun at his hip. Interesting that Porter had let him keep it.

Porter turned cold eyes his way. "I *recommend* that you select your words more carefully," he intoned, with an emphasis that was lost on Rhett.

Dr. Bray cleared her throat. "Are you implying that the items you showed me upstairs have been...*here*... since before the arrival of the European colonists?"

"Hardly." Porter's gaze softened. "Facilities like this one exist all over the world in various forms, and have for thousands of years. Over time, we've divided up our collections so that, should one vault be compromised, its collection will not be destroyed."

"You're an ancient order of treasure hunters, and yet I shot one of your agents in a mall plaza," the Frenchman said. "Have I got that right?"

Rhett choked on his apple. "You *shot* him?"

The man lifted one shoulder and dropped it again, as if the matter were inconsequential. "Her, actually. And not fatally."

Dr. Bray gulped, and the two guards exchanged a glance.

"Excuse me for my skepticism," Rhett said, "but I'm not following any of this."

Porter turned his gaze on him, and Rhett had to fight to keep from flinching. His eyes were cold.

"I work," Porter said in that cool voice of his, "for the Enforcement Network for Intelligence, Global Monitoring, and Assessment. We are a multinational organization dedicated to the preservation of ancient artifacts and the study thereof. It is our job—our *responsibility*—to keep those items from falling into the wrong hands."

"Such as?" Rhett prompted.

"Anyone with a skewed perspective, or with goals that benefit the few, rather than the many." Porter had yet to blink. "Government agencies. Military forces. Or even smaller organizations, such as..." He paused for what appeared to be dramatic emphasis. "The Hand of the Sun."

As far as dramatic reveals went, it fell a bit flat, presumably because none of them had the faintest idea what he was talking about. Rhett's gaze flicked to the Frenchman, then to Dr. Bray. The former was picking at his fingernails; the latter was scratching her chin.

"So you're not with a government?" Dr. Bray asked.

The Frenchman scoffed. "That's what he said, isn't it? Do try to keep up."

Dr. Bray narrowed her eyes. She'd seemed rather soft and inexperienced when she first spoke to Rhett, but the pinch of her lips and the low pull of her brow suggested that she was more spirited than he had first assumed.

"According to him, he's storing priceless antiques in a mall. Do you understand how much provenance matters? Do you have the faintest notion how many sacred objects have been removed from their home countries for the sake of financial gain?"

"Art gets stolen all the time," the Frenchman said in a tone that suggested that Dr. Bray was naïve, at best. "If Mr. Porter is looking to protect an investment—"

"We're not talking about art!" Dr. Bray thumped a fist on the table so sharply that Rhett jumped. The Frenchman had struck a nerve. "We're talking about sacred objects! Religious items! I don't know what your religious affiliations are, sir, but you must believe in something, and the items Mr. Porter showed me upstairs were meant to house their occupants through the afterlife. I want to know his intentions for them!"

Porter's lips twitched. An almost fatherly expression of affection stole over his features as he studied Dr. Bray.

"Dinah is quite right," he said, nodding his head to the professor. "And I believe she had you there, Fabien. You, too, believe in *something*, if I'm not mistaken. Why else would you be here?"

The Frenchman—Fabien—scowled and turned his head away.

"I am, of course, more than happy to answer your questions," Porter went on. He reached into the pocket of his coat and withdrew a small, flat black object no larger than a hockey puck. He set it on the table before him. Rhett's first thought was that it was some sort of remote device, like those Alexa things his brother-in-law sometimes bought. Porter tapped the top of the device with a single finger.

The room exploded with light, so bright that for a moment Rhett thought the small object might have been a bomb. He lifted one hand to shade his eyes against the glow and gasped when he registered just how wrong he was.

Rhett wasn't prone to gasping in surprise. In pain? Yes. In fury? On occasion. But years of training and experience had prepared him for just about any eventuality.

Just about, but not all of them. Because nothing had prepared him for this.

The room around them fell away. Their chairs and the table were still exactly as they had been. Everything around them, however, had vanished.

Instead of a dingy little office in Ohio, they were now positioned before the Great Pyramids of Giza. The ground beneath Rhett's feet was sand, and the imposing figure of the Sphinx loomed over them.

Slowly, in part because he didn't want to give away his curiosity, and in part because he didn't trust what his eyes showed him, Rhett bent down. He meant to run his fingers through the sand; instead, his fingertips met the scuffed linoleum of the office floor.

A hologram, then, or something like it. It was an illusion, but a good one. The sun above them was painfully bright, even if it wasn't hot.

"Good tech," he said begrudgingly.

"Oh!" Dr. Bray—or rather, Dinah—leapt to her feet and beamed at the sight before her. "This is very clever! Just think what we could do with this in a classroom setting."

Fabien glared up at the pyramids and leaned his chair back on two legs.

"I take it you don't approve?" Rhett asked.

Fabien didn't bother to turn his head, and when he spoke, it was low enough that Rhett assumed his answer was only meant for him. "I don't like anything that alters my sense of reality...especially not without my permission."

Porter ignored them, addressing Dinah instead. "I know that ancient Egypt is your specialty, so let's start here. I understand that you're concerned about the nature of our work. Are you aware of the history of grave robbing in this country? It is an ignoble profession that spans millennia."

The smile dropped off of Dinah's face at once. "Of course. It started in ancient times, even before the collapse of the dynastic empire."

"True." Porter turned to the pyramids with his hands folded behind his back. In the dusty desert landscape, his black coat was wildly out of place. "The elites, particularly the pharaohs, consolidated wealth and power, and used it to build structures such as these. Tombs that were aimed at the sky, built with the stars in mind. Monuments that dominated the landscape, and drew the eye of believers and thieves alike." He turned his head toward Dinah. "They buried so much of that wealth in their tombs that they nearly collapsed the economy of an empire. Without grave robbers, their civilization may have crumbled as much as four hundred years before it did."

"Sounds like an excuse for stealing whatever you like," Rhett observed.

Porter turned all the way around to face the table once more. "On the contrary. There's a difference between the Germans stealing the head of Nefertiti, and some Egyptian grave-robber reclaiming the wealth buried by his king, don't you think?"

Rhett crossed his arms. "Perhaps you could skip the history lesson and get to the point?"

Porter's lips twitched again. His coolness was unnerving, but

Rhett liked it better than *this*. He didn't want this man to think of him fondly.

Porter bowed his head. "I shall expedite my lecture, then." He tapped the little disc again, and the Egyptian landscape disappeared, only to be replaced with what Rhett thought might be Machu Picchu, only without any buildings or other signs of human habitation.

"Civilizations rise and fall," Porter said. Around him, the buildings Rhett knew from countless pictures rose from the ground block by block, speeding past in a dizzying time-lapse blur. "Its inhabitants live their lives, make their advancements, develop language and culture and music." The city thrived around them, bright and well-loved, before fading and crumbling before his very eyes. "It is inevitable, however, that they eventually break down. Sometimes they are colonized."

Porter tapped the puck, and the mountain city was replaced with a village at the base of a mountain. Like the former city it, too, rose and expanded.

"Others face natural disaster."

A plume of ash erupted from the mountain peak, smothering their party in a cloud of gray dust. On reflex, Rhett raised one hand to protect his mouth and eyes, but the ash passed through his fingers and never reached his lungs. It was only light, of course, but that momentary terror set his heart racing.

The ash vanished. Now their table stood on the Great Wall of China. Around them, the landscape changed just as swiftly and thoroughly as the others had, although the wall itself remained.

"Still others change naturally, over the course of time," Porter intoned. "Still, every culture develops treasured items. They create objects that are not merely beautiful, or merely sacred, but also immensely powerful."

Porter tapped the puck again. They were standing in an empty patch of grassland now, with only trees for company. Gradually, the landscape around them was altered by unseen hands; a hill rose as if from nowhere, but it was clearly being shaped, just as the cities of Pompeii and Machu Picchu had been.

"When civilizations fall, fade, or are threatened, their prized possessions run the risk of being lost, or destroyed... or stolen." Behind Porter, the landscape changed once more as trees fell, grasslands were cleared, and the familiar structure of the mall took shape. "ENIGMA was established by a coalition of people who refused to let that happen."

"So you didn't steal the items upstairs," Dinah said. "You...what? Preserved them?"

"We made trades with other ENIGMA strongholds," Porter replied. He tapped the puck a final time, and the room returned to normal. He scooped up the little object and tucked it back into his coat pocket. "If we were to keep objects in only one place, and that facility was compromised, we could lose our entire collection at once. Now, when a facility is compromised, the depth of that loss is minimized."

Rhett sat up a little straighter in his chair. "That's why you've called us in," he blurted.

Porter arched an eyebrow.

"Your facility was compromised," Rhett pressed on, growing surer of his conclusion by the moment.

"Indeed." Porter inclined his head. "Several items were taken. A member of an enemy organization, the Hand of the Sun, made an incursion into our facility. The agent stole several objects of value."

Rhett held back a smirk. "And how did this enemy organization manage to rob your mall?"

Porter didn't smile. "He procured a device that allowed him to walk through walls."

Fabien let out a bark of laughter and got to his feet. "I've had enough of this, Monsieur Porter. It's all been very entertaining, this little Illuminati-style explanation of yours, but it's clearly a prank of some kind. Walking through walls, ah? Very funny. I'm afraid that I don't have time for such absurdity, no matter how clever your devices are. All this talk of pyramids and cultures, and now you want me to listen to you talk nonsense about your nemesis, with its silly, dramatic name? No, thank you. I am a busy man."

"It's not *silly!*" The guards had been so quiet during Porter's little lecture that Rhett had almost forgotten that they were there until the taller of the two leapt to his feet. His lips curled back to show his teeth, and he drove one fist into the tabletop with such force that the legs creaked beneath the blow. "This was a mistake, sir. Carson is dead, this frog shot Parker, and now—"

"Who are you calling a *frog?*" Fabien demanded. He made a move toward the guard, and his shorter counterpart rose to block his path.

"Stand down," the man warned.

Fabien's hand twitched toward his gun. "Or...?"

"Enough," Porter snapped. "Ronnie, I expect better from you. Marcus, this man is our guest. As for you, Fabien." He let out a weary sigh, and his gaze traveled between each of them in turn. The lines in his face had deepened, and for the first time, he looked not only ordinary, but very tired. The veneer of smooth indifference fell away. "I suppose this all sounds quite unbelievable."

"Erm." Dinah scratched her chin again. "It does, yes."

When Porter's eyes found his, Rhett only shrugged. "I have no reason to believe you, or to disbelieve you," he said.

Fabien scoffed. "No? Even though it sounds like madness? Like a child's game?"

"Maybe it does," Rhett agreed. "But I've seen strange things in my line of work. And Porter here promised me something that I won't be so quick to throw away."

Fabien blanched. His hand fell away from his gun. *Interesting,* Rhett thought. Porter must have made him a similar promise. What did it take to lure in a man of his demeanor? More than money, surely.

Rhett turned his attention back to Porter. "It would take nothing short of a miracle for you to do what you've promised. Very well, then. Show me a miracle."

Porter's hesitant, paternal smile reemerged. "As you wish." He stepped back on one foot and waved a hand toward the door. "Right this way, and we'll see how close I can get."

6 DINAH

DINAH HAD long since learned that, from a purely academic perspective, it wasn't helpful to think of the world in terms of black and white. Even with regard to the study of history, theories were evolving all the time.

As much as Dinah was tempted to scoff along with Fabien about the idea of dueling secret organizations that shuffled and reshuffled ancient artifacts over the course of centuries, she couldn't quite bring herself to dismiss the sarcophagus she'd seen upstairs.

Of course, it might be a fake. But what if it wasn't?

That possibility was one reason that she found herself trailing after the others down one rather dull hallway after another until they ended abruptly in a set of doors, which Porter badged open. These led into a large elevator. They clustered inside before Porter pressed his thumbprint to a security scanner. The doors closed, and a soft hum filled the air around them. The mechanism was so smooth, Dinah barely felt it start. It wasn't like the elevator in her building at the university, which practically gave her whiplash every time she used it. She'd long since resorted to climbing all five flights of stairs.

When Porter scanned his eye on the far side of the elevator, Fabien let out a grunt.

"You take security seriously, at least," he observed.

"That we do." Porter led them through the doors. "Very seriously. But this is only preliminary. Come." He led them into the next room. It was as unremarkable as the corridors had been, despite its size. There were two men on duty, dressed in the same black SWAT-like uniforms as the other guards. They nodded to Porter, their expressions grim.

At the far end of the room stood a massive door, reminiscent of a bank vault, but with a dozen or so lights and sensors glinting on its face.

Fabien was the first to approach the door. "Well, well," he said, with a new note of enthusiasm in his voice. "This is interesting. Is this where you keep those items of yours?"

"Indeed." Porter stood back, studying Fabien with the same intensity that the other man watched the door. "I believe you have some experience with safecracking?"

"Mm." Fabien shifted closer to the door. "Among other things." He stopped a few paces from the door and brushed one of his thumbs across his lip in an absentminded sort of way. "I'm not familiar with this kind, though. It's a little above my pay grade, I think." He flashed a wry smile over one shoulder. "So if you want me to tell you how your thief got in, I'm afraid you've hired the wrong man."

"We know how he got in." The taller of the two guards that had followed them in kept his voice low, but the acoustics of the vault amplified it.

"Of course," Fabien chuckled. "He walked through the walls. How could I forget?"

The guard's jaw worked in silent anger, but he didn't reply.

"Why don't I show you?" Porter retrieved the little disc from his pocket. "We have recordings, after all, and it makes more sense to show you here." He set the disc on the ground and crouched beside it. "Ronnie, Marcus, if you'd like to excuse yourselves, that may be for the best."

"No." The taller guard, Ronnie, shook his head. "I'm staying."

His companion only nodded his agreement.

"Very well. Let's see." Porter tapped the top of the disc.

The change was neither as dramatic nor as breathtaking as before. The room itself remained unaltered, except for four new figures that appeared in their midst. Two were strangers; two were copies of Marcus and Ronnie.

"Oh, dear," Fabien said as he eyed up the two new faces. "I'm afraid I shot the smaller one."

Ronnie, the real one, growled. "She's been through enough, jackass."

Fabien blew him a kiss.

The hologram figures stood perfectly still, mid-discussion, like wax likenesses of their breathing counterparts. Dinah shivered and crossed her arms, tucking her hands into her armpits. For the first time, she wondered what it would mean if Porter was telling the truth—not just for her, but for all of them. Why would an organization like this need someone like her?

Maybe it will be a prank, she thought hopefully. *For a show, perhaps. Then I can go home and have a good laugh about it in the safety of my own bed.*

"Play," Porter intoned.

The hologram guards lurched to life, continuing whatever conversation they'd been having. Their mouths moved, and one of them even laughed, but they made no sound.

Then their eyes turned to the elevator.

A shimmering blue light danced over the door, and a figure robed in gold passed through. The hologram guards reached for their weapons.

"Pause," Porter said.

The hologram froze. The golden figure had passed almost the whole way through the door now. Dinah took a couple of shuffling steps forward, drawn to the intruder.

Fabien snorted. "He looks like C-3PO."

Dinah sputtered in disbelief. "What? His outfit is *clearly* a combination of Pre-Columbian iconography and the aesthetic of the Riace bronzes. And this part?" She indicated the crest of gold over the man's helmet. "It's a nod to the mask of Agamemnon."

"Obviously," Rhett chuckled, adjusting his stance so that he leaned a bit more heavily on his cane. "What she said."

Porter didn't share their amusement. He stood upright once more and strolled over to join Dinah, standing so close that the material of his dark coat almost brushed her elbow. "You are correct. The Hand of the Sun delights in borrowing imagery from the past. They feel that it gives them more credence. We've identified this as Agent Apollo."

Dinah blinked at him. "The Hand of the Sun," she repeated. It was embarrassing that she hadn't put it together sooner. "As in... Aten?"

Porter merely nodded.

"Aten?" Rhett repeated. He took a step closer, eyeing the figure with renewed interest. "The Egyptian god? But Apollo is Greek."

"The Hand of the Sun includes members from all across the globe." Porter reached out one hand toward the golden rays surrounding Agent Apollo's mask. His palm and fingertips slipped through the illusion, mingling with the projected light. "And indeed, their leader goes by the name Aten. There are others, of course. Ra. Belenos. Mithra. Sunna. And this one, Apollo, named after the Greek god as you suggest." He stepped away and folded his hands behind his back once more. "We have no way of knowing the agents' true identities. Their suits and names are essentially calling cards, a way of making themselves known without exposing themselves as individuals. Although that, of course, is not their only power. As you can see. Play."

The figure lurched into motion again, passing first through Porter, then through Dinah, who didn't have time to step aside before Apollo was upon her. Being inside the hologram was momentarily disorienting; from within, the recording of Apollo was a confusing array of pixels floating in midair, contained within the high-resolution 3D shell of his body.

She was still marveling at the tech when Rhett let out a small grunt of dismay. When Apollo finally stepped away, one of the hologram guards lay dead on the floor, his face half-melted.

Bile rose in Dinah's throat, and she slapped a hand to her mouth, squeezing her eyes shut as she did so. Even the fraction of a second that she'd spent looking at the man was enough that the image of his slack body and ruined head had been seared into her brain. *There should be more blood,* she thought. *That wasn't a bullet. What the hell did Apollo do to him?*

When she opened her eyes again, Marcus had turned away, but Ronnie's eyes were fixed on the dead man, even as his hologram-self fired on the intruder. The other two guards had turned a bit green. Dinah forced her gaze to follow Apollo, who was already striding through the vault door as that brilliant blue light from before rippled over his skin.

"How is he doing that?" Dinah asked.

"The Hand of the Sun has amassed powerful objects from all over the world," Porter explained. "I'm not familiar with this one, but I would like very much to get our hands on it—and keep it out of the possession of the Hand."

"What would you do with an object like that?" Rhett asked. He didn't seem horrified by the hologram of the dead man lying only a few feet from them. Fabien, too, had barely batted an eye.

Porter hummed. "You want to know if we would use it to harm our opponents, as Apollo did to us? No, Rhett. We're not trying to eradicate the Hand, merely to provide an alternative. There is value in studying history, and in preserving it. But we do not use it against our enemies."

"History?" Fabien asked. "Whatever he's using must be some of the most advanced tech on the market. I've certainly never seen anything like it."

Porter bobbed his head from one side to the other. "Many of the items we store here are one of a kind, based on a progression of technology that is long since lost. Technological developments are not consistently linear across human history."

Fabien opened his mouth, presumably to ask a follow-up question. Before he had the chance, Apollo emerged again.

"Pause!" Fabien snapped.

To Dinah's surprise, the projector did as he asked. The hologram of Apollo was perhaps halfway through the door, frozen in place, semi-translucent and glittering. Fabien crouched down to peer through the agent's body. After a momentary hesitation, he extended one hand to prod at the place where the vault door and Apollo's body converged.

The instant his fingers met the metal, a shockwave passed through the room. Fabien was thrown off his feet, and a dozen warning lights began to flash, accompanied by the deafening shrill of a siren. It only lasted about ten seconds, but the force of it left Dinah's ears ringing.

"Damn." Rhett pressed one hand to the side of his head and grimaced. "Did that happen when Apollo went through?"

"No." Porter's lips tugged up at the edges for a moment. "But your instincts were right, Fabien. When the agent is actively passing through solid walls, he doesn't appear to be able to touch anything. You will note that he did not fire on the late Carson Bentley until he was fully through the wall. I believe that the device, remarkable as it is, presents him with some limitations."

"Sir…" Ronnie's voice cracked. When Dinah glanced over her shoulder at him, he was still staring down at the dead man.

Porter quickly bent to power off the device, and the five holographic figures disappeared. "My apologies," he said, and seemed to mean it. "I thought it necessary to show our new hires what we're up against."

"*Potential* hires." Fabien clambered back to his feet and made a great show of dusting himself off. "I still don't know that I believe all of this, Monsieur Porter. You have shown us nothing real, only lights and colors. No proof. I am a man who requires proof, I'm afraid."

Ronnie growled. "He showed you—"

"Something that could have been manufactured to prove a point." Porter held up a hand to silence the guard. "He's right, of course. We're asking him to believe something that the general populace has been conditioned to believe is a fiction. A fantasy. It's only natural to ask for hard evidence."

Porter waved a hand to the guards. "I must insist that you wait for us. We shall require some privacy."

Marcus cleared his throat. "You're letting them in? Into the vault? Sir, are you sure that's—they don't even work for ENIGMA!"

"Not yet," Porter agreed. "But I have every faith that they will before the day is out. I'm an excellent judge of character." He waited until the guards withdrew.

Dinah had the impression that there was more to their resentful glares than mere mistrust. They seemed almost jealous. "Have they never been in the vault before?" she asked.

"They have," Porter told her. "But their clearance doesn't grant them unfettered access. That honor resides with only a few of us."

A headache was setting in behind Dinah's eyes, and her temples throbbed. The novelty of the situation had begun to wear off, only to be replaced by the dull ache of anxiety pooling in her gut. If this was a joke, Porter had long since taken it too far. If it wasn't...

If it wasn't, then *what on Earth had she gotten herself into?*

The elevator doors closed, and Porter turned to the vault door. His hands flew over the controls and sensors in a pattern that Dinah couldn't follow.

While their potential employer worked, Rhett shuffled closer to Dinah. "Never seen a man die before, huh?" he asked in a low voice.

She gulped; her eyes moved involuntarily to the spot on the floor where the dead man had lain. "Once," she grunted. "Not a man, though."

Rhett's brows rose, but he didn't press her.

"There." Porter stepped back as the heavy door swung wide, revealing the vault beyond. With a small smile of self-satisfaction, he nodded to Fabien. "Your proof awaits, sir."

Dinah's feet faltered, and Fabien held back as if unsure of himself. In the end, once again, it was Rhett who went first, the metal tip of his cane tapping against the floor with every step.

7 FABIEN

FOR ALL PORTER'S TALK, Fabien didn't really believe him. Why should he, after all? The man's explanation sounded like the storyline of an old comic book, or a conspiracy theory devised by a madman.

None of that stopped him from following Rhett into the vault. If Porter was willing to put on a show this good, there must be *something* good in here, even if it wasn't what the man had promised.

His first impression of the space was laughable. All that security, and yet the vault was filled with rows of the sort of warehouse shelving that he might have found at any loading dock in the world. Most of it was of the metal variety, the sort held together with struts that fit together to support the shelves, although there was a sort of kan-ban system along one wall for smaller items.

Fabien scoffed at the sight. "I can't say I'm impressed, Monsieur."

"Not yet." Porter's tone was perfectly amiable. "I'm certain that you would like a demonstration, though. Perhaps I should start with how I found you."

That caught Fabien's attention. He had been wondering that very thing. Years of running and hiding, more than a decade of experience of flying under the radar, and this man had tracked him down in what, a day? The sooner he worked out how that was done, the sooner he could avoid it in the future.

There was a large round table made from some dark wood standing off to one side. Porter gestured to it. "Please wait here a moment, and I'll show you your first miracle." His eyes flashed with amusement as he strode off between the shelves.

He was barely out of sight before Fabien approached the nearest rack of objects.

"I don't think you're meant to be doing that," Dinah fretted. For such a young woman, she seemed a remarkably reserved sort of person. Was that an American trait? Or an academic one?

"Are you going to tell me off, too?" Fabien asked Rhett.

Rhett shook his head and leaned on hip against the stable. "No. But I am going to stand out of range just in case you do something stupid and get knocked on your ass again."

Fabien glowered at Rhett for a moment before turning his attention to the shelf. The one at eye level contained a few curious items: something that looked like a taxidermied rabbit's foot, only *much* too large; a black-velvet-lined case containing a silver necklace set with blood-red gems; a small glass display box housing an antique pistol with a set of silver bullets; and a pair of old and rather careworn metal cuffs.

Fabien reached for the gun case.

"I wouldn't recommend starting there," Porter observed. He reappeared from between the shelves carrying a jewelry box and a large tube, of the sort architects might use to transport large blueprints. "That one isn't particularly safe. You can try the bracers, though, if you like."

Dinah flinched, as though she'd been caught in the act of doing something naughty, but Fabien lifted his chin. He slid the bracers onto his wrists. They were made for someone larger than he was, but the moment they were on, his whole body began to hum. It was as if every nerve ending had come alive at once. His muscles ached—not with weariness, but with the desire to be used.

"Well, go on, then," Porter said. "Try picking something up."

Deciding that it was better not to shake the shelving, Fabien turned to the large wooden table. He gripped the lip of the tabletop experimentally.

Judging by the table's size and the fact that it seemed to be made of hardwood, he guessed that it was easily five hundred pounds. He should have been barely able to budge it on its own.

And yet, to his astonishment, he lifted it. And it felt *easy*.

Dinah squeaked. "How—?"

"It's unclear if those bracers once belonged to Thor, or if they were made by the same smith," Porter observed. "Some of the texts refer to Thor's as gloves, rather than bracers. What I *can* tell you with some certainty is that they were the ones used by John Henry many centuries later."

"Thor?" Rhett chuckled to himself. "Another god. Is he one of the Hand's? Or one of yours?"

"He wasn't a god, merely a man, the stories of whom got a bit out of hand. Now, Fabien, if you wouldn't mind, could you please put that down? It's one of a kind."

Fabien returned the table to its place, taking a bit less care than he meant to. He was barely tired from an effort that should have been impossible.

Dinah stepped forward to try to move the table, but made no

headway at all. Her cheeks puffed out with the effort, and a sheen of sweat beaded on her forehead.

"Interesting." Fabien slid one of the bracers off. "Are you that out of shape, or am I simply…?"

The words died on his tongue. The instant the metal bracers were removed, his muscles screamed. He felt as if he'd done a thousand pull-ups back-to-back, and the pain of it traveled all the way through his shoulders and down his back. He fell forward with a gasp, catching himself on the edge of the table as he did so. The bracers fell from his hands and hit the floor with a clatter. One of them rolled beneath the tabletop.

"Mon dieu," he panted. Without the support of the table, he'd be a heap on the floor.

"I'm afraid that it's not possible to use these items without some consequence," Porter said. The bastard didn't need to sound so smug about it. He laid the tube and the little box on the table before bending to retrieve the metal bracers. "Sometimes the consequences are small, or can be counteracted. Other times they can be quite detrimental to the health of the user. I'm afraid that the smith who created these was far more interested in finding a way to augment his clients' physical capabilities than in ensuring their long-term health. The Rus wanted supersoldiers, and didn't care overmuch about the human cost." He placed the bracers back on the shelf where Fabien had found them. "You'll forgive me for saying so, but there were *centuries* of European technology that lagged behind the rest of the world."

Fabien massaged his wrists. His arms hurt so much that they could barely bend at the elbows. *He could have warned me before I tried them*, he thought bitterly. Then again, he *was* the one who had asked for proof. In a way, Porter's willingness to let him try things for himself earned the man a bit more of his respect.

Rhett cleared his throat. "You mention technology and myth in the same breath, once again."

"It's all the same thing. The stories have to come from somewhere. Do you find it easier to believe in magic than to believe that the great heroes of the past had access to technology that we've lost."

Rhett chuckled. "Fair enough. Show us your next miracle, then."

Porter uncapped the tube and removed an immense canvas painted with a map of the world. It had faded with age, and the outlines of the continents didn't seem entirely accurate. It reminded Fabien of the ancient maps he'd seen in museums or in the private collections he'd systematically looted, back when he spent his time on theft more often than assassination.

Porter laid the map out on the table, then opened the jewelry case. Inside lay what looked like a metal arrowhead on a chain. A small glass phial was seated inside the back of the arrowhead, away from the tip. A complicated mechanism, rather like the interlocking interior of a watch fitting, stood out from the side of the arrowhead.

"Might I trouble one of you for... ah, yes." Porter's eyes landed on the collar of Rhett's shirt. He produced a set of tweezers seemingly from nowhere and used them to pluck a short red-blond hair off of Rhett's clothes. "The locator and the map are attuned to one another. Some might call this sympathetic magic; of course, there are all sorts of stories about witches using hair for evil ends. Others might call it alchemy. And what differentiates alchemy from chemistry? Or from genetic testing? *Any sufficiently advanced technology...*"

"*Is indistinguishable from magic,*" Fabien finished. When Dinah shot him a look of surprise, he smirked despite his pain.

"What? I read. Besides, Clarke coined that law when he was arguing with a Frenchman. Know your enemy, oui?"

Dinah rolled her eyes.

"And now..." Porter turned the small knob on the arrow's side. A faint clicking accompanied the motion, and the arrowhead jerked in his hands. He let it drop so that it pulled the long chain taut; the arrowhead spun like a dowser above the map. The chain ended in a ring that tugged at one of Porter's fingers. At length, the chain stopped moving altogether, with the point of the arrow pulling the chain to an angle that didn't make sense, given the natural pull of gravity.

Fabien leaned over the map to study the place where the arrow's point had settled. It was clearly indicating California, although without the state lines drawn, Fabien was not quite sure what area it indicated. He was only personally familiar with San Francisco and LA; he didn't take much work in the United States. Too troublesome all around.

"McNugget," Rhett breathed.

Dinah tipped her head to one side in bewilderment. "McNugget...?"

"My sister's dog." Rhett took a step back. "That was one of his hairs. I'd appreciate it if you wouldn't dox my loved ones to strangers." The hand clenched over the handle of his cane was trembling.

Porter tugged the glass phial free from the arrowhead, and the chain went limp. "I understand your concerns, and I do apologize, but you're going to have to trust one another. This is quite a dangerous mission. Let me offer one more item of proof. Dinah, if you please." He bent to retrieve a rather clunky pair of boots. They were mostly formed from leather and stitching, surrounded by a metal skeleton. "They may not fit quite right, but that won't matter for our purposes."

Dinah's gaze darted from Fabien to Rhett, then back to Porter. "That's quite all right, I'm happy to let someone else—"

"I want all three of you to understand the stakes of what we're doing here." Porter fiddled with a dial on the side of one boot's support structure. "I'll set them to, let me see, five hundred miles a step? Just make sure that you take one step forward and one single step back, or else we might have to locate you."

"Five hundred *what?*" Dinah squeaked.

"Miles. Don't worry, the settings will bring you right back once you've had a chance to look around. They're often called seven-league boots, but that's a gross oversimplification of their ability to traverse space. Make sure not to touch the time dial, though. It would be much easier to rescue you from, say, Canada than from the seventeenth century." He stood back and ushered Dinah to step into the boots.

Under other circumstances, Fabien would have been curious to try them for himself, but his arms still felt like they weighed a hundred pounds each. Let Dinah try the time/space boots.

When no one came to her aid, Dinah knelt to remove her shoes before slipping her stocking feet into the boots. She took a deep breath, flexed her hands, extended one foot experimentally, and disappeared.

Porter lifted a small plastic tub from the floor and held it in his arms while they waited.

"What's that?" Rhett asked. "Magic cauldron?"

"Trash can," Porter said. "Using the boots tends to make people..."

An ashen, windswept Dinah reappeared. Her jacket was dotted with dark splotches of water. Porter shoved the trash can into her hands; then Dinah fell to her knees, already retching.

She cradled the trashcan to her chest. "Oh, God."

Rhett crouched beside her and rubbed his palm across her back in large circles. "Where did you disappear to?"

"Wisconsin." Dinah heaved again. "Dairy farm. It was… raining." She kicked her feet until the boots came off. "I never want to do that again."

"Wisconsin was that bad?" Fabien asked.

Dinah's dark complexion still had a faint greenish tinge, but that didn't stop her from glaring up at Fabien. "Not Wisconsin. The boots. It's like being seasick, but worse."

"Wouldn't know." Fabien sniffed. "Never been seasick."

Porter collected the boots from where they'd fallen and returned them to their place on the shelf. "Is it safe to say that the three of you believe me now?"

Dinah nodded enthusiastically, but Rhett was looking at Fabien. His lips were pressed into a thin, pale line.

"Enough to do the job," Rhett said at last.

Fabien crossed his arms. His estimation of the young woman lying on the floor at his feet wasn't terribly high. She didn't look as though she'd ever handled a firearm. Rhett was more interesting, but he was ten years too old for the job and had an injured leg. Clearly, he himself was the most experienced person on their little team.

Still, if Porter could deliver what he'd promised…

Fabien nodded once. "Agreed."

"Hold on." Dinah was midway through struggling back to her feet. She had to grip the strut of the shelf for support. "Apollo broke into this vault. What did he take? It must have been pretty important, right?"

Porter sucked his teeth.

"You don't know," Fabien observed. "Don't you keep a catalog of items in the vault?"

"We do. Unfortunately, some of our records were… damaged. I

have reason to think that the Hand hacked our systems, and I haven't had time to go through the hard copy of our inventory line by line. We know *who* broke in, and our intel suggests that the agent plans to target another vault. That's why we're hiring you. Between the three of you, your skillsets should be ideal for not only intercepting Agent Apollo, but also recovering the device he used to break in, along with whatever he stole."

On the surface, it was a simple enough assignment. Fabien, however, had enough experience with understanding the things that weren't being said to read between the lines.

I haven't had the time. Porter had sent the guards away rather than allow them access to the vault. He had brought in three outsiders to help him, rather than reassigning personnel from within the organization. And he was going through the inventory personally.

Either he believed that there was a mole among ENIGMA's ranks, or he was hiding something.

Rather than address any of that, however, Fabien only offered a half bow. "Understood, Monsieur Porter. I am happy to be of service. When do we start?"

8 RHETT

THERE WAS a part of Rhett that had hoped Porter would give them some sort of high-profile tech to aid them in their mission. He would never have admitted it, but when Porter, Ronnie, and Marcus escorted them to ENIGMA's armory, Rhett's inner child shivered with delight.

Fabien, of course, went right to the guns. Rhett had already assessed him as the sort who thought carrying a big gun made him more of a man. Tiresome, but unsurprising.

Dinah gravitated toward the items that allowed for on-the-go research options. That, too, was predictable, but he suspected that it might be a bit more useful in the long run. Porter's rundown of ENIGMA's history and their rivalry with the Hand of the Sun was woefully incomplete. Besides, what if Apollo was carrying some other, more powerful weapon now? No one knew what he had lifted from the vault... or so Porter claimed. Instantaneous access to information could prove vital to their very survival, never mind the success of the mission.

For his part, Rhett gravitated toward the more subtle items. He studied a handful of what looked like small flash-bombs, each no larger than a grape, trying to determine what they were for. He was no closer to working it out when a voice spoke up from behind him.

"Time bombs." The guard, Ronnie, was standing just behind him. "They're not as helpful as you'd think."

Rhett couldn't bite back the small laugh before it escaped him. "Time bombs?" he repeated.

"Yup. Crush one in your hand and you'll get about ten, maybe twelve seconds of time where everything else is frozen—"

Rhett crushed one of the small objects between his fingers. It had felt firm when he was first holding it, but it crumbled when he tightened his grip.

It reminded him of when Porter had paused the recording down in the vault, except that Rhett was the only person in the room to continue moving. Silence fell over him, and a slight stuffiness filled his lungs, as if he was holding his breath against his will. It was a bit like being underwater, or in the part of a dream where he realized that he needed to run, but his muscles strained to obey him. It wasn't *painful* to move, just tedious. Rhett turned his head a fraction to see Fabien holding a massive rifle, then to the other side where Dinah was halfway through pulling a headset on. He could see, and think, and analyze, but he couldn't have lunged at Ronnie if he wanted to.

"—in place," Ronnie finished, as the sound came rushing back. "They're still in development, I think."

Rhett held up a handful of them. "Mind if I take these?"

Ronnie frowned. "Uh, sure."

"I appreciate it. Never know when taking a few seconds to think something over might come in handy. Now, let's say I'm interested in some protection."

Ronnie indicated his partner, Marcus, who was currently

fitting Fabien for what seemed to be a lightweight Kevlar vest. "Like that?"

His first instinct was to nod, but he stopped halfway through. "On second thought, maybe something... lighter?" Rhett shifted his weight so that he could tap the side of his boot with his cane. "I haven't done heavy combat in a long time, and I tend to prefer things with a bit more, hm. *Nuance.*"

Since Rhett's arrival, Ronnie's expression had been bitter and guarded, but his face lit up for the first time. "I've got a couple of things you might like, then. Wait right here." He left Rhett standing alone as he hurried off.

Rhett rolled the time bombs in his palm like marbles, pretending not to listen in on the other conversations. Marcus was explaining the large rifle's settings to Fabien, while Porter was walking Dinah through all the features of her headset. They were so quick to outfit strangers with their tech.

What if one of us had been approached by the Hand? he wondered. *For all they know, we're double agents. If ENIGMA is capable of delivering on promises like the one Porter made me, what might the Hand offer?*

Why trust us at all?

Unless the whole point of this mission is that the three of us are disposable.

"Here you are." Ronnie reappeared with a hip harness in one hand and a long jacket slung over the other. On Rhett's build, it draped like a trenchcoat.

Ronnie helped him into it, which unnecessary but greatly appreciated. Being on his feet so long wouldn't have been an issue, but that little stunt in the mall entrance had done a number on Rhett.

Get it together, Zappotis. You're on a mission. There's no time to whine about aches and pains. Once he got a moment alone, he could down a couple of painkillers and numb the whole thing.

"You seem to be taking this in stride," Ronnie observed, then grimaced at his choice of words. "What I mean, is..."

"I've had odd jobs in the past." Rhett pulled the jacket around him and smoothed out the thin material.

"Odder than this?"

"You'd be surprised." Rhett extended his arms to make sure that the sleeves of the coat wouldn't restrict his movement too much. It was incredibly light and somewhat stretchy, and an unexpectedly perfect fit. The material was silvery-gray, light as silk and breathable as linen, with a soap-bubble sheen to the fabric. "What is this?"

Ronnie grinned. "It's a chameleon coat. If you stand perfectly still for three seconds, you'll blend in with your surroundings. Not completely—it's not like it makes you invisible or anything. You're still a three dimensional object in space, and you'll still cast a shadow and everything, but it works pretty well. I do recommend pulling up the hood when you try it. Otherwise you'll look like a floating head, which is *not* subtle. There are boots and gloves, too. I'll have them sent to the jet for you."

"Interesting." Rhett massaged the lapel. It didn't move like vinyl, but it had a slightly plastic texture beneath the pad of his thumb. "Thank you."

"And this is for you, too." Ronnie held up the pistol.

Rhett took it from his gingerly. It looked less like a gun and more like a handheld massager, like the one Zoe had gotten him for Christmas a few years ago that was currently stashed in the storage unit along with everything else Rhett never used but couldn't bring himself to throw away.

"Is this for my leg?" he asked.

Ronnie snorted. "Hardly. You'd hurt yourself pretty badly if you used it on yourself. If you're up close and personal with an opponent, press it against them and fire." He smirked and jerked his head toward Fabien. "Remember when he got knocked on his ass earlier? Well, this'll do worse, and it'll hurt like hell, too."

Rhett chuckled to himself. "Maybe I should use it on him as a trial run."

Ronnie rolled his eyes and sighed wistfully. "*Please.*"

It was easy enough to get the harness in place around his hips and thighs. When he was done, between his everyday clothes—God, he still reeked of airport—and the jacket and the harness, he looked quite absurd. Rhett stared down at himself in dismay, and only realized how still he'd been when his legs suddenly vanished, leaving only a pair of boots behind. The rest of him quite suddenly became the color of the floor.

Rhett yelped, then laughed at himself for forgetting. "You weren't lying about the coat."

"No, he was not." Porter was only a few paces away, evidently waiting for their conversation to end. "I took the liberty of having something special made for you, by the way." He was holding a cane in both hands, and when Rhett turned to him, he offered it with a gravitas that suggested it was more than it seemed.

Rhett took it from him and held it up for inspection. The knob handle tapered slightly so that it could be held either like a cane or more upright like a sword. At first, he thought that indicated that it might come apart, like a sword cane perhaps, but the smooth exterior was one solid piece, and didn't appear to be something that could disassemble.

"Am I just supposed to use this as a club?" he asked.

"You could, in a pinch. It's quite durable. There are other factors to recommend it, though. May I?" When he passed it back to him, Porter showed a small depression in the handle. "Pressing this with your thumb will—" He demonstrated, and the length of the cane began to hum. Sparks jumped along its length. "—will reveal its hidden properties," he finished.

Rhett took it back and studied it. "And it won't fry me by accident?"

"It's quite safe, so long as you handle it properly." Porter pivoted on one foot, and Rhett realized that the others were waiting for him. He slipped the handful of time bombs into one of the chameleon coat's large pockets and squared his shoulders.

"I trust we are all ready," Porter said, "and time is of the essence. Are you all ready to begin?"

Rhett nodded, and the others did as well.

As ready as I'm going to get, he amended, *without having the whole story.* If there was anything he'd learned over the years, however, it was that men handing out odd jobs to people they barely knew weren't in the market for uncomfortable questions. Porter had work that needed to be done, and he'd offered to pay them handsomely enough. Whether or not he really was one of the good guys didn't matter. What mattered was that he had something Rhett wanted.

And given everything Rhett had seen, between the vault and the armory, he was starting to think that Porter was capable of delivering on miracles after all.

ALL THAT TIME indoors and underground had thrown off Rhett's sense of time. He was surprised to find that, when Porter and the guards led them to the mall roof, it was still light outside. Dusk was approaching as the sun fell toward the western horizon.

Rhett covered his eyes and stared out across the empty parking lot toward the barren field beyond. It was dinnertime in California. He hadn't given Zoe much of an explanation when he left, and the kids were probably wondering where he'd gone. Kosta and Anna liked him a lot more than Cliff did, and even he had more patience for his antics than Zoe.

He'd sent a text before he boarded his flight, and his phone had been off ever since. He'd left it in a locker, along with his old cane. Dinah had been forced to leave her luggage, too. Only Fabien hadn't been carrying anything with him when he arrived.

Other than his gun, of course. He still had it, along with his new toys. He hadn't said a word to Rhett since they'd left the vault.

The small silver aircraft waiting for them on the roof resembled a jet, although according to Porter, it was self-manned.

"No need for pilots," he explained. "We can handle any issues remotely."

Dinah didn't seem convinced, but Rhett only nodded. Fabien didn't even listen to the explanation before boarding.

"Good luck," Porter told them. Behind his back, Ronnie and Marcus stood at attention, although Ronnie did smile briefly when Rhett caught his eye.

"See you on the other side," Rhett told Porter, before slipping through the door of the jet. Dinah followed.

True to Ronnie's word, the boots and the gloves that matched the chameleon coat were waiting in the jet. Rhett busied himself with changing into them while the door of the jet slid closed. Dinah settled in the seat across from him as the engine hummed to life.

It was only a matter of moments before they took off for unknown territory, leaving the ground, and the vault, behind.

9 DINAH

SILENCE WAS, in Dinah's opinion, only good for two things.

First, it allowed her to focus while she was meant to be studying, or reading, or writing papers, or *grading* papers, or occupying her mind in some significant and productive way. This was highly desirable, and often necessary when it came to her work.

The other option was much less desirable: silence made her extremely, paralyzingly, and uselessly nervous. Silence was the long stretch of time spent at faculty parties while she tried to decide who to approach and what to say to them when she did. Silence was the awkward pause after she called someone to pay a bill and accidentally told them *I love you* rather than *Thanks, and have a good one*. Silence was sitting in front of a cooling cup of coffee while the fellow PhD student she sort of, maybe, *definitely* liked looked for the words that would most politely communicate that he wasn't similarly interested in her and never would be.

Put bluntly, silence was a bitch, and Dinah hated it. And yet, for reasons she could never quite articulate, she was terrible at ending it.

Which was why she had been sitting in her seat on the jet for approximately the last two hours trying to think of something to say.

Her companions hadn't seemed bothered by it. Rhett had taken some pills from a bottle he'd slipped into his pocket and then stared out the window. He was still staring. What could possibly be down there that was worth looking at for so long?

Fabien, on the other hand, had been constantly in motion. He'd examined the cockpit for ages, and was still making his way systematically through the aircraft, studying each detail. The seams of the interior panels. The vents for the AC. The lights. The seats. The little dining area. To Dinah, it looked like the sort of posh but efficient interior one might expect from a private jet—not that she had any experience with those, but still, she had expectations. Fabien was going over the whole place with a fine-toothed comb, and Dinah couldn't for the life of her work out why.

In the end, it was Rhett who spoke up first. "What are you doing?" he asked. He was still sitting with his elbow on the arm rest, his chin on his palm, gazing downward. They were approaching the coast, and a wide stretch of sea was just coming into view along the horizon.

"Checking for..." Fabien twisted around to face them and mouthed a word that Dinah couldn't make out.

"What?" she asked.

Fabien shot her a disapproving glance.

"Bugs," Rhett said, unmoving. "He's looking for bugs."

Fabien's head whipped toward him. "You can't just *say* that!" he snapped.

"Of course I can, because the jet *is* bugged, and I guarantee you that Porter or whoever's watching the feed just saw you mouth the word anyway. They're in the entertainment consoles, by the way."

Fabien scoffed. "They're not even on!"

"The consoles aren't," Rhett told him. "But I promise you there are more sensors down there than that kind of screen needs. One of them's an out-feed. Also, if they're smart, they'll have bugged the headrests for audio, where it'll be clearest."

Fabien hurried over to investigate the TV, muttering curses to himself in French. Dinah couldn't tell what he was looking at, but evidently Fabien knew what he was after, because he swore again. "Why didn't you say so earlier?"

"Because there's no point." Rhett didn't seem the least bit bothered by it. "I'm sure they have tech you and I wouldn't even recognize as such. We'll never find it all."

It hurt Dinah, irrationally, to be left out of the conversation. She was young. She knew about tech. Maybe she could be helpful. Besides, with the headset, she might be able to get a leg up on them.

She was tempted to point this out, but Fabien spoke first. "What are *you* looking for, then?"

"Watching our trajectory." At last, Rhett lowered his arm and turned away from the window. "Porter told us that we're being transported to another vault, but he didn't say where. I was wondering if I could figure out where he's sending us, but all I can tell you is that we're headed east. That's New York down there, and I'm not going to be able to learn much by watching the ocean."

"So we're headed almost directly east." Fabien did the thing with his thumb again, rubbing it over his bottom lip. Dinah wondered if he even realized he was doing it. "Hmm. Maybe he's sending us to Europe, then?"

"Maybe, but there's no point in speculating just yet." Rhett leaned back in his chair, examining each of them in turn with the same intensity with which he'd stared out of the window. "So. What did Porter offer you?"

Fabien scoffed. "As if I'd tell you. We've just met."

"Hmm." Rhett's gaze shifted to Dinah. "I suppose you won't want to discuss your offer, either."

"Erm—" Dinah fidgeted in her seat. She couldn't think of any reason not to tell, but the fact that Fabien was being so defensive made her wonder if she was being foolish for even considering it.

"Fair enough," Rhett sighed, misinterpreting her discomfort. "I don't particularly want to talk about my offer, either. But I do have to ask." He leaned forward, and his pale eyes sparked with mischief. "Do you think that round table in the vault was, you know...?"

Dinah stared at him.

Rhett's eyebrows rose higher. "*The* Round Table?"

"Oh, goodness." Dinah slumped in her seat. "I wasn't even thinking." She tilted her head toward Fabien. "You *bench-pressed* the *Round Table*."

"Come on, now." Fabien clicked his tongue. "That's reaching, don't you think?" He was about to say something else when the jet shuddered and began to list to one side.

Dinah grabbed the armrests and braced herself for impact, although they were still high over the ocean. "What was that?"

"Don't know." Fabien shot to his feet, but when the jet shuddered again, he was sent toppling sideways. He had to catch himself on the table across the aisle.

"Interference?" Rhett asked. His olive complexion had taken on a greenish undertone. "Supposedly they're controlling this thing from the ground, but I—"

The jet lurched again. Dinah shrieked as it slowed, tipped nose-down, and plummeted toward the sea.

10 FABIEN

I SHOULD NEVER HAVE BOARDED *this damn ship,* Fabien thought bitterly as he tried to regain his footing. *I should have shot Porter the moment he turned up in the hotel room.* At the time, he'd been worried what would happen if he did so—after all, if Porter could find him, there must be other people who could find him, too. Now, he figured that he probably would have been better off if he'd just shot the man then and there and saved himself the trouble.

They were going to end up dead either way, and it was all because ENIGMA used some stupid remote jet whose power had been knocked out over the ocean.

Behind him, Rhett was swearing, and Dinah had curled up like a helpless shrimp, muttering to herself in low and incomprehensible tones. If they weren't on a mission together, Fabien might have felt sorry for her. As it stood, he was only angry that he'd been paired up with such a sorry excuse for backup.

Rather than carrying them all on a slow swan dive beneath the breakers, however, the jet shifted again. The nose tilted upright, almost as if some unseen hand was trying to overcompensate for a shift in weight. As the floor beneath his feet evened out, Fabien staggered up to the empty cockpit. He'd already given it a thorough examination earlier, in large part because he didn't trust the remote flight capabilities.

He'd been expecting to find a small fire, or a shower of sparks to rival that symbol of American wilderness, Old Faithful. Instead, what he found was much more disturbing: a series of dents in the wall of the cockpit, as though something had collided with the exterior wall at a ninety-degree angle. Something round.

"Rhett?" he called. "Dinah? I think we might be in..."

He was going to say *trouble*, but the word died on his lips as his prediction was confirmed. The wall danced with blue light, and before his very eyes, a man stepped through.

Porter had shown them the recording of Apollo's incursion into the vault only hours before. Fabien hadn't trusted it; after all, an image was easy to fake.

If *this* was a fake, however, it did a great deal more to fool his senses: from the rush of wind to the subtle shift in cabin pressure to the fact that he could see all the way through Apollo into the little podlike craft that was now fastened onto the side of the jet. That explained the crash and the shift in their trajectory, and at the same time it explained nothing at all because *a man had just walked through the wall*. Porter's projector hadn't captured the full range of sensory overload that came with witnessing the impossible in real life. There was even a bright scent of hot metal and a faint whiff of ozone that followed Apollo into the cockpit, all of it adding up to form the proof of what Fabien's rational mind wanted to dismiss. The world was not as he'd thought it was.

His astonishment paralyzed him for a full two seconds, during which Apollo passed fully through the wall. The blue light around him died, leaving only his gold metal skin, as solid and tangible as anything else onboard the craft.

Stop staring, Fabien told himself. *Porter said he can't hurt you when he's intangible, but you saw what he did to that guard. If you don't want to get your face melted, you'd better move fast.*

He ducked just as Apollo reached for his gun.

For the most part, Fabien liked to keep his combat long-distance. It was safer that way, to move through the shadows and cover his face. Most of his targets didn't get the chance to fight back. By the time the recoil settled in his hand, they were already dead.

Still, that wasn't the *only* way he knew how to fight. Apollo's gun was barely in his hand before Fabien came in swinging. With all that metal armor, he wouldn't be able to land a good hit, but he might be able to get the man pinned.

Apollo was bigger, but Fabien was fast. He caught Apollo by the wrist and twisted the other man's arm behind his back. After a brief tussle, he was able to drive the agent's chest against the wall between the cockpit and the cabin, with his own weight holding the man in place. Apollo didn't have enough room to get any momentum going, and his leverage was stunted by the placement of Fabien's feet.

"Got you," Fabien hissed.

Apollo spoke, although he must have had a voice scrambled built into that helmet of his, because his voice came out low and tinny when he asked, "Do you?"

Then he pitched forward through the wall, dragging Fabien along with him.

Fabien's skin tingled as they went, and a rushing whine built in his ears, somewhere between static and the roar of the ocean trapped in a seashell. He opened his mouth to cry out, but the whine built, along with the watery *thu-thump* of his own heart.

They seemed to be falling in slow motion. Even before he was all the way through the wall, he could see through Apollo and into the cabin. Dinah was staring at them, her mouth open in disbelief, her hands still clenched on the arms of her seat.

Rhett had vanished.

Then they were through the wall, and Apollo made them solid again. Fabien landed hard, striking his chin against the floor with such force that his teeth rattled.

The gun that Marcus had given him had been leaning against the wall. When the jet started to go down, it had slid forward and gotten tangled up in the legs of the chairs. *Should have been carrying it,* he thought, but he hadn't believed that he'd need it in midair. He'd been too focused on searching for wires and bugs.

Now he tried to reach for it, but Apollo brought his boot down hard on Fabien's wrist. His bones creaked beneath the sole, and he bit his tongue to stifle a groan of pain. That small hurt was forgotten a moment later when Apollo dropped to one knee, driving his full armored weight into Fabien's kidneys.

For a moment, his vision went black as Apollo rose again and kicked him onto his back. Black and red star clusters danced across his vision.

Apollo drew the pistol from his belt.

The pistol was unlike any Fabien had seen before, with a round mouth like a blunderbuss, too wide for any caliber of ammo Fabien had ever used. He thought of the guard, writhing in pain as the flesh melted away from his skull.

This is it, he thought. *Dinah won't help me, and Rhett's gone. I'm going to get my face melted off by a man dressed like C-3PO, and I'll never—*

And then, quite suddenly, Rhett was there, rising from his seat in a single smooth movement. He'd pulled his hood up so that it obscured his face.

The chameleon coat, Fabien realized. Rhett hadn't vanished. He'd blended in.

The black pistol Rhett had chosen was already in his hands. He reached Apollo, pressed the rounded end of the handgun between his shoulder blades, and pulled the trigger.

Visions of the jet's demise flashed before his eyes: a hole blown through the siding, so large that it sucked Apollo through before taking the rest of them with it.

Instead, Apollo was thrown against the far wall with such force that he went limp with the impact.

"Thanks," Fabien wheezed.

"Anytime." Rather than reach to help him up, Rhett spun toward Dinah. "Cockpit. Now."

Dinah recoiled from him. "Why?"

"Because we need you to see if you can figure out how to keep us in the air, even if the remote controls go down."

Dinah sputtered helplessly and flailed her arms. "I don't know the first thing about how to—"

"You don't need to." Rhett pointed to her headset. "Can't you pull up the manual on that gadget of yours?"

"Oh." Dinah raised one hand to touch the ENGIMA headset. "Maybe."

"Either use the headset, or trade Fabien for the rifle," Rhett barked.

Fabien hadn't approved this message, and he certainly wasn't about to hand his rifle over to Dinah, but the threat worked. Dinah scrambled to her feet and bolted toward the cockpit so fast, it was a wonder she didn't leave a dust cloud in her wake.

Apollo was already moving, so Fabien made a swipe for his rifle. *I'm never leaving this behind again,* he thought as he braced himself against the table in the little dining space. *This is sleeping with me.*

There were three manual settings on the rifle: stun, laser, and live rounds. According to Marcus, the live rounds were the most deadly, but the laser never ran out of ammo.

With some reluctance, he clicked the switch to stun and locked it. The more he damaged the jet, the more danger they would be in. Besides, if they could stun Apollo and restrain him, ENIGMA might be able to determine his identity and stop... whatever he was up to. None of that was Fabien's business. His job would be done.

To his immense frustration, Apollo's body shimmered blue and translucent just as he took aim. *What keeps him from falling through the floor of the jet?* Fabien wondered. *Or sinking into the floor of the vault as he robbed it?*

With a bit of tech like that, Fabien could do his own job with astonishing accuracy and very little fanfare. If they did manage to subdue Apollo, perhaps that clever little device of his could get conveniently 'lost' in the process.

Fabien fired two pulses anyway, just to be sure. With each blast, the rifle kicked in his hands. The air between himself and Apollo rippled silver, like heat rising from tarmac on a summer day, and the jet wall behind Apollo bowed outward.

The mask hid the agent's face, but Fabien was certain he was grinning. Taunting them.

"Nice try," Apollo growled.

He lunged forward, resolidifying alongside the gun. He bashed it aside with one arm, only to choke when Rhett clotheslined him with a swing of his cane. The agent fell back, clutching at his throat, his limbs spasming with the electric charge it carried.

Rhett plunged again, driving the top of his cane forward like a sword, but by the time it reached him, Apollo was intangible once more. He ducked away from Rhett's blow even as he swung his fist toward Rhett's temple.

The impact was a bloody mess. Rhett's eyes sprang wide as Apollo's metal-clad knuckles met his face, and his head snapped sideways with such force that Fabien feared his neck was broken. He let out a choking cough as he collapsed.

Apollo ignored Fabien and strode back toward the wall he and Fabien had tumbled through. Fabien scrambled forward and pressed his fingers to Rhett's throat. To his relief, he was still breathing, although the wound in his head was oozing blood at an alarming rate.

In one last attempt to slow Apollo, Fabien fired at the man's retreating back.

His timing couldn't have been worse. Apollo was already stepping through the wall to the cockpit, where Dinah was bent over the controls.

Fabien wasn't thinking about the physics of it. All he was thinking was, *I have to stop Apollo.*

He fired; Apollo, moving through the wall, had opened up a space through the wall toward Dinah; and the latter, no longer protected by the physical barrier of the wall, flopped sideways like a fish out of water. She hit the ground in a boneless heap.

And then, quite abruptly, Fabien was staring at a blank wall, through which he could not give chase.

He swore to himself as he turned and bounded over Rhett's fallen form. He'd been so confident when Marcus gave him the gun, fully aware of the advantages it provided him, that he hadn't stopped to think about all the advantages Apollo had, too.

A blast of gunfire erupted from the cockpit before Fabien could reach it. He braced for the sight of Dinah's melted flesh, and was momentarily relieved to find that Apollo had turned his weapon on the jet's controls instead.

The jet shuddered and resumed its reckless descent with a heap of dripping plastic and twisted metal where its manual controls had been. Apollo barely spared them a glance before darting through the outer wall, back into his own ship.

"Son of a bitch!" Fabien screamed. He flung himself after the enemy agent and collided with the wall for his troubles. He snarled. Screamed. Beat his fists against the plastic lining.

All to no avail. The jet spun sideways as Apollo's craft detached, leaving them in freefall as they plummeted toward the sea.

How did he find us? Fabien wondered. Had Apollo been tracking them since takeoff? Or did he have one of those maps, like the one Porter had shown them? Because it seemed awfully convenient that he should find them so quickly…

Apollo's one-man vessel sailed off through the sky, even as the vast expanse of empty ocean rose to fill the glass. Fabien squeezed his eyes shut, thinking of all the promises he'd be breaking by dying now, out in the middle of nowhere, in the service of people who didn't care about him.

He felt the jet shift again, and opened his eyes. Instead of water, sky again filled the cockpit window. Some automated system, he thought absently, had come back online and raised the nose. Perhaps it had been a mistake for Apollo to destroy the controls. It seemed to have freed the plane from its dive. But the reprieve lasted only a moment before gravity overcame the efforts of the jet and water once again dominated the cockpit view.

He should have cut a deal with Porter, told the man where to wire a severance fee in the event of his death.

Je suis désolée, he thought. *I'm so sorry.*

Then the world was nothing more than crumpled plastic and

shattered glass and a rush of water rising up to fill the cockpit. Dinah was swept away, and Fabien would have been, too, if he hadn't been holding on to the captain's chair for dear life. He rose up, buoyed by the water.

His last conscious thought, before the ocean overpowered him, was that he should have let someone else die for Porter's cause.

11 RHETT

"KELLY!" *he cried, yanking open the door of their battered one-room house.* "We've been found out. They got Afique. We need to go."

Kelly shook her head. "Nobody's answering, Rhett." *She held up her phone, showing him the list of calls.*

Rhett grabbed his own cell. "I've got a connection," *he said, already scrolling through his contacts. He tried Abdul first.* "See? It's ringing."

"Rhett."

He turned his back on Kelly and waited for Abdul to pick up. It rang through to voicemail, and he hung up before the robotic voice could finish telling him to leave a message. Fine, then, Abdul wasn't answering? He'd try Mazin.

"Rhett," *Kelly repeated.*

"Hush." *Rhett held up his free hand. He'd try Nasif next. Then Amira, just in case. Someone had to answer. One of them had to. Because if they didn't...*

"Rhett." *Kelly put her hand on his shoulder. The phone was still ringing. He couldn't put it down. Mazin was going to answer, and they were going to get out before anything worse happened. Before anyone else was taken.*

Kelly squeezed his shoulder until he turned, letting the arm holding the phone go slack. She was smiling that same patient smile, the one he'd gotten to know over the last six months, the one she always wore, even when things were bad. Her cheeks were sunburned. Her forehead was peeling. She looked the same as every other day.

This couldn't be happening.

"Rhett," she said, one last time. "Nobody's answering."

He'd known what she meant the first time she said it, but he couldn't believe it. Wouldn't believe it.

She wanted to tell him something. He knew she did. The words hung in the air, unspoken, thick between them. The silence was so potent, he could barely breathe.

She didn't speak.

She never did.

There wasn't time.

The walls of the house opened up, tearing at the seams until the light came in, a deluge of desert daylight...

Water. Saltwater. He could have sworn that he remembered the sky, a cloudless blue partly obscured by the ruddy desert dust and bits of plaster. Instead of heat and light, Rhett was enveloped in a deep blue darkness that dragged him down.

And down.

And down.

―――

HE SAT UPRIGHT, gasping for breath, even though the air was plentiful. His mouth was dry.

For a few seconds, he wondered why his head hurt more badly than his leg. Hadn't he just been with Kelly? He could have sworn she was right there.

Instead, he found himself face-to-face with a short, curvy woman in a white coat, who boasted an abundance of curly black hair. The woman raised one eyebrow.

"So," she said, in a voice tinged with an unfamiliar accent, "you're awake."

"I am." Rhett swung his legs over the edge of the bed. The room was the size of an ordinary hospital ward, complete with an adjustable cot and sleek, softly-beeping machines. Sitting upright took its toll. His head throbbed, and he let out a hiss of pain, but when he lifted his hand to his temple, there was no blood. No bandages, even. Only a small patch where his head had been partly shaven.

"We got you all patched up." The woman scribbled something on her clipboard.

Rhett frowned. "Wouldn't *patching up* imply that there was something broken?" He prodded his temple a little more firmly. The ache persisted, but poking it didn't seem to make a difference.

The woman smirked. "See? That's how good a job we do. So fixed, you'd never know it was broken in the first place." She made one final note, then set her clipboard aside. "I'm guessing you're no stranger to this sort of thing, huh?"

Rhett closed his eyes. "What sort of thing?" Damn, did he have a concussion? What was wrong with his *head*?

"Waking up in strange hospitals." The woman crossed her arms and leaned one full hip against Rhett's cot. "'Cuz most people in your shoes would be freaking out right now."

"It... happens." He was thinking of Kelly.

"Your friends are fine, in case you were worried."

Rhett hadn't been, if only because he hadn't been thinking

about his companions at all. It came back to him suddenly: Porter, the mission, the jet. The blow to his temple, which was the last thing he remembered before he'd been back in that house with a woman he could never speak to again.

"Oh," he murmured. "Thank you." His hand dropped into his lap and he sat there, frowning. "Where are we? And who are you?" For all he knew, they'd been scooped up by a military vessel. Or worse, what if this woman worked for the Hand? Rhett had played his part in plenty of missions where he'd played the good cop, sometimes even the honey pot, in an attempt to break down an enemy agent. He wouldn't put it past this woman to say, *Rhett, I've helped you, and now it's your turn to help me...*

Instead, the stranger tapped her pen against her chin in thought. "That second question is easier to answer. I'm Doctor Cecília Moniz. As for where you are, that'll take some explanation. I'll introduce you to Captain Correia. He'll explain everything."

"Captain," Rhett repeated. "So this is a military facility? What branch?"

Dr. Moniz snorted. "Of course not. I work for ENIGMA. You weren't that far away when your jet went down, and we were able to get to you in time. Although we lost Apollo, *of course.*" Dr. Moniz wrinkled her nose in annoyance.

"Oh." Rhett bit the inside of his cheek as he reevaluated Dr. Moniz. He'd thought that the woman might be Brazilian, but maybe she was Portuguese...? Although they had been a long way from Portugal when the jet crashed, assuming the jet went down shortly after he was hit.

Dr. Moniz waved her hand as if swatting flies. "It's obvious that you don't believe me. Or, at the very least, that you don't trust me."

"If you were with the Hand, telling me that you work for

ENIGMA would be a smart move," Rhett said. "I wouldn't know whether to believe you or not."

Dr. Moniz's answering bellow of laughter nearly shook the walls. "Oh, I *like* you. Tell you what, why don't you get dressed, and I'll take you up to see Captain Correia. Let him try and talk to you. Sound good?"

Rhett nodded, and Dr. Moniz turned on her heel. She stopped just long enough to wave to the little mound of neatly-folded clothes waiting on the seat of the chair just beside the door.

They weren't all Rhett's clothes. The chameleon coat and its accessories were there, along with his pressure pistol, its hip holster, and the cane Porter had given him. When he slipped his hand into the coat pocket, he found the time bombs undamaged. Hopefully getting them wet wouldn't negate their effects, if and when he got a chance to use them.

The rest of his everyday clothing, however, was gone. His knee brace sat on top of a dark uniform that, when he went to lift it, nearly slithered through his fingers.

Rhett held it up, bemused by the cap sleeves and the short leggings that would reach perhaps midway down his thighs. It was a diving skin.

The rest of the clothes matched: there was a zip-up shirt cut from what felt like neoprene, although it breathed more easily, and was far lighter. There was also a pair of neoprene leggings, cut to a size that fit him perfectly, even over the brace. Impressive. Given his height, he usually had trouble finding things that fit him and didn't have an extra inch or two.

When he was done, he stepped through the door after Dr. Moniz. "For the record, I think I might believe you now, since you left me my weap—"

He stopped short, with his empty hand still on the doorknob.

Dr. Moniz was standing with her back to Rhett, hands clasped behind her, staring out through a glass wall that reached all the way from the floor to the ceiling. The lights from the hallway in which they both stood reflected off the glass, but in the dark expanse beyond, thousands of tiny silver lights swirled and danced.

"Are we..." Rhett took a tentative step forward, then another, until his hand rested against the glass. It was cool to the touch, and very thick; when he looked from just the right angle, he could see that an inch or more of it stood between him and the darkness. "Are we in space?"

"Underwater." Dr. Moniz smiled up at the spinning lights. "Marvelous, isn't it?"

Truly, it was. Over the course of his life, Rhett had seen wonders that stole his breath and horrors that threatened to bury him under their weight, but nothing quite like this. The darkness seemed to go on forever, and the creatures within it moved through their tiny lives without the smallest sense of humanity's comings and goings.

"What are they?" he asked.

"Plankton, mostly." Dr. Moniz pressed one finger to the glass. "But there are jellies out there, too. This is a good night for them; there usually aren't so many."

Rhett dragged his eyes away from the glass and made himself turn back to the corridor. It was a normal height, roughly eight feet, but the outer walls were slightly curved. The glass wasn't set into the wall; it *was* the wall, reinforced at intervals with curving steel ribs.

"Like it?" Dr. Moniz grinned and drummed her fingernails against the glass. "I'll tell you what, the bureaucracy wears on me sometimes, but I never get tired of the view."

Rhett tried to imagine what the building looked like from the outside. Or perhaps, the ship. Was it a ship? If so, it wasn't shaped like anything he'd seen before.

"This way." Dr. Moniz waved down the corridor. "I'll take you topside, and you can get a better view."

Rhett followed her, still watching the creatures that danced and undulated in the depths beyond. He'd accompanied Anna and Kosta to the Monterey Bay aquarium the summer before, and the thought of Anna's squealing delight made him smile.

There was an elevator at the end of the corridor, although it didn't require the same intense level of security that Porter's vault had, just a simple badge swipe. Rhett stared at the buttons on the control panel: twenty-eight floors. They were on floor twenty-three. Dr. Moniz jabbed her thumb at the one that said *D*. Beside it, a printed label clarified, *Topside Deck/Gardens*.

Instead of going down, as he'd expected, they rose. The elevator still allowed them a view of the outside, and with each floor, there were fewer plankton outside, and a bit more light.

On floor two, they broke the surface of the water, and Rhett gasped. They were, as he'd suspected, in the middle of the ocean. The water was rough, but the ship barely moved as the waves lapped its glass hull. Above them, the moon was a full disc of silver in the night sky.

They reached the deck at last, and the elevator door opened to reveal a sprawling garden beneath an immense geodesic dome, a greenhouse at sea.

"It's lovely." He craned his neck back, as entranced with the garden and the greenhouse structure as he had been with the life below the waves.

"Like I said, it's kind of hard to explain until you see it." Dr. Moniz followed him out, leading Rhett down the paths between the raised garden beds. "But now you have, so I can officially say it." She spread her arms wide and beamed. "Welcome to Atlantis."

12 DINAH

DINAH AND FABIEN had been waiting in the garden for a long time.

"Do they mean to keep us here indefinitely?" Fabien asked. He was walking around the otherwise empty table, as he had been for the last half hour, ever since one of the crewmembers had deposited them here and told them that the captain would be along shortly.

It said something about everything they'd seen so far that it had taken Dinah some time to work out that *Atlantis* was a codename and that this was not, in fact, *the actual mythical place.* Fabien had rolled his eyes when she'd admitted as much.

"It looks like you can leave whenever you want," Dinah said. She was more worried about Rhett than about being left unattended, to be perfectly frank.

Fabien snorted. "And go where? Can't leave the deck without a badge, and in case you haven't noticed, we're in the middle of the ocean. We are, quite literally, stranded here. So unless you believe that I can swim all the way to the coast, I think we can agree that our options are limited."

"I don't know why you're getting mad," Dinah told him. "After all, you're the one who shot *me*."

"On accident!" Fabien stopped pacing and threw his hands in the air. "How was I to know that the wall wouldn't stop the shot? You wouldn't have known it, either, unless your fancy headset told you."

"I was in the middle of teaching myself how to fly a jet," Dinah retorted. "I don't think it's too much to expect you to know how to fire a gun, given that it's your *literal job*." She scooted her chair at an angle so that she wouldn't have to look at Fabien anymore.

"Come on, now." Fabien stomped over so that he stood in Dinah's line of sight. "You can't expect me to do everything. It's obvious that I'm the most experienced member of this little crew—"

"It's not obvious to *me*," Dinah spat. "Since, as we were just discussing, *you shot me in the back*."

"I stunned you," Fabien corrected. "It's different."

Dinah rolled her eyes, got to her feet, and turned her chair away from Fabien again. The man was the worst. Besides, if anyone was going to be in charge, it should be Rhett. He had been calm under fire, he'd saved Fabien's sorry hide, and he'd taken one for the team, rather than shooting one *of* the team.

If it came down to a vote, she'd be voting for Rhett. She had no illusions about her own leadership qualities, and her combat qualities were nonexistent. At some point, she'd be useful. She hoped. Porter seemed to think so.

Not that she was feeling particularly charitable toward Porter at the moment, either.

Fabien resumed his pacing, and in his irritation, he nearly plowed headfirst into the doctor who'd looked them over when they first arrived. She appeared as if from nowhere, between a raised bed bristling with greens and another overflowing with squash vines. Corn stalks grew upright from the beds, and Dinah was pretty sure there were beans in there somewhere, too.

When she saw the person walking behind Dr. Moniz, she got to her feet. "Rhett!"

Fabien darted over to him and immediately began touching his face.

Rhett swatted his hand. "Do you mind?"

Fabien stepped back, frowning. "It looks good. Better than I would expect."

"We have good tech." Dr. Moniz dropped into one of the empty chairs. "The captain isn't up here yet?"

"No." Fabien huffed his displeasure. "We've been abandoned."

Rhett was touching his temple again, almost absently, as if he didn't realize what he was doing.

"That's unusual." Dr. Moniz pursed her lips and kicked her feet up onto the supports beneath the table.

The light fixtures on the metal struts above them were illuminated, as were the lights that lined the walking paths between the garden beds. Beyond that, the other plots were illuminated only by moonlight. A cool breeze wafted in across the water, which must mean that there was ventilation of some kind coming through the upper deck. Now that they had proof of Rhett's safety, Dinah allowed herself to relax and appreciate the beauty of the floating city.

"How does all this work?" she asked.

Dr. Moniz leaned back in her chair with her arms folded behind her head and peered up at the moon. "You mean, how is it powered? We've got a built-in hydroelectric system, an underwater seaweed garden, and a jellyfish farm for protein. Although you'd be surprised how much protein you can get from plants, too. What we don't use gets composted for the garden beds." She waved a hand to the rows of planters. "We've got a state-of-the-art rain collection system and an industrial-grade desalination tank."

"It's quite the setup," Dinah said.

Dr. Moniz nodded. "Only downside is that we don't make landfall, transport's restricted on account of the resources involved, and we mostly work in eight-month shifts, so some people start to get on your nerves after a while. Doesn't leave a lot of time for much else, but I don't mind. I like it out here."

"Is all this built just for the vault?" Rhett asked.

Dr. Moniz chuckled. "No way. It started out that way, though. Now we're also running tests on new equipment. Captain Correia swears that everyone's going to live in a place like this someday, all things considered. Even make our own uniforms out of seaweed pulp and protein chains. We're running at almost zero waste, except for personnel exchanges and emergencies."

The tread of boots along the walkway made all of them jump. Rhett reached for his pistol, and Fabien's hand twitched toward the rifle slung over his shoulder. Only Dr. Moniz seemed unconcerned, although she did get up from her chair.

A man strode across the deck toward them with his chin held high and his hands clasped behind his back. Dinah was first aware of his height, then of his girth: the person's presence was intimidating, and although he was heavy, it was clear that he could have bench-pressed her without so much as breaking a sweat. His black hair was combed back from his brow, while his chin was indiscernible beneath his thick beard. His black eyes blazed in the moonlight, visible well before he reached them and the well-lit area in which they stood. He had to be the captain. Even without the formality of a uniform, everything from his posture to the set of his shoulders made it clear that they were in his space.

In another lifetime, he might have been a pirate. Dr. Moniz

could easily be mistaken for an Army field doctor, but Correia would never be seen as a military man. There was too much wildness in him.

He moved between the rows of okra and sunflowers, and came to a stop a few strides away.

Dr. Moniz dipped her head. "Captain."

"Doctor," he replied, although he was staring at Fabien when he said it. His heavy brows were pulled low over his beady eyes.

Should I bow? Dinah wondered. *Or salute?* Surely she should do something other than just stand there and stare.

Correia shook his head slightly. "You're late," he told them.

Fabien bristled. "Actually, you're the one who kept us waiting. We've been waiting for you for the better part of an hour—"

Correia held up one hand to silence him. The big man strode to the nearest chair and dropped into it with a sigh. "I'm not accusing you of wasting my time," he said. "I'm telling you that I know why Porter sent you here, and you're too late. Apollo has already come and gone." He unclipped a small screen from his belt and tossed it face-up onto the table. "He removed five items from the vault."

Rhett and Dinah exchanged a worried glance, while Fabien reached for the little tablet. It was the size of a smartphone, but when he touched the screen, a 3D image of an amulet popped up, along with a scrolling text description.

"At least you've cataloged what you've got here," Fabien muttered.

"Doesn't Porter?" Captain Correia shook his head. "I wish I could say I was surprised. Porter's always been wary of keeping a database, but at least we know what we lost." He scrubbed his hand across his face and tugged his beard. "Not that it helps. Hands of the Sun, walking through walls... never thought I'd see the day. I wonder where they came up with that. According to the security footage, he walked right through the side of the ship. How are we supposed to stop a person who can pull a trick like that?"

Fabien shook his head. "I wish I knew."

Dr. Moniz fiddled with a curl of her hair. "Does this mean that he's likely to target other vaults?"

"I'm not even sure what he's after." Correia waved a hand in the general direction of the tablet. "He could have taken anything, but he took… trinkets. Objects of minimal value. I'm not sure why he even bothered."

"Why bother protecting useless things?" Fabien asked.

Correia opened his mouth to reply, but Dinah got there first. "Weren't you listening during Porter's whole speech? The vaults were built to protect historical items—even things that don't have obvious power are still valuable, from a cultural standpoint. Right?" She nodded to Correia.

The captain offered her a weary smile. "Precisely. The Hand is a small organization, even smaller than we are, only a few dozen people across the globe, although they're more influential than I'd like to admit. In the past, they've attempted to target individual vaults. We're prepared to fight off an attack, but this new device that allows them to come and go as they please… it's a disaster."

Dr. Moniz cocked her head. "And they're using it to steal junk?"

"Unless those trinkets are more useful than you think," Rhett pointed out. "Maybe they've discovered a new purpose for them."

"I know how to find out." Fabien shoved the tablet under Dinah's nose.

"If ENIGMA doesn't know the value of an item, the headset won't," Dinah warned him.

"Forget the headset," Fabien said. "Isn't that the whole point in bringing you along? You're an egghead. You know things. So figure it out."

Dinah stared at him for a moment, then glanced around the table. All of them were staring at her.

She scratched the back of her neck. "Fair enough," she said. "I'll see what I can figure out." Although, if ENIGMA couldn't figure out the significance of what the Hand was after, she couldn't begin to imagine why she would be able to make heads or tails of anything.

INTERLUDE

Apollo looked down at the handful of items he'd retrieved from the maritime vault. It had been almost painfully easy to sneak in while the crew was preoccupied with rescuing the personnel aboard the jet.

It was annoying to hear that they'd survived—ideally, the crash would have killed at least *one* of them—but the diversion had served its purpose. He turned the items over between his gloved fingers.

He was still lost in thought when the messenger in his control panel started to blink. *"Ray Six, do you copy?"*

He flicked his hand across the board, activating the speaker. "Ray Six here. I hear you loud and clear, Ray Twelve."

"Is the mission a success?"

Apollo lifted one of the objects between his fingers. He dropped the others in the receptacle that hung from the side of his chair. No doubt the Aten would find something to do with them, but the real prize was the fifth item, the one that perfectly matched one of the objects he'd lifted from the Ohio vault.

"It is," he said. "Are there any eyes on you?" The agent, known as Ray Twelve over their communications, or Ra among the other members of the Hand, had been tasked with the most difficult mission of all. Unlike Apollo, who only entered the vaults to take what the Hand wanted, Ra was in deep cover, working within ENIGMA itself.

Apollo never trusted moles. If an agent was willing to turn on one organization, what would stop them from turning on another? Still, Ra's assistance had been invaluable in the mission so far.

He didn't know Ra's identity. In their transmissions, Ra used a voice scrambler, so that they sounded exactly the same as Apollo did. They had met once, a few years before, at a meeting of the Hand. They'd both been in their uniforms, and neither of them would have been able to identify one another outside of the circle.

Which was the whole point. ENIGMA was too soft. Too trusting. Take this whole mess with the contractors. Someone had sneaked into the vaults, and what had ENIGMA done? Invited in *new* people. Widened their circle. The Hand was smaller. A closed fist, one that had survived the ages precisely because of its exclusivity.

"No," Ra told him. "*Not yet. I walk in shadows...*"

"That we may all walk in the light one day," Apollo finished. "Your assistance is appreciated, Ray Twelve. Do you have the new coordinates?"

"*I'm sending them now. This one is... different, Six.*"

The location populated on Apollo's map, and he leaned forward to examine the numbers. Just as there had been for Atlantis, there was a range of data. It was larger this time, but when he saw the approximate location, he sucked in a breath. The range was wide, and the terrain was treacherous. He'd have a much harder time getting close without being detected, and while his suit allowed him to walk through walls and evade gunfire, its field couldn't be extended to the ship. His vessel could still be blasted out of the sky, and if he crashed, his suit wouldn't save him from injury, or from being stranded in remote territory. There was no guarantee that the Hand would come to his rescue, either. The Aten, their leader, played the long game, and they wouldn't risk the lives of the other members to retrieve him.

"Be careful, Six," Ra told him. *"I'll get you more information if I can, but I won't risk discovery."*

"Nor should you," Apollo assured the other agent. "This is enough." He ended the transmission without a farewell. Pleasantries were a waste of time, and he had work to do.

With the new coordinates in his map, Apollo adjusted his course.

He had another vault to find.

13   FABIEN

DINAH HAD BEEN PORING over those damn listings for almost six hours. Captain Correia had taken them to their own quarters, with two bunks.

Fabien had planned on taking one of the bottom bunks, since it made for easier egress should the situation sour, but Dinah had beaten him to the first one, and Fabien would have felt guilty making Rhett climb after the beating he'd taken.

For the first few hours, Fabien had dozed. His distress over Porter's sudden appearance in his hideaway, and the subsequent adrenaline rush, had kept him going for almost two full days. Exhaustion was catching up with him at last. He drifted off into an uneasy sleep with the light of the holograms playing across his eyelids, and dreamed of almost drowning all over again.

He woke to the rumbling of his stomach. Rhett was sitting up in bed, watching Dinah study the tablet. Every so often she would flip to the next listing, stare at it without blinking for a few minutes, and then flip to the next.

The sun was up by the time Dr. Moniz returned for them. She

led them to a mess hall where they were served congee topped with shredded jellyfish floss, boiled seaweed, ginger, and green onion. Fabien was tempted to turn up his nose at the jellyfish, but his stomach said otherwise. It wasn't as bad as he'd expected. The other personnel shot them curious glances, but Fabien kept his head down. He'd been delirious when he was brought onboard, and the thought of anyone seeing him like that was... humiliating, to say the least. He hated relying on other people.

They so often let you down.

Dinah ate without looking up from her screen, repeating her ritual of flipping from one object to the next. It wasn't until she'd scraped her bowl clean that she looked up.

"I think I know what we're looking for," she said. "Is there a way to call Porter?"

"Sure." Dr. Moniz got to her feet. "I'll take you to the bridge."

Atlantis wasn't like any other ship Fabien had been aboard, but the bridge wasn't so different from what he was used to. Three other crew members were manning the controls, while a series of screens situated around them showed data about the ship's operations, incoming weather patterns, live video feeds from throughout the ship, and sonar views of the water around them.

According to the sonar, a dozen large objects were moving toward the vessel on a collision course. Fabien sucked in a breath when he realized they were whales.

He wouldn't have minded being stationed someplace like Atlantis. It would be all too easy to get comfortable here. Let the Hand have whatever they were after. Why worry about some old trinkets? In a place like this, Fabien would always be moving, always hidden from the people he might otherwise have to answer to someday.

Hiding out here would mean breaking his promises, however. That thought alone made him turn to the captain.

"Dinah thinks she has something." He hooked a thumb at the young professor. "Any way to give Porter a ring?"

With a sly grin, Correia reached into his pocket and produced one of the small, round holograph projectors that Porter had used back in Ohio. "Even better, we can get him here in the room with us... or close enough." He punched a few buttons on the top of the device as he led them through to a stateroom. Once the five of them were inside, he closed the door behind them and placed the projector on the floor.

A moment later, Porter's lean figure popped into view. He was dressed less formally than usual, in loose pants and an oversized shirt that hung off of his skinny shoulders. His hair was rumpled, and he yawned as the projection kicked on. He might as well have been standing in the room with them, he looked so real.

"We caught you early," Correia observed.

"Yes." Porter rubbed his eyes. "But after your message last night, I can only assume that this is of the utmost importance." He sat down in the middle of the room, perched against nothing, although Fabien assumed that he was sitting on the end of his own bed. "Please, continue. It's never too early for ENIGMA business."

Dinah held up the tablet she'd been studying since the night before. "Can you see this?" she asked.

Porter nodded. "I can."

"So I've been going through the items." Dinah pointed to the image of the amulet. It looked like a smooth black stone, with a hole worn through the middle the size of a human eye. "This is—allegedly—good for detecting quantum disturbances between neighboring dimensions. According to the records, hundreds of these exist, both in vault catalogs and in civilian hands."

"Right." Porter rubbed his eyes again. "They were said to be able to detect 'fairy rings' in the old days. It's a common enough artifact."

"So why take one?" Dinah asked.

Rhett shot Fabien a funny look. It took Fabien a moment to realize that he wondered what he thought of that information. Unfortunately, Fabien didn't think much of it at all.

Dinah flipped to the next object in the listing. It looked like a narrow stone, or a stick polished to a smooth shine. "And this is a petrified fingerbone…"

"Ew," Fabien muttered.

Dinah sighed. "It's thousands of years old. Anyway, it's carved with what the records say is a spell of fertility." She shook her head. "So I'm pretty sure that's not what Apollo was after, either."

"Then why take it?" Rhett asked.

"I think he wanted to cover his tracks. Make us wonder what he was really after. My guess is that he grabbed a couple of things at random, things that were easy to carry, things that you might want to recover but that meant nothing to him." Dinah flipped the image again, and the hologram changed to show a heavy metal ring, set with a rough-cut stone and inscribed with sigils Fabien didn't recognize. "This, supposedly, is a magic ring, meant for contacting spirits." Dinah looked at the others. "I assume that's not what it does, right?"

"An echo ring," Porter corrected. "King Solomon had one. So did Genghis Khan. And technically, it only allows the wearer to speak with unseen entities."

"So it's a finger-mounted radio?" Fabien asked dubiously.

"More or less," Correia said, "although we've never worked out where the signals come from. Not from beyond the grave, that's for certain."

"Then there's a small witch bottle." The tablet displayed the image of a round-bottomed glass bottle made of blue glass and filled with... were those human teeth? Fabien shuddered. "Supposedly they were used as protection spells, but having seen what Porter showed us in the vault, I suspect they had other uses." Dinah waved a dismissive hand. "But then, there's this."

With a dramatic flourish, she revealed the image of the fifth and final item.

Fabien leaned forward to see what all the fuss was about. The object was only a few inches long and appeared to be a curved piece of metal. One end had a small projection protruding from it, while the other had an indentation of similar size. Along the curved top of the object, strangely filigreed geometric protrusions rose like the pattern of a Greek key; what looked like Arabic script ran along the object's flattened sides, although Fabien knew enough Arabic to know that the words were nonsense writing.

"What is it?" Fabien asked, when nobody but Dinah seemed impressed.

"That's an excellent question," Dinah said, wagging a finger at Fabien. "And the thing is, nobody knows. Nobody who's ever contributed to ENIGMA's database, anyway. The record only states that it's one of five objects of this kind that were spread out and stored at various vaults across the globe for safekeeping. And look." She pointed to the two ends. "It looks like it would fit together with the rest of the pieces to make a circle." She beamed at them. "I kept wondering how all these items related to one another, but I don't think they do. I think Apollo is trying to collect whatever these things are. I bet you anything that the Hand knows what they're for, and they want it badly enough to break into three more vaults to get it."

If Dinah was expecting fanfare and a pat on the back, she must have been sorely disappointed by the flat, haunted stares of the others. Gradually, her smile wilted. "Do you think I'm wrong?"

Fabien shook his head. "That's not the problem. It sounds like you're onto something, Professor."

"But... I solved it." Dinah shrank into herself. "Isn't that what I was supposed to do?"

"It is," Rhett said. "And now the rest of us are wondering what a man who can walk through walls might need with whatever that is. More importantly, we're wondering how we're supposed to stop him before he gets what he wants."

Correia muttered something under his breath and wiped his brow. "If we can catch the bastard, we can find out what he wants those things for, assuming that Dr. Bray is right. The thing is, we'd need to get close enough to get his device away from him."

"Easier said than done." The memory of being dragged through the wall made Fabien's skin prickle. Apollo's abilities had left him feeling helpless in the moment, but with every passing moment he was more determined to put the agent in his place. The man's abilities made him complacent, and now that Fabien had tried and failed to stop him once, he would be able to recalibrate his attacks next time. They could use Apollo's intangibility against him. After all, he couldn't rob the vault if he couldn't touch it, and he couldn't steal the next fragment of the relic if he couldn't *get* to it.

All he had to do was stay one step ahead of the other man, and he'd have the satisfaction of kicking *Apollo* in *his* kidneys. The ultimate satisfaction.

Correia turned to the projection of Porter. "First things first. Does this look like anything you had in your vault?"

"It looks vaguely familiar," Porter admitted. "But I never paid it much attention, since I didn't know what it was for. As I recall, the object was retrieved in... Turkey?" He directed the question to Dinah, who nodded. "I can check the vault."

"In the meantime, we should see where the other pieces are stored," Correia said.

Dinah scrolled through the text of the listing. "According to this, they're in Laputa, Holy Land, and... El Dorado?" She cocked her head to one side like a confused dog. "Are all of these places real?"

"They're the code names we've adopted for the sites," Dr. Moniz explained. "Obviously, this isn't the Atlantis of legend. The tech didn't exist back then. But it gives us a way to talk about the vaults without giving away their geographic locations."

"El Dorado?" Correia's tone of disbelief made Fabien watch the captain more closely. "What do you make of that, Porter?"

The hologram of Porter massaged his temples. "I don't know what to think, Captain, but I can tell you this much... if I were Apollo, I wouldn't launch an attack on Holy Land until I was confident that I was close to achieving my goal."

"Not that Laputa's any easier to attack," Correia said. "If anything, the terrain makes it more difficult."

Fabien lifted both hands. "Hold on. I don't know what you mean with all this code name nonsense, but if the point is to keep Apollo from getting all five of these things—assuming that's even what he's after—we don't need to take them all. We just need to get to one of them before he does and lay a trap. Right?" He looked around at the others.

"I suppose that's true," Correia mused.

"In which case, we might as well start with the most vulnerable vault," Rhett reasoned. "It sounds like this Holy Land place is the most well-defended."

"And El Dorado is lost," Correia said. "Unless Apollo knows something we don't, he won't be going there."

"And even if he does," Porter added, "we can't intercept him."

"Wonderful." Rhett clapped his hands together. "Then

Laputa it is. I assume you have a way to get us there? One that doesn't end with us crash-landing in open water?" He glared at Porter.

"We can get you there," Correia promised. "Or at least, we can get you awfully damn close."

Porter rose from his perch on the unseen bed. "Very well. Captain, I will leave them in your care. In the meantime, I'll check the vault just to be sure that the object in question is missing from our collection. It would be a shame to get so swept up in this theory that we accidentally leave the other vaults vulnerable. I'll also alert the vaults in question."

"Hold on." Correia slid to the edge of his seat. The legs of his chair groaned, but he was too busy glaring at Porter to notice. "Do you mean to tell me that you haven't already alerted all of the other vaults about the Hand's actions?"

Porter had the good grace to look sheepish. He cut his eyes away from all of them, into the depths of a room they could not see. "You understand why that might be... less than desirable," he said. "To know that any of the vaults have been breached could cause panic."

"Or it could mean that the other vaults are able to ward off a similar incursion." Correia pointed an accusing finger at his compatriot. "I understand not wanting to admit defeat, especially after they almost shut your vault down, Porter, but this is bigger than your ego. The whole future of ENIGMA is at stake. Maybe more than that, given what the Hand has done in the past."

Fabien rocked back on his heels. This time, when Rhett glanced at him, Fabien caught his gaze and mouthed, *What?* Porter hadn't said anything about his vault almost being shut down.

No wonder he went outside the agency for help, if he's already on probation with ENIGMA. I wonder what caused that?

Rhett only shrugged in response, but Fabien could tell that he, too, was seeing their mission in a new light.

"I'll alert them," Porter promised. "In the meantime, you three should head to Laputa. I'll alert you when I've had a chance to review our inventory." The hologram abruptly cut out.

Dinah whistled to herself. "What was that about, Captain?"

"ENIGMA business," Correia grunted. "None of your concern." He rose to his feet and motioned to Dr. Moniz. "Stay with them. I'll pull a crew together and organize a transport out by 0800 hours." He stomped to the door and slammed it shut behind him when he left.

Fabien patted his gun absentmindedly. Every time he thought he found his footing on this mission, someone jerked the rug just a little bit more.

There was more to their assignment than Porter had told them. What else had he left out?

14 RHETT

RHETT DIDN'T REALIZE that he'd been bracing for another midair fight until he was told there wouldn't be one.

"I told you, we're trying to restrict resource expenditure," Dr. Moniz explained. "Jets are environmentally expensive. Unfortunately, the trip out is a one-way ticket, on account of... well, on account of ENIGMA trying to avoid the very thing that's happened here." She sighed and ran one hand over her curls. "I don't know what we're going to do now that the Hand can do things like this. I wonder if it's tech they stole, or something they developed? It wouldn't take many of them to turn our whole organization inside out."

Rhett fiddled with the handle of his cane. He was still thinking about Porter. Wondering about Porter. If the newfound abilities of the Hand represented a debilitating threat to his organization, why hadn't he reported it?

Dr. Moniz's new revelation, however, would likely be much easier to explain. "If we're not taking a jet, then how are we getting there? By ship?"

"I could tell you, but—"

"Let me guess. It would be easier to show me?"

Dr. Moniz aimed finger-guns at him. "Now you're getting it. Besides, if I'm being honest, this isn't my favorite bit of tech ENIGMA uses. As a doctor, I'm a bit skeptical of anything that relies on total cellular rearrangement of the human body, you know? The endocrine system alone is a delicate thing, never mind what it could do to your nerves if it malfunctioned."

Rhett blinked at her. "I'm sorry, *what?*"

"Nothing to worry about, I'm sure." Dr. Moniz patted his arm in a way that might have been comforting, had it not been preceded by such ominous phrasing. "We've never had a mishap with it. Not that I know of, anyway."

Rhett gripped his cane tighter. "Is this tech something Apollo could have messed with while he was onboard?"

"Um." Dr. Moniz winced. "Only if he knew about it?"

Again, not comforting.

"But since it's the only way you'll beat him to Laputa, if that's where he's headed next, it's not like you have a lot of options," Dr. Moniz added.

Rhett snapped his mouth shut. Understanding the danger more fully would only make him nervous, but it wasn't like there was anything he could do even if Apollo had sabotaged the transport. Ignorance, in this instance, might constitute relative bliss.

They waited among the garden beds, in the chairs where Correia had first greeted them the night before. Dinah was slumped in one of the chairs, her mouth open, snoring on occasion. Fabien, on the other hand, kept bouncing between the rows like a restless and unhelpful bee.

It was almost exactly 0800 hours when Correia returned with a trio of men, none of whom bothered to introduce themselves.

They hung back, eyeing the newcomers with mistrust, while the captain addressed all of them.

"I've made arrangements for your travel to the base near Laputa. A crew will be there to meet you. I can't get you the whole way, of course, but I can ensure you don't have a repeat of your voyage in. You have everything with you?"

Rhett nodded. Fabien did, too. Dinah, who had only just woken up when the captain started speaking, rubbed her eye with a knuckle and grunted.

"Very good." The captain met Rhett's gaze and frowned seriously. "Let us hope, for your sake and for ours, that the mission ends there. I don't know what that item does, but if the Hand wants it, it can't be a good thing."

THE TRANSPORT TURNED out to be a door.

Admittedly, it was a very unusual door. In fact, it appeared to be a doorframe, shaped like a freestanding torii gate.

"I've already set the coordinates," Correia told them. He stepped back to usher them through. "Good luck. I'll have someone contact you in Laputa once he finishes searching his vault."

Rhett stared at the empty gate, waiting for something to happen. Nothing did. It just sat there, bright red and inviting, a few paces from the outer wall of the greenhouse.

"What's the matter?" one of their guards asked under his breath. "Scared?"

Rhett couldn't see anything to be scared of, but when he turned his head, he caught Dr. Moniz's eye. The woman had said something about cellular arrangement, hadn't she?

Captain Correia nodded to the gate, and Rhett took a step

forward. As he did, something moved between the upright posts of the torii gate. It rippled, like spidersilk caught in a breeze.

The closer he got, the more he could feel it: pressure, building like a charge in the air. The temperature dropped sharply, and his ears popped. He was tempted to stop and reach out a hand, but Rhett wasn't so certain that he was among friends. Any show of weakness might come back later to bite him in the ass.

Instead, he kept walking, right through the gate.

The moment he stepped between the posts, he gasped. The temperature plunged, and the breath squeezed itself from his lungs. His ears popped again, and he stumbled, holding out one hand blindly to catch himself as he fell.

Someone spoke. Someone else answered. A moment later, a hand closed around his arm to steady him. Rhett's first instinct was to lash out, but even as he tensed his limbs, a weight fell around his shoulders, accompanied by a musty, mothball aroma. Off-white fur settled around his shoulders. It was like being hugged by an ancient and poorly-groomed polar bear.

"Put that on," a woman said, in an accent so thick it took Rhett a moment to process what had been said. The white fur no longer belonged to an animal. It was a coat. Rhett stuffed one arm into its sleeve, then grappled with the other. The warmth of the coat was a blessed relief, but getting it on meant letting go of his cane.

He took another step and nearly fell on his face. The roaring in his ears never quit, and the blinding whiteness around him didn't subside. *Maybe when I stepped through the gate, it scrambled my eyeballs,* he thought dizzily. *Maybe I'll be blind forever.*

The unseen hand grabbed him again and slipped something over his head. "Slow breaths," the woman said. "Don't panic. You're snowblind, and the altitude change can make you sick."

Rhett adjusted the goggles that the woman had mashed onto

his face. When he finally managed to get them in place, it took a moment for his vision to resolve.

No wonder he'd been blind, he realized. No wonder he'd been half-deaf. The whirling snow was blistering white in the sunlight, and it was *wind* roaring in his ears.

Only moments before, he'd been a few feet above sea level in the midst of the ocean, in the early hours. Now, somehow, it was late afternoon, and they were in the mountains.

And, judging by their altitude and the temperature, they weren't in any old mountain range. Rhett would have bet all the money Porter had offered him that a single step, with the help of the torii gate, had carried him all the way from the Atlantic to the Himalayas.

15 DINAH

DINAH HAD NEVER BEEN a big fan of winter. If she'd ever encountered teleportation before, she would have known she wasn't a fan of that, either. She stumbled out the far side of the torii gate with her stomach in knots, only to have strangers on the other side start stuffing her arms through sleeves, her hands into gloves, and swaddling her head with snow goggles and a hat that looked like something from a vintage Russian military uniform. Given that she was still wearing the headset that Porter had given her, it was hardly comfortable, but at least her ears weren't freezing anymore.

Their new escort was slightly friendlier than the guards who had followed them from Atlantis. The three of them accepted their new wardrobe without surprise.

"They could have warned us," Fabien muttered to Dinah.

"I don't think they like us," Dinah whispered back.

She thought she'd kept her voice down low enough that the Atlantean guards wouldn't hear, but she was wrong. The one standing nearest to them scowled.

"Never had a break-in before," he growled. "And then, while we're pulling you lot out of the waves, a Hand gets in?"

"Shouldn't be surprised," his friend added. "Another mess coming out of Porter's territory. Should be par for the course by now."

Dinah stood there, shivering, while the guards turned their backs. Fabien made a rude gesture. "What's their problem?" he demanded.

"It's no big deal." Dinah tucked her neck deeper into the coat's collar. *Happens all the time at the university,* she thought. *One guy vouches for a candidate he likes, and then everyone who's got an issue with the older prof transfers all their frustration to the new hire.* "They've got an issue with Porter."

"Which Porter didn't mention." Fabien stomped his feet in the snow. "Just like the captain didn't mention that he was shipping us off to yeti territory. Have you noticed just how much these people aren't telling us?"

"It had occurred to me, yes." Dinah didn't add that the list of people she didn't fully trust included Fabien himself. It wasn't just that the man had shot her in the back, although that certainly didn't help. The larger problem was just how close-lipped he was. The longer she spent with ENIGMA, the more out of her depth Dinah felt.

And then, there was the issue of the object Apollo had stolen. As their new hosts began packing the crew into large sleds, Dinah puzzled over the object once again. It hadn't taken her long to work out that, of all the trinkets Apollo had stolen, the fifth was an outlier. The trouble was that she had no idea what it did. Admittedly, she didn't know much about witch bottles, either, but at least she'd heard of them. She'd been brought along for her brains, hadn't she? And now she couldn't ID the one thing that mattered.

The sleds, it turned out, were meant to go uphill. She watched with interest as they were powered on; instead of being dragged along by humans or draft animals, they were solar-powered, and hovered a few inches above the snow. It was a bumpy ride, and the constant wind gusts forced them off-course as they skimmed over the brilliant landscape.

With no better way to pass the time, Dinah powered on her headset. She wasn't sure that it would work in the cold, but aside from the occasional flicker in the connection, it allowed her to browse smoothly.

There were no hits for image-matching on the web, but there was a second tab on the upper corner of the visor's screen. Dinah tried to select it, only to get a popup that said, *Security Clearance Required*, followed by two buttons, *Proceed* and *Cancel*. What the hell, she thought, might as well give it a go.

When she selected *Proceed*, a brilliant green light flared to life and scanned her retina. Dinah let out a squawk of surprise and nearly tumbled backward off of the sled. If Fabien hadn't caught her, she might very well have flopped head first into the snow.

"Sorry!" She righted herself with some effort and blinked a few times, half-blinded by the scanner. "I wasn't expecting that."

"Reflexes like a cat," Fabien muttered under his breath.

Dinah would have been more offended, but she was too preoccupied with the new tab. Her clearances had been approved, apparently, because a new setting was now outlining various objects in her field of vision in green. When she focused on them, a text box populated next to them, which adjusted her scrolling speed based on how quickly she read. She tried it with Fabien's weapon—*Smart-Target Rifle: This gun manually switches between three functionalities...*—then on the sled itself, although the manual appeared to be in a Tibetan dialect. There was, however, a translation feature, and once the text adjusted to English, she skimmed partway through the listing before growing bored. Very likely, the headset would only be able to tell her what ENIGMA already knew, but it was at least easier to access now.

"Wish I'd seen this before I became an experimental pilot," she grumbled.

Fabien cocked his head. "What was that?"

"Nothing," Dinah said, "I just..." She tipped her head back and paused when an outline appeared momentarily in the cloudy skies above them. Night was falling, and soon the snow goggles would no longer be necessary.

The outline flickered out, then in again, an incomplete silhouette in green. *Please don't let it be Apollo,* she thought.

The object, whatever it was, was much too large to be the Hand's aircraft. Dinah squinted in the hopes that the headset would zoom in for her or something, but it didn't.

"Earth to Dinah." Fabien snapped his fingers next to Dinah's ear. "Come in. What are you looking at?"

Dinah lifted a hand to point into the clouds. "Do you see that?"

"See what?" Fabien squinted, too. He leaned forward on his bench, angling his neck first one way and then the other, trying to see over the heads of their guides.

"That." Rhett, a row ahead of them, lifted his arm to point into the clouds. "I saw it, too."

The outline appeared again, stable this time, and Dinah sucked in a breath. It wasn't a ship up there. It was a *city*. It stood above them, removed from the mountainside but still mountainous in profile, with jagged spires that scraped like teeth against the star-speckled night above. The clouds broke open to reveal blunt-topped buildings with little caps of snow. Beneath the streets, a chute uncoiled, so narrow that when it reached the ground below it created the illusion that the whole construct floated above the slopes, balanced upright on that single slender strand.

A text box popped up to tell Dinah what she already knew: they had found Laputa.

———

RIDING the lift was far more disorienting than navigating the glass halls of Atlantis had been. The moment the sled situated itself beneath the flexible, translucent tube, it was drawn upward. It rolled up behind them as it sucked them skyward, so that no one could follow.

Dinah clutched the lip of her bench and closed her eyes. It was all too easy to imagine a failure in the lift system, such as it was, and the resulting fall into deep snow a dozen stories below. Would the snow break her fall? She suspected not. More likely, it would break *her*. The sensation of being stunned and helpless as the ocean washed through the jet had stayed with her, and would probably never fade. She'd been so helpless. Just thinking about another tumble through the skies made her stomach lurch. It didn't help that the headset could calculate the distance to the ground within a quarter of an inch.

Think of ancient poetry, she told herself. *List out the kings of Axum, or the monarchs of Elam.* Recitation always helped her take her mind off of things. Sure, this was a bit different from prepping for her PhD presentation, but the principle was the same.

When she opened her eyes again, they were sliding out of the chute and into a warm room the size of an auditorium. The entry door closed beneath them, the tug of the antigravity lift stopped, and the sled hit the ground with a dull thud.

Dinah barely had time to get to her feet before a door at the far end of the room opened and three figures strode through. Two of them were so swaddled in outerwear that she couldn't see their faces, but the third walked bare-headed, with her uncombed hair trailing loose around her windburned face. It was impossible to guess her age.

She greeted the ground crew in a Tibetan dialect, then swung toward Dinah. "Porter called," she said bluntly. "He told me what you're after, but you're not needed here. We have everything under control." She wrinkled his nose. "We'll send you downslope tomorrow. In the meantime, don't cause trouble." With that, she turned her back on them and stormed away.

16 FABIEN

ACCORDING TO THE GROUND CREW, the captain of Laputa was named Kunzang, and Fabien didn't like her one bit. Not that it mattered, since she'd refused to speak with them after that brief exchange in Laputa's landing bay.

"What's *her* problem?" Fabien grumbled to one of the men Correia had sent along with them.

The guard looked him over, and his lip curled as though he smelled something unpleasant. "She doesn't trust you. None of us do."

Fabien crossed his arms and glared right back. "Obviously. Because of Porter?"

"Because you're outsiders." The man shouldered his rifle, one that seemed to be a different model of the one Fabien had been given. "And yeah, because of Porter."

He stalked away, but Fabien kept pace with him. Rhett and Dinah were still trying to talk to the tight-lipped Tibetan ground crew that had picked them up on the mountainside, but this man was getting on Fabien's nerves. Either answers would be forthcoming, or he'd end up starting a brawl with Kunzang's people. Probably ill-advised, given their height. All she'd have to do was toss them over the wall, and their mission would come to a frozen, grisly end.

"What's your problem with Porter?" Fabien demanded.

The guard scoffed and kept walking.

"Hey." Fabien grabbed the man's arm and yanked him to a halt. "I don't know what your deal is, and I don't know what *Porter's* deal is. I only found out about your little Illuminati-style club a few days ago, and I'm doing my best here. I don't give a shit about the politics involved. I just want to know what the hell is going on."

The guard shook him off. "Touch me again. See what happens."

Fabien stifled a growl. As tempting as it was to escalate the situation into a fight and burn off some of this excess energy, he forced himself to take a deep breath and stand down. "Listen. What's your name?"

The guard braced his feet wide, in a fighting stance. "Severino. Why?"

"Because, *Severino,* there must have been a time when you were new to ENIGMA. A point where all this"— he waved his hands to encompass the walls of the floating city—"was still confusing. I'm not trying to start anything. I'm not trying to muscle in on anyone's territory. I just want to understand what I've gotten myself into. See if the job's worth it. *Entendeu?*"

Severino's answering snort was more amused than combative. "*Compreendo.* I'm not getting involved in this, but I'll ping Correia. See if he'll talk to Kunzang for you." He jerked his chin toward the middle of the large room. "See if I can't get you out of the landing bay, at least."

"Great." Fabien took a step back. "Appreciate it." He

wandered back to Rhett and Dinah, running his hand absentmindedly over the strap of his rifle as he did so. His usual policy was to not ask too many questions about a job when he took it, so that he wouldn't be implicated if and when things went sideways.

Maybe it was time to update that policy.

"...if it really *is* what Apollo's after," Dinah was saying, "then maybe we shouldn't leave it in the vault, you know what I mean? Walls won't keep him out, so the best way to keep it safe is to put it somewhere he won't think to look."

"That's not my call to make." Rhett rubbed his eyes, which were bloodshot beneath his snow goggles.

"Maybe if we present it to the scary lady?" Dinah hooked her thumb toward the door.

"Right." Fabien slumped against the side of the sled. "We, the three people nobody trusts, will suggest to the captain of Laputa that she let us borrow an object from her magical vault for safekeeping. Solid plan."

"It's not magical," Dinah said instantly. "Everything we've seen has a scientific explanation, and—"

"I was being sarcastic. For emphasis." Fabien flapped a hand at Rhett. "Back me up here."

"You don't have to convince me of anything," Rhett told him. "You have to convince *her*."

Fabien turned to see where he was looking and found Kunzang waiting in the doorway. Severino and one of those fur-clad associates hovered behind her.

"Well?" Kunzang called. "Are you coming?"

Fabien's feet were moving before he stopped to question what her motives might be.

———

THE VAULT in Ohio had been buried deep underground; the maritime vault had been placed in the midst of a many-storied floating fortress. The vault in the mountains, however, was housed in a squat building in the center of the city, connected by domed walkways beneath the curtain of snow.

"This place is pretty exposed, isn't it?" Fabien asked.

Kunzang snorted. She was five paces ahead of him, and despite her short legs, he was finding it difficult to keep up. "Exposed? Yes, that's the point. Aircraft can't get up here. In this climate, the wings ice over. People can't get here on foot without being visible from the watchtowers. And good luck getting an army up here... people have tried, believe me. On top of that, we have security measures throughout the floating city, so when I tell you that *we don't need your help,* I mean it."

No matter how fast he moved his legs, Fabien kept falling farther behind. So did the others. He was breathing much too hard for a man who was only speed walking. "Apollo has... a device that... I'm not sure you're... prepared to combat."

Kunzang stopped short and spun to face him. "You're not sure? Well then, by all means, let me turn my city inside-out for your benefit. You, an outsider, Porter's altitude-sick lapdog. Your opinion must be the one that matters."

"I just..." Fabien tried and failed to match her indignance, but he ended up wheezing instead. "I just... want to protect... the vault." Damn, when this was over, he'd need to do some altitude training. The thin air had left him all but useless.

Kunzang snorted again and kept moving.

The vault door itself was much like the one in the mall's underground, and Kunzang executed a similar sequence of incomprehensible button presses and hand gestures in order to open it. Fabien tried to keep track of the motion of her hands, but it was useless. He was too busy wiping cold sweat from his brow into the now-soggy lining of his borrowed coat and trying not to throw up.

When the door swung wide, Kunzang stepped through. "Wait here," she told Severino and her fur-clad associate. They both nodded, while Dinah, Fabien, and Rhett followed her into the vault.

The space was far more organized than the one under Porter's command. Instead of open shelving, each item was stored in its own special compartment in a backlit honeycomb of Plexiglas.

"Oh!" Despite her shortness of breath, Dinah stepped forward to admire the setup. "They're like modified tansu boxes."

"Indeed." Kunzang patted the front of the nearest box lovingly. Her anger had faded to something almost affectionate. "Each of them locks with a unique code that rotates at random, selected by ENIGMA's proprietary AI. Much safer than that mess in the States." She sniffed.

Fabien wasn't sure that he was loyal to Porter, per se, but it was hard to disagree with her assessment. This setup would slow the average thief down considerably, perhaps long enough to give security time to catch them.

If the thief couldn't reach through walls, that is.

Dinah, absent-minded as usual, wandered away down the wall of objects, trailing her fingers just far enough away from the sleek doors that she didn't leave fingerprints. She paused from time to time and stared at different objects intently.

"Here it is," she called from halfway down the row.

They moved to join her. Sure enough, a partial circle of metal was propped up for display, a perfect match of the one taken from Atlantis. Seeing it in person was different than on the screen. It had weight to it. Substance. Fabien could tell, even with a wall of Plexiglas between them, that it would be cool to the touch.

And for some reason, he wanted to touch it. When he'd put on the cuffs back in Porter's vault, he'd felt something in him change. A tingling rush of power.

This object, whatever it was, made the hairs on his arms stand on end. He wanted to run his fingers over the grooved top, press his thumb to the inscribed not-quite-Arabic on the side. He wanted to hold it.

He wanted to know what in God's name it did.

"As I said," Kunzang said, "perfectly safe. Nothing to worry about." She pointed to the door. "You can go now."

"But—" Dinah began.

"We're done here," Kunzang told her, and turned her back.

"Hang on." Fabien followed after her, somewhat rejuvenated by the two minutes they'd spent standing still. He caught up with her this time and darted ahead, cutting her off. "Shouldn't we at least set a guard or something? Try to trap Apollo?"

"*We* will," Kunzang said. She jabbed his chest with one finger. "My crew. The ones I can trust."

Rhett's gait rolled a bit more than usual as he loped up behind them. "Surely you can find something useful for us to do?"

"The best thing you can do for me is to lie low and respect my orders," Kunzang growled. "And while you're at it, get out of my vault. I don't trust Porter, and I don't trust you."

"What's the problem with Porter?" Rhett asked.

Kunzang's smile was all teeth and no humor. "What's the problem with Porter?" she echoed. "The *problem* is that after centuries of secrecy, his grandfather sold us out to the Hand. We lost an entire vault in the conflict that followed. *An entire vault.*" She looked Rhett up and down with undisguised disgust. "Bet he didn't tell you that, did he?"

Rhett, tight-lipped, shook his head.

"Well, it's true. Ask anyone." Kunzang took another step

toward the vault door. "And I'm not letting my vault go the same way. Now come on."

Dinah, who had been lingering by the artifacts, finally caught up with them. "What did I miss?" she asked.

Rhett shifted his weight to put more pressure on his cane. He shook his head once, then followed after Kunzang.

Dinah made pleading eyes at Fabien. "What happened?"

Fabien fumbled for the right words. He knew from bitter experience that people had a nasty tendency to hold sons accountable for their fathers' actions, and he'd long since vowed not to do the same. Still, doubt tugged at him.

Because Porter's vault had been the first to be plundered. And hadn't he already thought it a strange and unfortunate coincidence that Apollo found them in midair?

Maybe, the suspicious part of his mind suggested, *it wasn't a coincidence at all. Maybe Kunzang is onto something.*

17 RHETT

THE BUNKS in Laputa weren't as comfortable as they might have been, and Rhett's leg was bothering him after their brief stint in the snow. He lay on his back, staring up at the ceiling, and wondered.

As selfish as it might be, he wasn't wondering about Porter, or if he could be trusted, or why he had chosen them without telling them about the shaky footing he stood on with the rest of ENIGMA.

No, he was wondering if Porter would really be able to keep the promises he'd made when Rhett first accepted the mission.

The three of them had been assigned to one room—without stacked bunks this time, thank goodness. He could hear Dinah fidgeting around in her bed, no more asleep than he was.

"What are you doing?" Fabien demanded. Judging by his muffled voice, he was lying face-down in his pillow.

The movement in Dinah's bed abruptly stopped. "Nothing." She couldn't have sounded guiltier if she tried.

Fabien flopped around hard enough to make the bed squeak. "Liar."

"Evidently," Rhett murmured, "she's not the biggest liar involved."

"Still thinking about Porter, huh? Well, I don't care. I'm more worried about Apollo." Fabien sat up in bed, barely a silhouette in the far side of the room. "He tried to kill us once, and now we're locked in here, hemmed in by guards. You think we'll be safe if he strolls in? You think the relic will be safe?"

Dinah's sheets rustled again.

"Oh, for heaven's sake," Fabien barked, "will you just tell us what—"

He was cut off by the wail of a distant alarm.

In an instant, Rhett rolled to his feet, never mind the pain. He was still wearing the neoprene skin Dr. Moniz had given him back in Atlantis, mostly because it had eased his mind to know that he could roll out of bed at any moment and pull on the trousers that matched the chameleon coat.

"What do you think that is?" he asked.

"I think it's Apollo, here to take what he wants," Fabien replied grimly. He, too, was out of bed, already yanking his lightweight Kevlar over his head. "And I don't think Kunzang and her crew are ready for him."

"Nor do I." In the dark, Rhett fumbled for his cane, only to be blinded when a red light overhead flared to life. He blinked against the glare. "Fabien, do you think you can kick the door in? Or bash it down?" Damn Kunzang for taking his cane. All of their weapons had been confiscated, although they'd been allowed to keep their armor, and Dinah had been permitted her headset. In the cursory pat-down he'd been given, the Laputan guard had missed the cluster of time bombs stuffed in Rhett's pockets, although he wasn't sure what good they'd be to him now.

Fabien rocked from one foot to the other, shaking out his arms. After taking a few fortifying breaths, he dove toward the door, throwing his whole weight against it. The whole wall shuddered, but the door didn't budge.

"Screw this," Fabien grumbled. "If they think we're going to sit here and let that bastard—" He let out a roar of frustration and tried again, to no avail. When he saw that it was useless, the Frenchman drove his fist into the center of the door three times in quick succession. "Goddamn it!" he howled. "What was the point of all this? Now we've painted targets on our backs in the eyes of the Hand, and for what? For a man who won't even tell us the truth!" He whirled away from the door.

"This isn't Porter's fault," Dinah said softly. She was halfway out of bed, her headset still in place. Whatever she'd been doing over there, she certainly hadn't been sleeping. She looked like hell. They all did.

"Then whose is it?" Fabien thumped his chest. "I wouldn't be here if it wasn't for him. Do you think we're just going to be able to quit now? They know where to find us! And if they can find us—"

They can find our families. Rhett shivered. The thought was alarming enough, but a moment later, it was driven from his mind.

The doorknob rattled from the outside.

He immediately lifted a finger to his lips, and Fabien fell into a fighting stance. Admirable, he supposed, but useless. If it came to a fight, they wouldn't be waging war with their fists.

The door handle rattled again.

In the red glow of the emergency light, Rhett pointed to the door, then to Fabien. On the lightest steps he could muster these days, he slunk back, pressing his shoulder blades to the wall. Fabien did the same on the far side of the door, closest to the opening, while Rhett stood near the hinges. If only they'd been on the inside, they could have gotten out easily enough. Too bad.

Rhett had no sooner taken up his position than the door swung wide. Fabien tackled the interloper and wrapped one arm around his throat, while Rhett slammed the door after him.

"Hey!" The man they'd grabbed raised his hands in surrender even as he let loose a string of curses in Brazilian Portuguese.

Fabien let go of him. "Severino?"

"Yes, dammit." The Atlantean guard shook him off. "What the hell was that? I'm trying to help you." He rubbed his throat and glared at them.

Fabien shrugged, utterly unashamed. "You should have knocked first. We seem to have more enemies than friends here. What's happening out there?"

"Slaughter." Severino shook his head. "That agent, Apollo? There's no stopping him."

"Could have told you that for free," Rhett reminded him. "In fact, I seem to remember that we tried to do just that."

Severino's hands balled into fists. "Are you going to gloat? Or are you going to help now?"

Ordinarily, Rhett wouldn't have stood around waiting for someone else to answer. He wasn't sold on Fabien's better judgment. They hadn't known each other for long, and the lighting was terrible, and God only knew what was waiting for them on the other side of that door.

On the other hand, he'd made enough executive decisions that had gotten other people killed. Let Fabien take the lead on this one. That way, whatever blood they spilled would be on his hands.

"That depends," Fabien said slowly.

Severino exhaled sharply. "On what?"

"On whether you can get our weapons back."

THE HALLS of Laputa were bathed in the blood-red of the emergency lights, but they made it almost two hallways before they found the first body. It was one of Kunzang's guards—not the ground crew that had picked them up on the mountainside, but the fur-coated backup crewmen who'd flanked her everywhere she went. Rhett hadn't seen the man's face, and he still couldn't when they first stumbled across him, but it was obvious that he was dead.

People who'd been cut in half rarely pulled through. Especially when they'd been split in two the long way.

Fabien cursed and covered his nose, blocking the smell that should have accompanied the body. To Rhett's surprise, the air was stuffy, but not foul.

"Poor bastard," Fabien muttered.

Dinah held back, staring at the bisected corpse with bulging eyes. She looked as if she might be sick again.

Rhett, on the other hand, was wondering about the mess—or, more accurately, the lack of it. There was very little blood, just a small dark pool of congealing liquid staining his white fur coat.

"Come on," Severino said.

"One moment." Rhett stepped forward and prodded the dead man with his toe to nudge his coat aside.

The thing beneath wasn't a mess of ruined flesh. There was no flesh at all. Rhett crouched down to run his fingers through the blood. What should have been sticky was more like grease. Instead of organs, he was filled with wires.

"Is he a robot?" he mumbled.

"Android," Severino confirmed. "Good guards, with minimal needs. Usually, you wouldn't want to mess with them, but..." He gestured to the fallen one.

"I see." Rhett straightened up. "Carry on."

He had to fight to keep up with their rescuer, not only because of the low oxygen, but because he didn't have his cane. Or his painkillers. Or anything to keep him afloat when he felt so desperately in danger of crashing.

The armory door was open when they arrived. Most of its shelves had already been stripped bare, presumably by Kunzang's other automatons, but their weapons had been left behind. Fabien shouldered his gun, while Rhett reached for his cane with a sigh of relief.

The alarms were still blaring. Good. If Apollo had walked in and out as easily as he had done in Atlantis or the Ohio vault, they'd already have lost him. Apparently, Kunzang's people were putting up a fight.

"Can you take us to the vault?" Fabien asked.

Severino nodded. "It isn't far."

"Um." Dinah cleared her throat. "Maybe I should just stay here…?"

"Suit yourself," Fabien barked. "We won't have to keep an eye on you, then."

When Rhett spoke, he kept his tone kinder. "Lock the door after us. There are a few weapons left, and no reason for Apollo to come here."

Dinah cut her eyes away from him. "Right."

They left her there, following Severino through the tunnels beneath the snow. All of them looked the same to Rhett.

"I don't understand why we had to bring her," Fabien grumbled. "She's useless."

Rhett was too out of breath to correct him. Besides, they could hear the sounds of combat up ahead: the screech of gears, the blast of gunfire, the cries of the wounded. Apparently, not all of Kunzang's people were made of metal.

They rounded a bend into a warzone, or what was left of one. Three of the android guards had taken up defensive positions along the corridor, while their human counterparts watched their backs, firing in the direction of the vault door. The massive metal door stood open, and several sets of footprints, some charred, some bloody, marred the previously pristine floor of the hallway.

One of the other Atlantean guards was already in position. When he saw Severino, he lurched to his feet.

"He came so fast," the man blurted. "He was unstoppable. Nothing could hit him. Kunzang went in after him. Told us to cover her back." He ran his hands through his hair. "He melted Donato." The man mimed firing a pistol. "Gone."

Rhett swallowed hard. "Did she come back out?"

"Did she—?" The Atlantean stared at him with empty eyes.

"Kunzang. She went in after him. Did she come back out?"

He shook his head.

Rhett closed his eyes. Surely there must have been a better way to go about this. If only Kunzang had listened…

Well, no point in worrying about that now. She hadn't, and the vault was compromised, and for all they knew Apollo had killed her in the process. Instead of mourning what might have been, they had to move forward.

"Tell them to stand down," he said.

Severino gawked at him. "What?"

"They won't be able to shoot him if he's…" Rhett flapped a hand in irritation. "Phased out, or whatever. Tell them to stand back and guard themselves. He'll be vulnerable if he tries to fire on them. Otherwise, shooting at him is like trying to shoot at a ghost."

"And what will you do?" he asked.

Rhett squared his shoulders. "I'm going to talk to him."

Severino's disbelieving laughter died when Rhett swung back toward the vault door and started walking. The longer they waited, the higher the likelihood that everyone would be dead by the time he walked through the vault door. Dinah's brains had failed them.

Fabien's gunfire had, too. Well, then. Time for Rhett to do what he did best and see if that changed anything.

Besides, he had questions for Apollo. He knew more about him now. It was possible, if he played his cards right, that he might be able to reach a stalemate with him, at least in the short term.

Fabien moved to follow him, but Rhett shook his head. "Stay here," he said. "If this goes wrong, I don't want us both dead."

The Laputans lowered their weapons as he strode past; one of the still-functioning mechanical men turned blue-screen eyes on him, but let him go. He tried to keep his limp from showing, since he had an audience. He was pretty sure he was doing a shit job of it.

At the door of the vault, he hesitated. "Apollo?" he called. "I'm coming in. I want to talk."

Someone moaned from the depths of the vault, but that was the only answer he got. He was unlikely to receive anything more.

There was more blood in the vault's entrance, and an android, without its coat, lay half-melted near the first row of display cases. The lights had gone out, and there were no emergency lights in the vault. Walking forward meant walking into darkness.

He went anyway. When his foot hit something solid, Rhett froze, swallowing his fear. If he was going to reason with Apollo, he needed him to think he was perfectly at ease.

"Apollo?" he called again. Slowly, he inched forward, feeling his way in the dark with his cane and his feet. "I want to talk to you. I'm alone. We know what you're here for." Another object in his path. Something that crunched this time. He stepped over it.

The moan came again. There was a word inside it this time, hardly more than a bubbling breath. Rhett, who'd heard people speaking with a mouthful of blood, knew exactly what he would find.

"Kunzang?" he asked next.

The sound came again, slightly louder, but he still didn't understand. It was a Tibetan word.

In the end, he almost tripped over Kunzang, startling a cry out of the captain's lips. Rhett knelt beside her, fumbling with the woman's coat. Kunzang grasped his hands; her palms were wet with something thicker than blood. Rhett thought of the guard in the Ohio vault, his face melting away from the bone.

"Kunzang." Despite his revulsion, he gripped the captain's hands. Several of her fingers felt like nothing more than bone and tendon, although without light, Rhett could only imagine the extent of her injuries. "What happened?"

"Gone," Kunzang rasped.

"Who's gone? Apollo?"

"Gone," Kunzang said again. She let out another too-wet breath. "Door... open."

"The vault door is open, yes," Rhett agreed. "I should get you help." There was no evidence that Apollo was still here.

"No!" Kunzang clung to him. "It's gone."

"The relic?" Rhett shouldn't have been surprised. No wonder Apollo took off. He'd gotten what he came for. They were alone in the vault. "Let him have it. We'll alert the other vaults." He started to stand up and slipped on whatever coated the floor. In his attempt to catch himself, he fell back against the wall of tansu boxes and caught his chin on an open door. The force of the impact brought his teeth sharply together, and he bit his tongue hard. He could feel the heat of the blood trickling down his jaw even before the pain set in.

He clambered back to his feet. "I'll be back, Kunzang." He could hear the captain's heavy breathing, the only sign that she was still alive.

18 DINAH

THERE ARE A FEW WEAPONS LEFT, *and no reason for Apollo to come here.* She knew that Rhett had been trying to be nice when he said it, but the words kept rattling around inside Dinah's skull. They were mostly true. They should have been true. In fact, they would have been true, if Dinah hadn't done something tremendously stupid without telling the others.

She reached into the pocket over the oversized coat the ground crew had thrown over her shoulders and pulled out the relic she'd stolen from Kunzang's vault.

It had been too much to resist. According to Kunzang, the keypad combinations were generated by ENIGMA's proprietary AI. The same AI, presumably, that powered her headset. If they weren't the same, then at least they were connected, as proven by the fact that she'd stood there staring right at the keypad, only to see the text box populate with the ten-digit code.

Too easy. Which meant, on the bright side, that Apollo didn't have the relic. It was sitting right there, in Dinah's palm.

On the downside, she was currently the only thing keeping it out of Apollo's grasp.

Her PhD had prepared her for a lot of things, but the information about what to do when you were being chased by a murderous thief was sadly lacking. For a long time after Rhett and Fabien left her, she sat in the corner with the relic cradled in her palms and wondered what in the hell she was meant to do now.

When she was a kid, her mother had told her that when she was lost, the best thing to do was stand still, because someone would find her eventually. By that logic, crouching in an enclosed space while a madman rampaged through a floating city was probably the worst thing she could do. With that in mind, Dinah pushed herself to her feet, slipped the relic back into her pocket, and reached for a weapon.

There were two kinds of guns, according to the text boxes on her headset. She didn't have the training to fight with anything that would require finesse and experience. She could probably manage to point and shoot, though. None of them were like the multi-setting rifle Fabien used, so she had to pause a minute to think. The auto-targeting rifles would take the guesswork out of aiming, but the likelihood that she'd end up shooting the wrong person in a moment of surprise was uncomfortably high. Better to take the pulse rifle.

Having something to fight back with made her feel better. With a newfound sense of security, Dinah slipped out of the armory and into the hall. The red emergency lights were on, but the sirens had stopped, and the stillness of the corridors took on an eerie feel in the low light. She looked in the direction that Fabien and Rhett had gone—but no, they were headed into trouble. She ought to be heading away from it. Dinah didn't know the layout of the city well, but if Apollo was on the move, the last place he'd be likely to look for a stolen artifact was a place that he'd already been.

Instead of diving deeper into the city, Dinah retreated. A virtual setting in her headset allowed her to retrace their steps to the hallway where they'd found the dead android. Did androids die? Perhaps decommissioned was more accurate, but either way, it was proof that Apollo had already come and gone.

There were two doors off the hallway, but Dinah didn't like the idea of hiding inside a room. Apollo could easily come and go, but she would be trapped.

Instead, she sat down with her back to the wall, so that she could see both directions. Of course, Apollo could walk through the wall at any time, but if he did, Dinah would have a few seconds to start running before he solidified and opened fire.

As she crouched next to the corpse of the android, Dinah slipped her hand into her pocket again. To her surprise, the relic was no longer a cool hunk of dead metal. It was warm.

She pulled it out again and stared at it. Not only was it growing warmer by the minute, but the inscribed text stood out stark against the metal, like a backlit screen. The light was pale green, and it pulsed off and on, like a heartbeat.

As the letters grew brighter, it began to vibrate, humming gently against her skin, almost alive. Dinah squinted at the writing. It still meant nothing to her. And why would the relic be doing this now? What had changed?

This was almost certainly a very bad sign.

She startled at the tread of boots in the hallway, and ducked into one of the open doorways. Even if Apollo was coming, there was no reason for anyone to think she had the object. Someone would eventually notice that it was gone, and she'd have to explain to Kunzang why she'd stolen it to begin with, but at least it would buy the others time to come up with a plan.

Dinah held her breath as a solitary figure walked through the hall, carrying a gun like the one she had passed up. Her headset outlined it in green: *SureFire Target Seeker™, a rifle guaranteed to hit...* She flicked her gaze to the soldier's face, expecting the figure to pop up in outline as well. It wasn't an automaton this time, but a man. One of Kunzang's people.

When the man saw the broken android, he muttered something under his breath and dropped into a crouch, sweeping the hall, keeping his rifle in line with his eyes. Dinah toyed with the idea of asking him for help. *Seems like a good way to get shot*, she decided, and kept her mouth closed. She moved deeper into the room and held perfectly still.

The man was just outside of her line of sight, so she didn't see what happened next. All she saw was a silvery blue glow emanating from the hallway. She'd seen that light before, when Apollo strode through solid objects. She bit back a curse and stuffed her knuckles into her mouth to ensure her own silence. *Should have run when I had the chance. Maybe I'll get lucky and he'll just keep moving, like he did in the Ohio vault.* Sure, Apollo had killed one of the guards on that mission, and injured another when he walked right through the man, but he'd left three people alive. He clearly wasn't concerned about leaving witnesses.

In the hallway, the Laputan guard snarled something and opened fire. Dinah counted the shots: one, two, three. Maybe a SureFire had a better chance of hitting Apollo, even with that gadget of his. Did one bit of shiny tech cancel out another?

The Laputan guard stumbled back a pace, right into Dinah's line of sight. He shouted again.

Then a blast of return fire rippled the air, and the man dropped like a stone, his voice tearing out of his throat in an agonized scream. The SureFire rifle fell from his hands as he pressed both hands to his face, the way someone might put pressure on a wound to keep from bleeding out.

It was no good. Dinah watched in horror as the flesh on the man's jaw bubbled and sagged, dripping away from his teeth to reveal his teeth and the bare mandible. His howling trailed away into a wretched, squelching mewl.

Out of sight, Apollo fired again, and the man went still.

Dinah was frozen. The smell that filled the hallway turned her stomach, part smoked pork, part sewage. She would have retched, but she couldn't afford that now, not with Apollo out there.

The red emergency lights glinted off Apollo's gold suit as he stepped over the fallen man and bent to dig through his clothes. Dinah slid aside and pressed her spine to the wall.

Don't move. Don't twitch. Don't make a sound. If she sees you, it's over, even if he doesn't know what you have.

"I know you're there," Apollo said.

Dinah closed her eyes. *He's trying to draw you out. If he knew you were here, he wouldn't be talking, he'd just shoot.*

She should have run when she had the chance. Should have been smarter.

At least she'd never have to admit to her teammates how badly she'd screwed up.

"They can sense each other. Did you know that?" Apollo kicked the dead man, but didn't move. Dinah's hearing had never been so attuned to another person's movements. Her heart pounded in her chest like an out-of-sync metronome.

"I know you've got it." Apollo took a step. "And you're close, whoever you are. Are you in the walls?" There was a ringing thump as his fist met the side of the corridor. "The ceiling?" Thump. "Because I can feel how close you are. And you can't hide for long."

Dinah's hand dropped to her pocket. The relic inside was

warm now, buzzing so steadily that if it had been sitting on a desk, Apollo would have heard it. No doubt the writing was brighter, too.

"Hand it over," Apollo said. "Maybe we can make a deal."

It was tempting. This was only the third piece of the relic. There were two more out there.

But it didn't take a genius to work out that Apollo was lying. No deal would work out in Dinah's favor.

Besides, she'd already made one deal with a person she couldn't trust, and look where it had gotten her.

19 FABIEN

RHETT STOOD BEFORE HIM, bleeding from his chin, with his hands covered in gore, and said, "I'm not going back in there."

The Laputans were already moving in to retrieve their fallen commander, but Severino, his Atlantean companion, and one of the androids stayed with them.

Fabien tipped his chin toward Rhett's face. "You should clean that up."

"When we've caught Apollo," he insisted. He wiped his hands against the sides of his fur coat. "Besides, whoever's in charge of medical care is going to have their hands full, don't you think? Right now, we need to go back for Dinah."

"Let her hide," Fabien muttered under his breath. He didn't want to end up babysitting the scholar any more than they already were.

Rhett held his ground. "You didn't see—didn't feel—what Apollo did to Kunzang. I'm not going to leave Dinah to a fate like that. We're a team, Fabien. We don't leave each other behind."

He wasn't sure what it was, but there was something in Rhett's tone that made it clear that he wasn't going to take no for an answer. This wasn't negotiable.

And people didn't die on hills like that unless they were speaking from personal experience.

"Fine, we'll go back for her." Fabien wrinkled his nose. "But if we run into Apollo, I'm throwing everything I've got at him."

"He's probably long gone by now, anyway," Rhett said as they turned back the way they'd come. "He got what he came for. The compartment was—"

Rhett stopped short without warning, and Severino walked right into him. *"Que diabos?"* he demanded.

"The compartment was open." Rhett lifted his fingers to the bloody laceration on his chin. "Apollo wouldn't have been able to open it without the code, and there's no way Kunzang would tell him. And he couldn't have taken it out of the compartment without knowing the code, because he can't touch things when he's intangible."

"So?" Severino snapped.

"So Apollo doesn't have the relic," he said.

Fabien pressed his hand to his forehead and swore. "Dinah was talking about hiding it. And she was fooling around in the room earlier. You don't think—?"

Rhett broke into a run, and it didn't take Fabien long to catch up with him. The thin air wasn't bothering him so much as before. Either he was acclimating, or the realization of what their idiot companion had done was giving him the adrenaline boost he needed in order to override his overtaxed lungs.

How did she even get the code? he wondered. It never failed to amaze him that some people could be so smart in one moment and so foolish the next. Dinah wasn't a marksman or a trained soldier. How did she think she was going to ward off Apollo? With her fists?

Fabien reached the door of the armory before Rhett and flung it open. *What happened to locking the door?* The woman couldn't even get that part right.

"Dinah!" Fabien bellowed. "*Crétin*! What were you thinking? You should have at least told us!"

The room was empty.

"*Roi des cons!*" Fabien thumped his boot against the wall in an ineffectual display of anger. "Where did Porter find her? If she's still alive when we track her down, I'm going to kill her myself."

Rhett had come to a stop outside the door, breathing so hard that Fabien was afraid he might collapse. Even in the red light, it was clear that he'd gone pale, and that the wound in his face was bleeding worse than it had been before.

"Where would you go?" Rhett panted. "If you were her?"

"Do you want to explain what's happening?" Severino demanded as the other three caught up. The android moved in long, loping strides, keeping pace with the Atlanteans.

Rhett held up a finger as he tried to catch his breath. "We need to find our friend."

"But—"

"Now," Fabien snapped. "Does this place have a security system? Cameras? Any way we can track her?"

Severino's eyes flicked to the automaton. It had shed its outwear during the battle, revealing slender silver limbs, mechanized joints, and androgynous features that bore little resemblance to any human Fabien had ever seen. Whoever had designed them was clearly more interested in function than in making them look like people.

Probably for the best. As unsettling as the automaton was, it would have been much more disturbing with skin.

"Can you locate Dr. Dinah Bray?" Severino asked.

The android's flat blue eyes flashed with static. When it spoke, its mouth didn't move, and its voice was as androgynous as its form. "Dr. Dinah Bray is located near Corridor 31C, in the engine room."

"Is she alone?" Fabien asked.

The android's eyes flickered again. "Yes," it said. "No. Yes. System error. That data is not available."

"Great." Fabien kicked the wall again for good measure. "Then why don't you point me in the direction of 31C?"

They all ducked when three sharp reports echoed down through the corridor to the right, followed by a prolonged scream.

The android lifted its arm to point in the direction the sounds had come from. "That way," it said.

"Of course it is," Fabien snapped. He gripped his rifle to his chest and took off running.

20 RHETT

DON'T TRIP. *Don't trip. Don't trip.* With each step, Rhett had to hold his body together, as if the impact might send his various parts scattering in every direction. He would kill for a handful of painkillers. Literally kill. The exertion of the last three days had nearly pulled him apart at the seams, and he doubted that there was an item in any of these vaults magical enough to put him back together.

It's tech, Dinah would have corrected him, but for all he knew, she was already dead.

The android took the lead, guiding them through the corridor on steps so smooth that Rhett couldn't help but hate it, even if it was just a machine. It led them back to the place where they'd found that first slaughtered mechanical man, the one in the coat.

There was another body, now, alongside him, perhaps a dozen paces away. The face was a horror, but it clear that it wasn't Dinah. Rhett slumped forward and braced one palm on his knee as he tried to catch his breath. The other clung to his cane.

Severino swore to himself as he crouched over the fallen man. "What did Apollo do to him?" he murmured.

"Shot him," Rhett said.

"With what?" Severino's hands hovered over the dead man's melted flesh. "I've never seen a gun that can do that."

Great. Rhett straightened up. *So Apollo's got a bit of tech nobody knows how to handle, a gun they've never seen before that can melt flesh off the bone. Lovely.*

Fabien crept forward. "Dinah?" he hissed. He kept to the middle of the hallway, away from the walls. "Dinah, are you here? What did you do?"

"Maybe she's in here." Severino's friend circled one of the open doors, keeping the far wall to his back.

It would have been a smart move under most circumstances, when a wall behind you meant that your enemy couldn't get the jump on you. Now, Rhett clicked his tongue at him. "Get away from the wall," he snapped.

The Atlantean jerked his chin toward the open door. "For all we know, Apollo's in there."

Severino nodded. "Diego's got a point. We should—"

The wall behind the Atlantean shimmered blue as Apollo lunged through.

"Get back!" Rhett snapped. He plunged his hand into the pocket of his chameleon coat even as Apollo's hand thrust into Diego's back. He knew what would happen before it did. Apollo would materialize with his fist in Diego's chest and crush the other man's organs from the inside. Diego's eyes widened. He'd seen what happened to Marcus when Apollo walked through him, back in the recording from the Ohio vault. It must hurt like hell to have the Hand's agent overlap with his physical body.

Not as much as it would hurt when Apollo materialized, though. He could crush the man's heart in his fist if he wanted.

But only if he materialized in time.

Rhett grabbed the whole fistful of time bombs—there were only five of them now, since he'd crushed one during Ronnie's debrief—and crumbled one between his fingers before his hand was even out of his pocket.

The world froze. Fabien was already taking aim at Apollo, although he'd shoot Diego in the process if he pulled the trigger now. Severino was gawking at his companion, his own gun useless at his side. The android was dropping into a crouch, ready to lunge at the agent.

Rhett took the first elongated second to evaluate the situation, playing it out in his mind. Then he started moving.

Walking in suspended time was harder than he'd anticipated, but it could be done. He pushed off with one leg and moved through the room as though it was filled with molasses. Despite the added effort, it didn't hurt. He took two steps toward Diego, leaned his full weight in, and gave him a mighty, if slow-moving, shove.

Before the effects of the time bomb could wear off, he crushed a second one between his fingers and turned toward Fabien. He was far enough away that he needed to crush a third bomb before he reached him. When he did, he adjusted the angle of his rifle a few degrees. On second thought, he switched the manual setting from stun to live rounds.

The world sprang back to life. Agony seared through him, as if he'd just run a marathon. Was this how Fabien had felt after using those bracers in the Ohio vault? Rhett's leg gave way beneath him, and he collapsed with a mewl of pain.

At least Rhett's calculations were dead on. Even before he went down, Diego was thrown sideways at what must have seemed like a totally random angle to anyone else watching. He let out a yelp of surprise as he was flung down the hallway, leaving Apollo wide open. The agent must have already powered down his tech in anticipation of killing Diego, because his fist clenched in air that was suddenly empty.

A second later, Fabien's live round hit Apollo square in the chest, crumpling his suit inward to leave a concave hollow right between his ribs. He staggered back.

Then the android was on him.

Fabien lowered his rifle and crouched by Rhett's side. "What the—? How the hell did you do that?"

"Doesn't matter," Rhett wheezed. He slipped the last two time bombs back into his pocket. "We need to get to Dinah."

Fabien pursed his lips, probably thinking that he'd just as soon kill Apollo while he had the chance, but the agent had already phased out again. This time, he'd taken the android with him; they were still grappling with one another as they collapsed through the floor.

"Right," he said. "Can you stand?"

Rhett tried to sit up, but there was no way he'd be able to make a run for it with them.

"Find Dinah," he told Fabien. "Apollo won't bother with me if he's trying to find... you know." He lifted his eyebrows meaningfully.

He wasn't sure that it was true, but in the Ohio vault, and during their ill-fated jet flight, Apollo had prioritized any opportunity that brought him closer to the relic over killing. It was a calculated risk.

Fabien seemed to understand that, because he got to his feet and stared down at him for a fraction of a second before he nodded and took off. "Severino, Diego," he barked, "you're with me. Check the rooms, and for God's sake, stay away from the walls."

The Atlanteans did as he commanded, and within moments the hallway fell silent. Left to his own devices, Rhett began the painstaking process of dragging himself back down the corridor. Someone would come looking for them eventually, and they needed all the backup they could get.

21 DINAH

WHEN DINAH HEARD the voices in the hallway, she started crawling. There was no telling where Apollo was, and the Laputans probably wouldn't be impressed by the fact that she'd broken into their vault.

Really should have thought that part through, she scolded herself. *Now everyone's going to be pissed at you. Great job.*

The hum of the relic echoed in her ears, but it grew softer by the second as she scrambled deeper into the control room. Soon it was lost altogether among the shifting of the machinery and the hiss of pressure valves somewhere beyond.

Atlantis had been sleek and new, but Laputa was clearly an older construction. A messy criss-cross of pipes, cables, and fuse boxes threaded between sections that had been updated with newer equipment. It was a bit like visiting an old city that had been continuously occupied for centuries, with layers of development eating into each other or dropping away beneath the streets in the form of old aqueducts or hidden catacombs. Everywhere she looked, descriptions popped up on her headset. *Central Heating*

Duct Power Cable. Gyroscope Stabilizer. Fuel Line. Thruster Control. Auto-Navigation Switchboard. She didn't bother scrolling through the textboxes. After a while, she stopped reading the headings altogether.

There were fewer lights down here, spaced intermittently along the narrow walkways left for engineers. Deep in the bowels of Laputa, Dinah stopped crawling and curled in on herself as she planned her next move.

According to Apollo, the pieces of the relic could sense each other. At the moment, Dinah's fragment had gone cool and quiet once more. What kind of range did these things have? Clearly it wasn't a perfect science, because Apollo hadn't pounced on her earlier. If Apollo could use the fragment to track her, then Dinah could do the reverse, and use the information it provided to elude the Hand.

She settled down with her back against a branching conduit of cables as big around as a tree trunk and took a deep breath. The air was stuffy and much warmer than the rest of the city, thick with the scent of oil and hot metal and spilled grease. She reached into her pocket and pulled out the relic again.

If only she could work out what it was for, maybe all this chaos wouldn't be a waste of time.

Dinah turned it in her fingers, over and over. The shape itself meant nothing to her, and the words inscribed on the side were meaningless.

What would you think it was if you found it at a dig site? People found strange objects all the time. Dinah bounced the relic in her hand, weighing it. It felt solid and sturdy. Pure metal, as far as she could tell, although there must be something inside of it that could power the lights and make it hum. It clearly wasn't an ornament, and it must have some distinct purpose. The extrusion on one end and the indentation on the other implied that it interlocked with other items that had male and female fittings, almost like—

Dinah almost dropped the relic in surprise. *Almost like a battery.*

If she'd found it at a dig, her first thought wouldn't have been, *I wonder what ancient item this artifact could be used to power.* She'd have tried to ascribe it a function that made sense in a historical context. But according to Porter, Dinah's whole grasp of the historical record was iffy in the larger context ENIGMA provided.

If she was going to be of any use on this mission at all, she'd have to stop limiting herself to what she thought she knew and get with the program.

A shout from one of the walkways made her flinch, and she tucked the relic back into her coat pocket, bracing for a fight. It wasn't Apollo, which was good news. It also wasn't Fabien or Rhett, which was not.

She squinted between the pipes and cables and spotted one of the Atlanteans moving down the walk. Not Severino, either, so it could go either way in terms of friendliness. Better not to risk it.

Besides, more people meant more distractions, and Dinah already had to watch her back.

Moving deeper into the belly of Laputa might end in her getting cornered. Retracing her steps would bring her back to the last place she'd seen Apollo. Either way, she'd be walking into trouble, so for the moment Dinah just held her breath and watched the Atlantean pass her.

The man was only a hundred yards or so away before the relic started humming again.

"*Quiet,*" Dinah mouthed. She pressed her hand over her pocket from the outside so that the relic's hum would be smothered by the layers of fur and lining.

In the dim light, the blue glow of Apollo's intangible presence glowed for an instant, then burnt out. The Atlantean rotated on the spot, clearly just as wary as Dinah, but lacking a few tools to warn him of the Hand's approach.

He's coming, Dinah thought. She wished she could call out to the guard without giving her position away. Letting the other man face Apollo on his own felt like cowardice... but after all, Dinah was protecting the relic.

It wasn't her fault that she couldn't get involved.

It wasn't.

Wherever Apollo was now, he was solid. This would be the perfect time to fight him. Maybe, if Dinah hid the relic among the cables and tried to sneak up on Apollo, she could get in a shot? Although that would leave the relic unguarded and easier for the Hand to find.

Her indecision lasted too long. Apollo moved among the machines, a silent shadow in the half-dark, until he was upon the Atlantean.

The guard saw him just in time and started firing, and Apollo phased out again, giving his position away. He didn't hit the Hand. Instead, his ammo peppered the equipment around where Apollo stood. The scream of rending metal and the snap-crackle of sparks wasn't loud enough to drown out the man's cursing. Beneath Dinah's feet, Laputa lurched as its stabilizers struggled to compensate for the equipment that had just been destroyed.

In the chaos that followed, Dinah scrambled away, back toward the door and the hallway beyond.

"Diego!" someone yelled. More footsteps pounded against the metal catwalk a floor above as Severino charged into the fray. Dinah kept her head down and crawled as fast as she could.

She wasn't watching where she was going, so when she crawled practically underfoot of someone running the other way, they ended up on the floor in a tangled heap.

"Dinah!" Fabien barked. "What are you—"

Dinah snatched the relic from her pocket and pressed it into Fabien's palm. "Run," she said.

Fabien's mouth opened.

"Apollo's back there," Dinah blurted. "He's coming, and you're faster than I am, and better at planning. He can track the relic. This is what he's here for. So *run*."

Behind them, the gunfire dropped by half. One of the Atlanteans was down, and Dinah was pretty sure he wouldn't be getting up again.

She gripped Fabien's fist in hers. *"Run,"* she said again.

Fabien yanked his hand away, turned on his heel, and ran. In his wake, Dinah crawled back into Laputa's damaged organs and curled in on herself.

Without the relic, she was untraceable. Apollo could pass within inches of her and never know she was there.

You should try to help Severino and his friend, Dinah thought. Once again, she hesitated until the firefight in the depths of Laputa's belly fell silent at last. There was no way to fool herself into thinking that this was anything but cowardice. No way to spin it that would excuse her behavior as anything other than self-preservation.

She waited until she was sure that Apollo was gone, tracking the pale blue glow as the agent of the Hand strode through the cords and cables and screens and engines and circuit breakers of Laputa's nervous system. Only then did she get to her feet, while the city tilted on its axis and the loose spanners and bits of dropped hardware, forgotten by the engineers from whose fingers they'd slipped, skittered across the floor away from her.

Rivulets of blood reached her feet long before she found what remained of the Atlanteans.

22 FABIEN

GODDAMN WHOEVER HAD DECIDED to build a city in the air. As the floor sloped beneath his feet, Fabien was thrown into the wall. He nearly dropped the relic in the process.

Goddamn Dinah, too. What was Fabien supposed to do with this thing now that he had it? He stuffed it into one of the zippered pockets of the Atlantean trousers he was wearing.

The one good thing about all this was that Apollo would, as Rhett said, do anything for the relic. The surly, stupid part of Fabien's brain that wanted a rematch thought, *Excellent. Maybe now he'll stop running away every chance he gets, and we'll see what he's got for me.*

He stumbled back into the hallway, only for Laputa to lurch again, this time slanting the other way. Fabien fell backward and only managed to catch himself by flipping his rifle sideways, catching it on the far side of the door. The strap around his shoulder snapped taut, but he was able to drag himself forward and catch his elbow on the door as well.

In the hall, the bisected android rolled against the wall. Fabien got a bit less lucky with the Laputan's partially liquefied corpse, which rolled into his legs. The stench was unbearable.

Not that his borrowed fur coat smelled all that great, either.

The ship stayed slanted, tipping him back into the engineering sector, toward Apollo. Fabien untangled his feet from around the corpse, which sloshed away wetly behind him.

Disgusting.

Using his elbow for leverage, Fabien dragged himself out into the hallway. Laputa was tilted much more sharply than before, with the floor almost at a ninety degree angle. With one foot braced on the floor, and the other against the wall, Fabien set out at a waddling jog.

I need to get Apollo someplace where I can actually fight him. The narrow halls of Laputa made combat almost impossible. Apollo would be forever fading through them, intangible as a ghost. If he could only get Apollo out in the open, he might be able to get in another shot.

Too bad he didn't have Rhett around to help. Whatever he'd done in the hall had allowed Fabien to get in his first *real* shot at Apollo. One more like that, and they'd be golden, so to speak.

With a groan, Laputa righted itself again, rolling beneath Fabien's feet like the deck of a ship at sea. He pinwheeled his arms, and the momentum forced him back against the floor.

Beside him, the wall shimmered blue.

No, he thought, *I'm not ready,* but Apollo was already coming. Fabien shifted his center of gravity lower as he whipped his rifle into position. Apollo was almost through the wall by the time his eye met the scope.

Only, Laputa kept tilting. Apollo topped forward. Both men swore.

When they overlapped, Fabien's whole body screamed in protest. Apollo wasn't there, but *enough* of him was that every molecule in Fabien's body felt scrambled and thinned. He wanted to dig his fingernails into his skin, and his stomach heaved in rejection of this painful and deeply personal invasion.

Then they hit the wall. Or rather, Fabien hit it, and Apollo just kept going.

He lay there for a moment, breathing hard, as a warm trickle of blood trailed from his nose. His eyes seemed to have trouble focusing.

Get up, he told himself. *You've got the relic, and you need to get outside. Get up.*

It took a bit longer for his limbs to obey him, and at first he could do little more than crawl. Another attack like that, and he'd be down for the count.

All the more reason to keep moving.

He was almost to the end of the hallway when a handful of androids rounded the corner. They seemed utterly unperturbed by the rocking floor beneath them; whatever gyroscopic systems guided their movements were able to keep up with the ever-changing angle of the city.

"Wait," he called after them. He extended one arm toward them, but they must only have been taking orders from Kunzang, or from the city itself, because only one of them stopped to look at him, and that only briefly. They made their way to the door of the engine room, presumably *en route* to fix whatever had been damaged in the ship's core.

That didn't leave Fabien with a lot of options, and there was no way he'd be able to outrun Apollo at this rate.

Well, to hell with it. He didn't need his pride. He set the safety on his rifle, wrapped his arms around the stock, and rolled into the hallway.

As a child, Fabien had enjoyed rolling down hills in the bright summer grass of Ariège province. He'd revisited the experience only a few years ago and found it just as freeing and joyful as he remembered.

Rolling down the corridors of Laputa was like being beaten all over with a bag full of Euros—an experience that Fabien had endured only once, but which stood out vividly in his memory. Still, if he closed his eyes and pretended, he could almost convince himself that he was back in the rolling landscape of his childhood home.

At the very least, he could remember why he was here in the first place.

The next time Laputa swung, Fabien spread out his legs and threw one arm wide, in an ungainly and face-down likeness of someone making a snow angel. He bashed his thigh on the corner of the wall in the process, but at least it was enough to arrest his progress. Otherwise, he might have kept tumbling forever, like the ball bearing in a city-sized pinball machine. Once he'd finally stopped moving, he scrambled to his feet and kept running, uphill now, as the angle of the floor deepened.

Without the relic, he'd likely have lost Apollo by now, but if Dinah was right then he needn't worry about that. His target would come to him. All he had to do was be ready.

No one had taken them *outside* the city, but there had to be a way out. What if something got damaged? They'd need to be able to send someone out to do repairs, even if it was just the androids, and that would require a door. The Laputans couldn't walk through walls, after all.

But no matter how far he ran, he couldn't find one, and he wasn't exactly in peak fighting form at the moment.

Fabien pulled up short and pressed his finger against his pocket. The relic inside vibrated like a muted phone. Could that mean—?

Apollo lurched through the wall behind Fabien and to his

right. It was, whether the Hand knew it or not, the angle from which Fabien would have the most difficulty firing on him.

The next thought that occurred to him was a very stupid one indeed. When Apollo phased out while touching people, those people were able to follow him through solid objects.

But that wasn't the *only* way that the Hand could make a door.

Fabien grinned to himself and wiped the back of his hand beneath his nose. It came away bloody.

He pushed off the floor with his left foot, spinning to face Apollo. If he was going to do this right, he'd either need to grab Apollo between phases, or time his movements perfectly.

The agent of the Hand still shimmered blue. He couldn't make out Apollo's face behind that inscrutable, pompous mask, but the man had to be in pain. The chestplate of his suit was still caved in from Fabien's earlier shot, and the marksman said a silent prayer of thanks to Rhett. That was almost certainly the reason that Apollo hadn't caught up with him earlier—the Hand was hurting, and that concave chestplate wouldn't make it any easier to breathe.

Apollo stood there, one gloved hand pressed to his golden chest, and stared at Fabien in silence.

"Go on," Fabien said. His rifle was pressed to his shaking shoulder, the safety off. No doubt Apollo could see the way his arms shook as he stood there. "You need to phase in to shoot me, don't you? Or else your weapon won't work."

Apollo, too, was trembling. His suit, and whatever tech he was carrying, might allow him to move through walls, but it didn't fully compensate for the thin air, or his obvious injuries.

What kind of toll did it take on a man, to spend so much time not quite in the world? Fabien had only followed him once, and falling through the cockpit wall hadn't *hurt* the way Apollo walking into him had. Still, it would mess with a guy's head, wouldn't it?

Fabien knew a thing or two about that.

"If I deactivate the destabilizer," Apollo said in his deep, digitally scrambled voice, "then you will shoot me."

"And if you don't, you can't take the relic." Fabien's lips quirked into a wry smile. He pressed one hand to the pocket of his coat, still aiming his rifle with the other. "I think we might reasonably call this an impasse, don't you?" *Come on, take the bait.* He wasn't sure how accurately Apollo could track the relic, but if he was using the ones he'd already stolen as lodestones, he wouldn't be able to tell the difference of a few inches between Fabien's coat pocket and the zippered pocket of his trousers.

"Impasse?" Apollo repeated. His knees bent in anticipation of a leap. "I prefer to think of it as a deadlock."

He hurled himself toward Fabien, phasing in—or perhaps *stabilizing?*—just before impact. He was too close to shoot by then, and the two of them tumbled to the ground, wrestling over Fabien's oversized coat. In close quarters, Apollo's blows came hard and fast, catching Fabien in the collarbone, the gut, and the ribs in swift succession.

It was almost enough to make him lose the thread of his little plan, but Fabien was already two steps ahead. He managed to hold onto his rifle as Apollo yanked at his coat and, he hoped, make the Hand's win look believable. When the coat ripped and came away in Apollo's hands, the agent let out a laugh of triumph. He drove his knee into Fabien's stomach for good measure before launching to his feet. Fabien made one feeble swipe at the coat before Apollo destabilized.

Perfect. Now he just had to keep up.

Apollo took a step back, right through the wall of Laputa, and Fabien went with him.

Every atom, every molecule of his being screamed at him, but he managed to force himself forward. If the stunning blast of his rifle had been able to follow Apollo through a solid wall, then it stood to reason that Fabien could do the same. By the time they were outside the tunnel and most of the way through the snow, his steps faltered, and he tripped over the snow that gathered in drifts at his feet.

He tumbled face-first in the white drifts, already cursing himself as an idiot. *Great idea, Fabien, let him take the coat before you follow him through the wall! Now you can freeze to death outside.* It was even colder on Laputa than it had been on the mountainside below, and the winds whipped around him with enough force to lift him right off the island if he wasn't careful.

Still, he'd made it out. At least here, he'd be able to have a better view and couldn't get hemmed in. It was dark, and the air was brutally cold, but at least it had stopped snowing. There was enough moonlight for him to see clearly, casting the frozen city in an unearthly, shadowless glow.

Somewhere to his right, Apollo cursed.

"Wasn't in there, huh?" Fabien called back. He felt like death, there was bloody mucus in his eyes, and his hands were already turning blue, but he just needed one lucky shot. One more lucky shot.

"That was foolish." Apollo made no attempt to hide. He strode through the snow toward Fabien, glittering blue. "I'm going to kill you. You know that, don't you? You and your friends have made this mission *so* much more tedious."

Fabien licked his lips. He kept his eye ever so slightly away from the scope, afraid that his face might freeze to it otherwise. "Guess Porter shouldn't have hired us, then," he croaked. His breath all but turned to snow on the frigid wind.

"It would have been better," Apollo growled. "For both our

sakes. But the mistake is easily remedied." He took another step forward, and Fabien took an instinctive step back, just as Laputa lurched once more.

"It'd be a shame if the city crashed into the mountains," Fabien said. The cold didn't seem to bother Apollo as much as it bothered him, perhaps a side effect of the destabilizer, but the other man was struggling with every step. "Would the Hand send someone for you if it did?"

"Not for me," Apollo said. "For the relic. I know I'm replaceable." He took another step.

The blue light running over his armor flickered, just for a moment. Apollo didn't seem to notice, but Fabien did. *Maybe that tech of his doesn't like the cold… or he's been using it too much and the power's running out.* He sucked in a breath that seared his lungs from the inside, and stifled a cough. If one of them was going to make a move, they'd better do it soon.

When Apollo took another step forward, he braced his feet and held his ground. *One lucky shot.* No more tricks. No more slipping through solid matter. No more mistakes.

The light flickered again, and Fabien's finger jerked on the trigger, just as Laputa scraped against the mountainside. His shot went wide, and Fabien stumbled back. The rifle slipped through his frozen fingers.

Apollo laughed. The stabilizer had either died, or he'd turned it off altogether. He strode forward and reached for the pistol at his hip.

Great, Fabien thought dimly as he tried to right himself. Laputa was tilting hard now as its lip slid further up the mountainside. What were those androids *doing* in there?

Apollo took aim, and Fabien let himself fall. Rolling didn't hurt so badly this time. It didn't feel like much of anything at all.

You're going to die out here, he thought.

Maybe it was the lack of oxygen, maybe the delirium, but he could have sworn he heard another voice, soft and sweet and very far away, tell him, *No. You're not.*

"Erek?" He came to rest against a low wall. When he finally managed to sit up, he saw the slope spread out below him, down to the little hut where they'd arrived the day before, and into the darkness beyond.

A cloud passed over the moon, plunging the city into shadow.

He could just make out the figure moving against the sky. Apollo stumbled forward on unsteady legs. He was holding his pistol, the one that would leave Fabien looking like wet silly putty by the time it was done with him.

He can't phase out now, Fabien thought. *If you're going to fight him, now's the time.* Too bad his rifle was a dozen yards away. Too bad he could barely move.

Apollo lifted his pistol in quaking fingers. "*Au revoir,* Fabien LeRoux," he said.

Fabien chuckled weakly. "Your French is shitty," he said. As he spoke, he dug his freezing hand into the pocket of his trousers and retrieved the relic, which now felt like it had its own heartbeat. The light from the glowing inscriptions cast strange shadows in the snow.

Apollo took another stumbling step forward. "What are you doing?"

Fabien's lips were so cold he could barely manage a smile. The insides of his nostrils felt as if they'd already iced over. It was probably a very bad thing that the weather wasn't bothering him so much anymore.

"Catch," he breathed, and flicked the relic over his shoulder into open air.

Apollo lunged for it in a vain attempt to catch the artifact before it fell, and Fabien used the last of his strength to sweep the agent's feet out from under him. With a wordless cry, Apollo went over the wall and tumbled, face-first, through the numbing winds.

Left alone, Fabien curled in on himself. He wanted to look down, to know for sure if there would be a flash of blue below him, if Apollo had met his end or if he'd had one last trick up his gilded sleeves.

He wanted to, but he couldn't. All he could do was curl up in the snow alongside Apollo's footprint and close his eyes as the first layer of snow blew over him.

23 RHETT

RHETT DOZED to the dull pulse of the medical equipment, which was as good a lullaby as any he'd heard in years. It had been almost three hours since the engines of Laputa were finally restored to working order, and the dull red of the emergency lights was replaced with the glow of clear LEDs.

Nearby, Kunzang rested in a covered pod, her vitals faint but steady as the machine did its work. It was amazing that she'd survived his encounter in the vault, and she still looked like she'd been chewed up and spit out, but her wounds were already looking better with the artificially grown skin grafts the medical team had applied when they first brought her in.

Fabien, too, slept in a pod of his own. Both of them were hooked up to oxygen masks. Fabien still looked like hell, too, but the color was slowly coming back into his face and limbs.

Rhett shifted in his chair, and his new position brought Dinah into his line of sight. The professor sat with her head in her hands as her shoulders shook.

"What's wrong?" he murmured, rallying a little despite the fact that he was only half awake.

"I froze up," she whispered.

He smiled sleepily. "Makes sense. It's colder than a witch's tit up here."

She lowered her hands a little. "Seriously?" Her accusing glare roused a sigh out of him, and he sat up a little straighter. Whatever the med droid had given him was working its magic. He felt almost human again, as opposed to the barely-conscious ball of endless pain he'd been when they brought him in.

"You're not combat-ready," he said, rubbing one knuckle in his eye. "You knew that coming into this. We knew it, too. Nobody expects you to be. Look at what happened to the folks who were trained." He waved one hand at Kunzang, although he was certain that they were both thinking of the bodies that had already been sent down to the morgue on the lower floors.

"I had no business pocketing that *stupid* relic." She shook her head, and her throat bobbed.

Rhett covered his laugh with a cough. Leave it to a professor to use the word 'stupid' with all the vehemence of a curse. "You kept it away from Apollo for almost thirty-eight minutes longer than the vault doors could have," he pointed out.

"Exactly! Thirty-eight extra minutes of bloodshed, two more androids destroyed, at least three more people dead than there would have been, and Fabien almost frozen alive! And in the end, the relic is still gone."

"They might find him, you know." Rhett patted her shoulder. "They're doing sweeps on the slopes right now. For all we know, Apollo is dead, the relic is safe, and we got back the two he stole before. In which case"— he spread his hands wide in a gesture of triumph—"we succeeded. All thanks to you."

Dinah bit her bottom lip. "You really think so?"

"I think you did the best you could have with the information available," he assured her.

She smiled, albeit weakly. "Thank you."

"We'll decide what to do next when we know more. And when Fabien's up." He said it confidently, so that Dinah wouldn't lose even more sleep fretting over their teammate's wellbeing. "In the meantime, I need rest, and so do you. We'll be no good to anyone if we don't get some sleep." He got to his feet and held out one hand to her. "Come on. Let's go back to our room and get some shuteye."

Dinah took his hand, and he pulled her upright. He knew for a fact that the moment his head hit the pillow, he was going to sleep like the dead.

RHETT HAD LOST all sense of time. When he finally emerged from their room—the door of which had been left unlocked this time—Dinah was still snoring.

His tongue felt furry, and the inside of his mouth had that tacky, viscous sensation born of dehydration and too much time spent breathing too-dry air.

The halls of Laputa were populated only by the occasional android and the even rarer human. The androids paid him no mind at all, but the first human he passed stopped short. "Where are you going?" they asked.

"Er." Rhett unconsciously lifted his fingers to the plaster patch covering the gash on his chin. "The mess hall?"

The woman nodded once, her face as inscrutable as Kunzang's had been when they first arrived. "Come." She set off down the hall at a brisk pace, leaving Rhett to do his best to keep up.

He'd wondered if the woman was leading him off to a cell, in light of everything that had happened. If the Laputans took

Dinah's view of the events of the previous night, they'd surely more than worn out their welcome.

Instead, he was escorted through to a common area. The area was a mess—the tables and chairs had been set up again since the city's equilibrium was restored, and the smells from the kitchen suggested that it, too, had been brought back up to speed. The rest of the decorations, games, and common room furniture were still strewn against the walls like debris washed up after a storm at sea.

Fabien was sitting at one of the tables, next to a man Rhett didn't recognize. He was dressed like the other Laputans, and when his eyes found Rhett, they were cold as winter stars.

Rhett hurried over to meet them, muttering a distracted thank you to the woman who'd shown him the way. He dropped into the chair across from Fabien, eyeing up his new companion.

The Laputan pushed a plate toward him, filled with dried meat and little mounds of what looked like uncooked dough. "Tea?" he asked gruffly.

Rhett nodded.

He poured him some, although it didn't look much like any tea he'd ever seen before. It was thick and pale, with an oily film over the top. Rhett hesitated before lifting his cup, but if the Laputans were going to poison him, they might as well get on with it. He lifted the cup to his lips and took a tiny sip.

A creamy, buttery flavor sloshed over his tongue, and he took another sip at once. The man was watching him, perhaps as some sort of test, and he drained his cup before setting it back on the table.

Evidently satisfied, the man poured him another cup. "We haven't met before. I'm Tenzin." He rotated to face Rhett more directly, and Rhett realized that he was young. Younger than Dinah, even, almost certainly in his twenties. "Kunzang's son. My mother—" His lips tightened, and his dark eyes flicked away from his, just for a moment. "My mother voiced some... opinions about you."

Rhett picked at a piece of dried meat, already feeling fortified by the buttery tea. "Is she awake?"

"Not yet," Tenzin told him. "In the meantime, you'll have to work with me. I agree with her on some things... but not everything." He clenched his fist. "You tried to keep the relic from Apollo."

"And nearly wrecked the city in the process," Fabien muttered.

Rhett glared at him over his tea. He wasn't wrong, but at least he could have the good sense not to point it out in front of their host.

"And you did so at great personal risk." Tenzin shrugged one shoulder. "Clearly, we could do no better than you did. It's the effort that matters. You've proven—at least to me—that you are loyal to ENIGMA."

Fabien snorted and let the strip of dried meat he'd been picking at drop from his fingers. "Can I ask you something? Why didn't Apollo kill your mother?"

Tenzin flinched, and Rhett narrowed his eyes even further. Fabien, however, carried on as if he hadn't noticed.

"Apollo keeps breaking into vaults and leaving witnesses. Why? I saw the state Kunzang was in. He could have killed her easily. And yet, she lives. Why?"

Tenzin's eyes slid between Rhett and Fabien, taking their measure again. "He's in a rush? He's one man in hostile territory, and based on what you described, there seems to be a limit to how long he can use that device of his before it needs time to recharge."

"Hm. Maybe." Fabien leaned closer. "Or maybe he has another reason for leaving people alive. How do you know we risked our lives to save the relic? Maybe we risked our lives to help him steal it." He shoved his plate away from him. "You have no reason to trust us, Tenzin. Just as we have no reason to trust you."

Silence fell over their little group. It would have been deafening except for the steady thump of Tenzin's fingers drumming against the tabletop.

"I suppose you have a point," he said at last.

"A point," Rhett added, "that will be rendered moot when you find Apollo's body and recover all three relics."

Fabien groaned, and Tenzin cleared his throat. "Unfortunately, Apollo seems to have escaped. The ground crew found evidence that he survived the fall and made it back to his ship."

"And I'm sure he has all three pieces," Fabien added. "They can sense each other. He would have been able to home in on the location of the one I threw before he left."

Rhett swore under his breath. He hadn't realized how badly he wanted to get back to his family in California until he realized that it wouldn't be happening.

Of course, they had bigger problems to worry about. The mounting suspicion that there was a mole in their ranks had burrowed its way under his skin. Kunzang had reasons to mistrust Porter.

And if Porter couldn't be trusted, who was to say that the people he'd hired were any better?

24 DINAH

DINAH WAS JUST PULLING on her headset when the door to their quarters burst open and Fabien shoved his way through.

"I'm just saying," Rhett's voice snapped from the hallway, "that if he is working with someone in ENIGMA, maybe telling him that you're suspicious isn't the smartest move." He followed Fabien into the room and closed the door behind them.

"Maybe not," Fabien barked back as he turned to face him, "but I think we're all wary of Porter, and I'm starting to think we ought to be. He can't have sent us on this wild goose chase without knowing more than he's told us. It doesn't add up."

Speaking of Porter, there was a message waiting on Dinah's headset. She opened it, tuning out the squabbling of her teammates. It was a brief message, confirming what Dinah already knew by now: one of the items taken from the Ohio vault matched the relic Apollo had taken from Laputa the night before. There was no new information, only the text box that Dinah had read through a hundred times by now.

"—don't see why we'd be any more effective next time around," Fabien was saying. "He almost killed me last night."

"Maybe Tenzin will vouch for us this time." Rhett settled on the end of the bed. "We might be able to get some backup from the crew of the... what was it called? Holy Land?"

"Are you still thinking of going?" Dinah blurted.

The two turned to look at her, as if surprised to find that she was still there. Their gazes made her shrink away. She hadn't exactly been the most helpful member of their little group, had she?

Rhett spoke first, running his hand over the length of his chameleon coat as he did. It was a subtle tic, one of the rare signs that he was as out of his depth as she was. "I think we—no, let me speak for myself. I need to see this through. What are my options? Go home, with nothing to show for this? Besides, Apollo knows my face now. There's no reason to think that leaving now will protect us from him when he's gotten what he wants."

Dinah's shoulders drooped. "Apollo's still alive?" It was all too easy to imagine sitting down to dinner with her family at some holiday or other, only for Apollo to walk through the walls and start shooting.

She'd found Diego and Severino before the androids did. Or rather, what was left of them.

"Alive, and off somewhere celebrating the success of his mission." Fabien kicked one of his bedposts. "Which is why I'm not backing out. I'm going to see this through, and if Porter tries to wiggle out of what he promised me, I'm going to hold his feet to the fire until he follows through."

"Right." Dinah folded her hands in her lap. When Porter had first contacted her, the man had made promises that seemed far too good to be true. Now, she was confident that Porter could deliver, but the things Dinah had wanted seemed small by comparison to everything she knew now.

"What about you?" Rhett asked.

Dinah whipped her head up. "What?"

His smile was almost kindly. "You could go home. Or stay here, maybe, until the mission's over. I'm sure we could twist someone's arm into making sure that you're kept safe from the Hand."

It was a tempting prospect. She thought of the way her heart had threatened to pound out of her chest during her mad scramble through the engineering sector, and the way she'd hesitated at nearly every critical moment. Perhaps it would be better for everyone if she just pulled out of the mission and let the other two fight Apollo on their own.

But.

Dinah met Rhett's gaze. "It's a battery."

A small frown pinched at his lips and his brows. "What is?"

"The relic. I think it's a battery. And I think that when all of them are connected, they'll be able to power… something. I think he needs all five pieces, and when he has them, he'll be able to put them to use."

Rhett rocked back in his seat on the bed. He turned to Fabien, waving one hand as if to pull him into the conversation. "Didn't Tenzin say something about Apollo's device running out of power?"

"The destabilizer." Fabien tapped his thumb against his lips. "That's what he called it."

"Did you see what it was?" Rhett asked.

"No. But I think it must be small, for him to be able to turn it on and off whenever it suits him."

The three of them sat in silence for a long moment, each thinking their private thoughts. Dinah was trying to imagine how the five relic pieces would come together to fit with another bit of tech. It would have to be something that would fit in the middle, most likely, unless the last two pieces of the relic were a very different shape...

Fabien interrupted her train of thought. "If he can add even more power to that destabilizer of his, then nothing we can do will even slow him down."

"Then I guess we'll have to stop him from getting the last two pieces," Rhett agreed.

He looked to Dinah for confirmation, and this time, she nodded without a moment's hesitation.

If they were going to derail Apollo's quest to reunite the pieces of the relic, they'd need all the help they could get.

INTERLUDE

Apollo had to land his craft in a low, desolate portion of the steppes. He'd managed to arrest his fall through the Himalayan sky using the last little pulses of power afforded him by the destabilizer, but without the snow drifts below him, he'd still have been crushed under his own momentum. It had taken him a long time to drag himself upright and dig through the acres of white powder, following the pulse of the relics he already possessed.

At least the heating in his transport craft was fully functional. He was afraid he might lose one of his fingers to frostbite, and even now, his hand wouldn't move the way he wanted it to.

If that arrogant sniper costs me a finger, I will take his whole hand in exchange, Apollo thought bitterly.

The more pressing issue, however, was the damaged chestplate of his golden suit. Every breath cost him, and the pressure against his ribs was excruciating. They were bruised at best, and he was certain that at least one of them was cracked.

So he'd landed, and now he was lying in his reclined seat with a MendMe pressed to his side. He drifted in and out of consciousness, through dreams filled with blood and bone and the grating vibration of the destabilizer that let him move through the world like a ghost.

It was so much easier to breathe without that damned mask.

He was roused to wakefulness by the alert of an incoming transmission. *"Ray Six, this is Ray Twelve, do you copy?"*

He groaned as he lifted himself up to reach the controls. "I hear you loud and clear."

"Well," Ra said into the mic, *"that was a bit of a disaster, wasn't it?"*

Apollo laughed to himself as he flopped backward again. "Did you really call to berate me? Because my hands are full right now."

"I'll bet they are." Ra's digitally deepened voice still managed to sound pissy and irritable. *"They know what you're after by now. According to my intel, Holy Land is going on lockdown. And I hear you left Kunzang alive."*

"We agreed that it would be the best course of action." He rubbed one hand over his ribs. The pressure was already fading. The MendMe was working, at least. Once he was more or less functional again, he'd have to find a way to beat the dent out of the chestplate. Of course, it would never be like new again, but at least it would work.

"We?" Ra grumbled. *"I didn't hear anything about that."*

"You weren't part of the conversation," Apollo murmured. "It was Ray One's idea."

At the mention of Aten, Ra fell silent. Good. Apollo needed to rest before he moved on to the next mission, and Ra's whining didn't help. Apollo's patience with the other agent was running thin. Ra had the easy job, after all.

"Regardless, they're getting twitchy. It would be better to move fast, and—"

It came to him, in a rush, that Aten hadn't authorized this

message. Ra was operating in the dark, probably terrified that they would be found out before Apollo managed to collect the last two artifacts before their cover was blown.

"I'm doing what I'm meant to do, Ray Twelve. Perhaps instead of pestering me, you should focus on your own mission." Without signing off, Apollo killed the comm. When a new message came in, he ignored it.

His chest still ached, but Ra was right about one thing: the sooner he finished his mission, the sooner the Hand of the Sun would get the upper hand. ENIGMA was running scared. Its vaults had been compromised for the first time in two generations. If he struck now, the organization might never fully recover from the blow.

Apollo peeled the MendMe off of his chest and reached for his chestplate. Aten, after all, had chosen his name well. He was meant to be the chariot of the sun, the one who would usher in the dawn of a new era for the Hand, scattering the shadows of ENIGMA to the darkened corners of the Earth where they belonged.

25 FABIEN

RHETT PULLED the straps of his pack tighter until the bag molded to his back. "Admit it," he said with a smirk. "You're afraid of heights."

"I'm not," Fabien shot back. He adjusted the cap of his wing-suit self-consciously. "I just don't feel the need to fling myself off of mountains for sport, that's all."

The most irritating part of the whole affair was the fact that Dinah didn't seem fazed by any of this. She was already standing on the edge of the launch pad, marveling at the wonder before them. How could she take the idea of leaping into empty air so easily, when she was so useless in a firefight?

To be fair, the view was breathtaking, and not just because the wind seemed to steal the oxygen from Fabien's lungs. The icy peaks glowed in the thin sunlight, highlighting blue glaciers that sparkled like sapphires beneath them. He'd been forced to don his snow goggles again, which meant that the lower steppes, with the blank, brown landscape, barely looked like anything at all. They were so far away, so dull in comparison to the slopes themselves.

And Fabien was, essentially, supposed to *fall* there.

Tenzin came up behind him and gripped his shoulder, pointing to a spot far below. "We need to get you there, to where your helicopter is waiting. I see your reluctance to do this, but any other transport would take days to retrieve you. This will take you no time at all. Depending on how much of a lead Apollo has over you, you may still be able to beat him to Holy Land."

Fabien bit down on the inside of his cheek. The man had a point. That didn't mean that he had to like it, but it *did* mean that his alternatives were limited.

"I never said I wouldn't do it," he muttered.

"Very good." Tenzin slapped his back. "One of our androids will lead the way, and will accompany you on the next leg of your mission as backup, along with the ground crew that is already waiting for you. Are you ready?"

"Ready." Dinah spread her arms, testing the range of the material beneath. She looked absolutely ridiculous. They all did.

I'm going to be sent home in a body bag dressed like a human parachute, Fabien thought grimly. The humiliation might very well make him roll in his grave.

"Then follow your guide," Tenzin said, "and good luck."

At his words, the android who would be guiding them strode to the edge of the platform and executed a perfect swan dive into the open sky.

With a whoop of excitement, Dinah ran after it. She didn't move with the same grace—if anything, she looked more like a child leaping off a diving board into the deep end of the pool for the first time—and followed the android into empty air.

Fabien turned to Rhett, secretly hoping that he'd choke at the last moment, but he only reached around to pat his backpack and make sure that his cane was still strapped into place. He caught his eye and grinned.

"See you down there, LeRoux," he shouted over the roar of the wind. Then he, too, was falling, and Fabien was the only one left.

Tenzin watched him silently, and it occurred to Fabien that this would be the perfect opportunity for the man to get revenge for his mother's injuries. All he had to do was sabotage their squirrel suits, and the three of them would be gone for good. They'd leapt from the city ramparts like lemmings, eager to prove themselves.

Well, if that were the case, there was no point in staying. Fabien forced his legs into motion, striding off the platform without another backward glance.

For a moment, he was frozen, the instructions Tenzin had given them earlier pushed from his brain by the rush of adrenaline. The slopes were coming up too fast, and he'd lost sight of their guide, and of his companions. Was this what Apollo had felt as he tumbled toward the drifts? Helpless, paralyzed, and utterly nauseated?

What an awful way to die. Too bad the bastard hadn't finished the job.

After a few seconds that felt like a century, Fabien's brain kicked back into gear. He spread his arms and legs wide and let out a grunt as his fall slowed dramatically. It was nothing like flying in a jet, but at least he wasn't scared out of his mind anymore.

Now that he was properly face-down, he could see the others. Dinah was on her back, gazing up at the sky, tracking the movements of the android that was hovering above them. Rhett was even higher than that, and Fabien had to crane his neck as far as it would go to get a good look at him. He seemed peaceful, despite the winds that buffeted them.

Fabien was too close to the ground, and he could already tell that his angle was all off. He'd need to adjust course. What had Tenzin said about that?

Ah, right, the whistle.

On the platform of the city, he'd been able to reach up and grab the whistle with ease. Now, he had to twitch his shoulder and nudge the pipe toward his lips, which was harder than it sounded, given the fact that he could barely move his limbs. In the end, he had to extend his lips and use his tongue to flip the whistle the right way. Even then, finding the breath to blow it took a moment's preparation.

The whistle was an old one, made from some sort of glazed clay. When he blew on the pipe, it let out a bird-like burble, reminiscent of one of those old water whistles from his grandparents' collection at their farmhouse in Ariège.

The wind changed immediately, and a warm puff of air buoyed him higher, lifting him above Rhett and the others, almost in line with the height of the city. He'd have to blow more carefully in the future, but for now he kept the end of the whistle clamped between his teeth, just so that he wouldn't have to go through the trouble of catching it again.

The longer they flew, the more Fabien relaxed. For the first time, he let himself consider the full implications of what people could do with objects like the ones contained in the vault. People like *him*.

It had been ages since he'd done anything productive, since he'd built something to last rather than destroying everything that came in reach. How was he supposed to go back to his old life, knowing what he knew now? Was he just supposed to forget that tech like this existed?

Impossible.

26 RHETT

THE LANDING, when it came, nearly rattled Rhett's bones apart despite the ground crew's precautions. The android, of course, executed a flawless touchdown, and Dinah managed pretty well, too. Rhett, by contrast, more or less belly-flopped onto the landing pad. He'd meant to land upright, but at the last moment, his instincts warned him against it, and he curled his legs beneath him to spare his knee and hip the jarring impact.

"Smooth," Fabien said as he helped Rhett to his feet.

"I seem to recall that you're the one who was almost too scared to jump," he snapped back. The painkillers from Laputa were wearing off, and his mood was quickly souring as the adrenaline of their flight faded.

There were three military-grade helicopters waiting for them. The crew of Laputa had been mostly Tibetan, aside from the androids, but the soldiers who awaited them at the bottom of the mountain were multinational, although they all wore the same equipment.

It didn't take long for him to locate the man in charge. He was standing next to one of the helicopters, a black ballcap crowning his clean-shaven head, directing the rest of the crew. His skin was darker than Dinah's and deeply lined, and there was something so normal about his presence that it made Rhett's steps falter in surprise. He could have been directing any crew at any military base he'd ever visited. Aside from the unusual gun he carried, he would never have guessed that this man worked with ENIGMA.

"Greetings!" he called when he caught Rhett staring. He lifted one hand above his head and grinned at them, as if they hadn't witnessed a bloodbath the night before, as if they weren't in the middle of the strangest mission of his life. "You are the Greek, yes? Brett?"

"Rhett," he corrected, striding toward him. His cane was still strapped to his back, but he didn't want to fuss with it just yet. "Rhett Zappotis. And you are?"

"Commander Bemnet Fassil." He extended his hand to Rhett's. He had a good handshake. Firm. Reassuring. "Although you may just call me Fassil. No titles needed among friends, ha?" He waved him toward the chopper. "Come, come, we must get going. I will walk you through the debrief as we fly."

The android lingered behind, exchanging words with a few of the ground crew. "Should we give our suits back?" Dinah asked as she wandered over to where Rhett and Commander Fassil stood. "Is there a way to send them back up the slope?"

"I don't think that will be necessary. They're still in ENIGMA possession, after all." Fassil grinned at her. "And from what I hear, you've had some trouble with aircraft—so the suits may serve as a reassurance, yeah?"

"Yeah," Fabien grumbled as he stomped over to the chopper. "Wish I'd had one last night... I might have been able to keep the relic out of Apollo's hands."

"Maybe," Fassil said. "Or maybe not. The Hand are relentless, and thinking of what you might have done in one case or another may not be the most helpful use of your time. At any rate, Laputa relies on its remote location to offer security. The city was not built to be defended." The commander squinted up the slope, and Rhett turned just in time to see the android fold its long limbs inward as it stepped into one of the other helicopters.

"I take it Holy Land is easier to defend?" Dinah asked.

Fassil laughed and patted the young professor's back. "Many have tried to breach our vault before, and all of them have failed. There's a reason that Agent Apollo saved it for last."

"Next-to-last," Rhett reminded him.

Fassil's smile slipped. "Well. Yes." Without further explanation, he turned his back to them and hopped up into the belly of the helicopter, leaving the three of them to follow.

THE MOUNTAINS SLIPPED AWAY behind them, and Rhett dozed. All of them were still reeling from the after-effects of the battle in Laputa, and Rhett suspected that given the chance, he'd easily be able to sleep for a week straight through.

He woke once—somewhere over India, he thought—and peered down at the world below for a while. Fassil was awake, watching them, his gun across his lap.

"Why didn't we use something from one of the vaults to travel faster?" he asked. He would have whispered to avoid waking Fabien and Dinah, but if they could sleep through the noise of the chopper, his voice wouldn't be enough to wake them.

Fassil's mouth formed a smile, but Rhett could already tell the difference between a real grin and this one. "We could get you close, if we used the right objects," he said. "But..."

"But you don't trust us with them?" Rhett asked.

Fassil nodded to Dinah. "Your friend tried to steal one."

"To keep it from Apollo," Rhett said.

He let his head wag back and forth. "Maybe. And yet Apollo still has it. On top of that..." He trailed off.

On top of that, we were hired by Porter, and you don't trust our motives. Rhett crossed his arms. His neck ached from sleeping upright, and he was far more disturbed by his mounting paranoia. It was a terrible thing, not to be able to trust the people you were fighting with.

Once again, his thoughts veered toward Kelly. Trust among soldiers was hard-won and easily fractured. If Porter really was involved in all of this...

Then why hire us? Not us in particular, but anyone? He'd assumed it was to cover Porter's tracks, but he could just as easily have failed to report the break-in. Unless he was trying to make himself look innocent by showing himself as a victim? But that clearly wasn't working, and it was equally possible that the Hand had targeted him first in order to sow dissent among the ranks of ENIGMA.

Or he wanted an excuse to send someone into the other vaults who looked like an outsider... but is really working for the Hand. He eyed Fabien, who was sleeping with his head thrown back and his mouth open. How did Rhett know that he hadn't orchestrated his fight with Apollo to make it seem like he'd fought for his life?

"Now you're getting it," Fassil said. He was still watching Rhett, but without a hint of the fatherly attentiveness he'd shown earlier.

"And yet you're still inviting us in."

"Yes. Because what if we're wrong?" The commander lifted one hand to rub the little knot of wrinkles between his eyebrows.

"The last time that the Hand got this close to a vault, it was lost. Wiped off the map. We can't risk that happening again. Either you're dedicated assets, or you're dangerous liabilities."

Rhett slumped back in his seat with his arms crossed and studied him. "And either way, you can't very well let us go."

"You see our predicament exactly," Fassil said.

Rhett considered telling him and his paranoia to piss off, but where would that leave him? If Porter was going to betray them, he knew exactly where to find Rhett's family and how to hurt him most. And if Porter *was* on their side, and his offer was still good...?

It will be worth it, he decided.

Some debts couldn't be repaid without a little assistance.

THEY REFUELED and ate a cursory meal somewhere in Gujarat, and again in what he thought must be Yemen after passing over a vast expanse of sea. The dusty steppes below them made him think of Kelly, and the house in the desert where it had all gone to shit.

Rhett hoped it wasn't an omen.

"I thought we might be heading to the Mediterranean coast." Fabien had finally woken up and was looking much more himself than he had in Laputa that morning. "But we're heading south now, aren't we?"

Dinah yawned and stretched. "I assume we're going to Ethiopia."

Commander Fassil's jovial mood had returned, and he nodded. "Precisely. The vault at Holy Land is the oldest continually staffed repository in use today. Some say it was the original vault, in fact. That ENIGMA was born here, long before it took on that name."

Fabien glanced at Rhett, who only shrugged. "I thought," the Frenchman said slowly, "with all that talk of Egypt..."

"Oh, but even the Egyptians respected the early civilizations of Ethiopia." Dinah rubbed one knuckle in her eye and sat up straighter. "We have New Kingdom records from the reign of Hatshepsut that speak highly of their trading partners to the south. Of course, it's not an entirely linear progression from those kingdoms to its current iteration. Residents of Punt wouldn't recognize the present-day country of Ethiopia any more than the ancient Hellenes would recognize the modern country of Greece."

"Get to the point," Fabien snapped.

Dinah glowered at him. "It's a fascinating country," she grumbled. "And they possess a lot of interesting things. Including, supposedly, the Ark of the Covenant."

Fabien brightened. "Oh, good. Maybe we can open it and make Apollo look inside."

"Does all of your understanding of history come from action films?" Dinah demanded.

Fabien turned up his nose. "And? Look at where we find ourselves now." He reached up to the whistle on his shoulder and shook it a few times. "We can call up wind with a puff of breath. We can travel hundreds of miles in a single step. I think we can stop assuming that reality is quite as rigid as common sentiment would imply, don't you?"

"The Ark of the Covenant still won't melt people's faces off." Dinah paused and turned to Fassil. "Will it?"

Fassil laughed, a deep belly-laugh that made Rhett smile in spite of misgivings. "Hardly, although ENIGMA does not possess the Ark. We have other items, though. Our collection is unparalleled, which is why we're taking such precautions now. We don't want to end up with a situation like Kunzang's."

Rhett's hands clenched involuntarily at the memory of

Kunzang's slick fingers beneath his own, the shift of blood and exposed muscle evident with every breath. Of course no vault would want a repeat of that nightmare.

Would Kunzang's reputation suffer for what had been done to her? Would her reputation crumble beneath ENIGMA's scrutiny, just as Porter's had?

The choppers were flying faster than any he'd flown in before, but even so, night was nipping at their heels as they crossed a narrower stretch of ocean, separating the Horn of Africa from the Middle East. It overtook them at last, sweeping over the Earth below them in a dark wave and leaving only the glow of electric lights in its wake.

"Almost there." Fassil leaned toward the window. "The lights of Holy Land will be the only ones visible for many miles. There, see them? That orange glow? That is the compound."

Rhett could indeed make out the gleam of the compound in the midst of what otherwise appeared to be grassy scrubland. The chopper dipped lower, and he heard the pilot speaking into the radio with a question. He recognized the cadence, but not the language.

The radio was silent.

The pilot tried again. When he squinted at the lights, they seemed to flicker against the star-freckled sky. Someone answered the radio, but the pilot's tone suggested that something was wrong. After a hurried exchange, the pilot turned to speak to Fassil.

"Sir," she said in English, "the other pilots and I have tried to radio ground control, but nobody is answering."

"You're on the right frequency?" Fassil asked.

"Yes, Commander. And the other pilots can hear me, so this signal is working, but..."

They were close enough now for Rhett to see for himself why

ground control wa'n't answering. The lights of the compound were not the steady, unwavering results of filaments and electricity, but the guttering consequence of unchecked flame.

Holy Land was burning.

27 DINAH

DINAH WAS STILL STARING through the window of the chopper in horror when Fabien lurched to his feet, shrugged the top half of his flight suit back on, and reached for the door. Fassil made no move to stop him as he yanked the bay door wide, slipped the whistle into his mouth, reached for his rifle, and dove into the night sky.

If she'd been thinking clearly, Dinah would have stopped to ask herself what exactly she hoped to accomplish by following her teammate. She'd hardly been an asset the previous evening, and none of them knew what was happening.

But Dinah wasn't thinking clearly. She was barely thinking at all. Her body might as well have been making choices without her, because the next thing she knew she was yanking her own squirrel suit up her legs and wriggling her arms into the sleeves.

There were times when she wondered if her brain was wired all wrong. How come the chemicals that had rendered her lizard brain practically inert the night before weren't flooding her system as she flung herself face-first out of a helicopter over a burning city? Surely evolution favored those whose self-preservation was consistent from one moment to the next?

Then she was falling, and her mind went mercifully blank.

Fabien was ahead of her, well below the trajectory of the helicopter now. Too bad the whistles only called wind up enough to aid their ascent and not to propel them forward. When her attempts to catch up failed altogether, Dinah turned her attention to the ravaged compound beneath them.

Atlantis had been larger than any ship she'd encountered, larger than most ordinary buildings, but according to Dr. Moniz, it had been crewed exclusively by members of ENIGMA.

Holy Land seemed different. There was one sprawling primary building in the center of the compound, but a small settlement had sprung up around it, and fortified walls stood beyond that. The walls themselves were undamaged, and she could make out the silhouettes of people running to and fro between the residences. Only the building in the middle of the compound was destroyed, with every wooden element consumed by flame, while the stone and earthen supports had begun to collapse under their own weight. The ident system on her headset flickered green a few times in an attempt to highlight the structure, but it was too far gone for the AI to recognize.

It must have been a beautiful structure, Dinah thought sadly, before the Hand arrived.

She followed Fabien to a patch of ground near the central compound. The moment Fabien's feet touched the ground, he began to yank at the material of the flight suit.

"Should we be more careful with these?" Dinah asked. "They're ENIGMA property."

"I'd think ENIGMA would be more worried about *that*." Fabien jerked his head toward the blaze.

He had a point. According to her headset's AI, the whistles

weren't particularly uncommon items, and the suits were difficult to maneuver in. Dinah followed her teammate's lead and stripped the material away, even as they began to hobble toward the blaze.

They had only made it a few yards when they were greeted by angry voices, and a trio of armed soldiers emerged from the darkness with rifles trained on them.

"Who are you?" their leader barked.

"Fabien LeRoux," the Frenchman replied. "And Dr. Dinah Bray. We're with you. Fassil brought us in." He didn't seem alarmed to be at the wrong end of a rifle held by strangers, in the midst of a crisis. It seemed Dinah wasn't the only one whose sense of self-preservation was at least a little bit out of whack.

The soldier snorted and said something to one of his companions. Dinah didn't recognize the language, although she assumed it was Oromo, but she did make out the word 'Porter' in among the unfamiliar arrangement of vowels and consonants.

"The radio was down," Fabien said. "Our pilot couldn't make contact."

"Because the bloody Hand turned our own systems against us," the soldier spat back.

The air was thick with smoke, and even at this distance, the fire was hot enough to make sweat trickle down Dinah's forehead and the curve of her spine. She wiped her hand across her brow and used her arm to blow the glow. "He's in there?" The idea of a person forcing their way through that inferno, even with the destabilizer, was grim.

Fabien cocked his head. "Wait, *is* he?"

The English-speaking soldier nodded.

"Then we need to go *now*," Fabien said. "If he's counting on that tech to keep him alive, then its power will be draining fast. If we can stall him on the way out and run the battery down—"

Fabien was still talking, but Dinah had stopped listening.

Battery. She remembered the crescent curve of the relic, its weight in his palms. What if that curve in the middle was meant to lock around something? If the batteries were all fit together, they would be able to seat around a round object, or at least a round projection *from* an object...

Oh, she was an idiot. Why hadn't she thought to look through the headset's records earlier? She'd been so worried about Fabien, and then distracted by their travel, that it hadn't occurred to her that she might be able to get answers. She opened the visually-operated search function on her keyboard and typed in the word *destabilizer,* but got no results.

She grabbed Fabien's arm and squeezed, cutting him off mid-sentence. "Did you ever see what Apollo was using? Do you know what the destabilizer looks like?"

Fabien blinked and shrugged her off. "No?"

"Then you're right," Dinah said. "We *do* need to get to him. Because I think I know what the relics are meant to do."

What she didn't know, what she *couldn't* know without holding all of the objects in her hands and experimenting, was whether Apollo could use the relics individually, or if he needed all five of them at once. And if he *had* all five, would that mean that he could use the destabilizer indefinitely? Or would it be capable of something more?

Something worse?

She couldn't marshal her thoughts, but Fabien must have been able to read the desperation in her expression, because he turned to the Holy Land soldiers. "Take us to whoever's in charge," he told them. "*Now.*"

———

A DOZEN or so people were gathered near what must have once been the compound's entrance, in a high-tech metal building apart from the main complex. Their reluctant guide called out to the other guards, and they spoke for a moment before they were waved inside.

Dinah breathed a sigh of relief as they stumbled into the little building. The temperature dropped sharply, as did the humidity. It was better than air conditioning—it was like stepping into a cave.

Her newfound relief was cut short when the door slammed shut behind them. None of the guards had followed them in.

There were, however, two figures already waiting inside. One was a woman, perhaps in her late forties, with her hair pulled up in the ridged and braided Shuruba style that Dinah's cousin, Layla, often wore to family gatherings. The man was older, perhaps in his sixties, and his tightly-coiled hair was more salt than pepper. Both of them were dressed as if they'd recently been pulled from their beds, and the woman's eyes were red-rimmed.

On one wall stood an array of screens, which the two of them were watching intently. Below the screens was what looked like a computer console of some kind. In the middle, a circular screen projected an elaborate hologram, although Dinah couldn't tell what the display represented. It was a jumble of lines and edges, narrow at the base and widening at the top, like an inverted cone.

None of it meant anything to Dinah, and she was too worried about the people to focus on the textbox her headset provided.

Her gaze met the woman's as she turned to her, and the woman's jaw clenched. "You are the ones Porter sent?"

Dinah nodded. "Yes. Well, uh, we're two of them. I think Rhett's still with Commander Fassil. Last I checked."

The woman inclined her head and frowned bitterly at the ground. "Sent by Porter, and here you are, come to witness the fall of Holy Land. I should not be surprised—"

"Peace, Azmera." The old man raised his hand. "All is not lost yet." He turned to face Fabien and Dinah, offering them a weary nod. "My daughter carries a great weight on her shoulders, gentlemen. Her mother oversaw the vault before her, and it pains us both greatly to see my late wife's work come to this. We have all made sacrifices for ENIGMA, and now..." He gestured to the screens.

Nearly a third of them were dark, and flames burned bright in most of the others, although a few seemed to show parts of the compound that were still undamaged.

"I am Demeke," the man said. "And you... you are Dinah Bray." He nodded to Dinah, who scratched her chin sheepishly.

"I've read your work," Azmera said. She was watching the screens again.

"You have?" It was, without a doubt, the wrong moment to be self-conscious about her academic career, but she couldn't help wondering what the other woman thought of it.

Azmera trailed one hand over the controls. "You must understand my reluctance to trust you, especially *him*." She cast Fabien a dirty glance. "But time is short, and I cannot operate Holy Land alone."

Fabien made a disgruntled noise in the back of his throat, but Dinah stepped forward. "*Operate* Holy Land? You mean, command the troops?"

Azmera shook her head. "The Hand hacked our systems, dismantled our drones, and used our own defenses against themselves. The fires you see here? They are the result of our tech firing on *itself*. Apollo slipped through untouched. The compound burns, but Holy Land itself is still operational." She pointed to the hologram.

Dinah squinted at it, giving herself time to read the text. *Remote Operational System: Holy Land Tiered Labyrinth.*

It still didn't click until she looked even closer and saw the tiny numbering on the layers of the cone, stacked wafer-thin like tiers on an infinite cake.

"My God." She extended one trembling finger toward the hologram.

Azmera's hand flicked out, as though she intended to catch Dinah's wrist and stop her, but she didn't. Dinah prodded a layer with her fingertip.

The ground beneath their feet shuddered, and the layer rotated slightly.

It was a maze above a maze above a maze, interlocking like the layers of a Rubik's cube. A puzzle separating the surface from the vault entrance many stories below.

It was the most remarkable creation Dinah had ever seen.

28 FABIEN

FABIEN WASN'T USED to feeling like a third wheel, and he hated it.

"You see this dot here? This little point of light?" Azmera pointed one finger on the bottom floor of the hologram, although she was careful not to touch it.

"Yes, yes." Dinah bobbed her head eagerly. "Is that the vault?"

The woman smiled faintly. "Dr. Bray, you fail to understand. This whole construction is the vault."

Dinah whistled and braced her hands against her knees. "Amazing. How many artifacts does it house?"

"Millions." Azmera's pride was evident in her voice. "And all of them are cataloged by location, not by number, though as you can see, the locations are ever-changing." Her earlier hostility had been swept away in the conversation. People liked talking about the things that mattered to them, and Dinah was good at talking.

Whereas Fabien was standing there like an idiot, about as useful as a lump of old clay.

"But this light here?" Azmera pointed again. "This is our bead on the agent of the Hand. He appears to have gone to the bottom and started working his way up."

"He's conserving the battery on his destabilizer," Fabien said, relieved to have something to contribute. "I bet he let himself fall right through the floors to the bottom… although I still don't understand why he doesn't fall through the floor every time he uses that thing."

Azmera lifted her chin so that she could look down her nose at him. She was tall, though not quite as tall as Porter. "The destabilizer is a highly specialized device," she sniffed. "Of course you don't understand."

"You know how it works?" Dinah asked, surprised.

"I know enough for now. And I know that Apollo is close to gathering all the components he needs to make it into a much more powerful weapon than it already is. I will explain more, even more than the ENIGMA-wide records show, should I decide to trust you."

Fabien let out a little huff of annoyance. "Great. So how do we stop him now?"

Azmera pulled over a stool and perched on it as she indicated the hologram. "As you saw, we can move the levels independently of one another. Each floor has multiple possible exits to the floor below it, and one set of stairs below that can connect to the one above. If we rotate the levels"—she moved one, and the ground beneath their feet shuddered again, while the layers she was spinning realigned—"we can line up the steps with the appropriate entrance above to help anyone who might be inside to reach the next floor down. But if we spin it so that none of the exits align, the access to that level will be cut off. Any ordinary intruder would be trapped. The exits would be sealed. Apollo, however…"

"Can stroll right through any solid object in his path," Dinah finished.

"So long as that device of his has power," Fabien added.

"Precisely. I cannot stop him yet, but I can slow him down by rotating the floors and keeping him away from the relic he's after for as long as possible. He'll also struggle to make the climb between floors unless he can find the stairs up. It's difficult work to do alone, however. There are too many angles, too many options to consider. Usually I would have the luxury of time as he searched through the displays at random…"

"But the batteries can sense one another," Dinah added eagerly, cutting Azmera off again. "So he'll be able to tell when he's getting closer. It's like an incredibly complicated game of hot potato."

Fabien rolled his eyes at her back. *Péter plus haut de son cul.* If they'd been in school together, they would not have gotten on.

"Will you help me, then? My father—" Azmera bowed her head toward Demeke. "His hands shake, and his eyesight is going. I need someone to be another pair of eyes, and to work with me."

"Of course." Dinah found another stool and hurried to Azmera's side. "Where is he trying to go?"

"The relic is here, on Floor 33." Azmera pointed. "There are forty-nine floors altogether. The one just below the surface is Floor 49, all the way down to one at the point. Here, let me make it easier to see." Instead of touching the hologram itself, she laid her fingers on the round screen and dragged them apart, causing the hologram to zoom, providing even finer detail.

Dinah inspected it closely, then frowned as two new blips appeared on the top layer, Floor 49. "Who's that?"

Demeke took a step closer. "Another member of the Hand? Surely not."

Fabien, however, was watching the screens, and he broke into a grin. "No. Look." He pointed, and their eyes followed. Three figures, in fact, were making their way across Floor 49, although it was immediately obvious why only two of them gave off the life signs necessary to alert the system of their presence. One was, after all, not alive.

Rhett, Fassil, and the borrowed Laputan android pelted across the screen.

"It's Rhett!" Dinah pumped her fists, then spun back to the hologram. "Come on, Azmera. Let's get him where he needs to go."

"You work on that," Azmera said, crouching lower to examine Apollo's blinking dot. "I'll focus on seeing what I can do to slow this one down."

29 RHETT

"WE SHOULD HAVE CONSULTED MY SUPERIORS," Commander Fassil panted. "Navigating the vault without guidance is almost impossible."

The android, which was loping along on its long, graceful legs, looked down at him. "Communications are out," it intoned in a flat, monotonous voice. "And my readings indicate that many of Holy Land's other systems are down as well. We cannot say with any certainty that your superiors are still alive."

Can't confirm that my teammates are alive either, Rhett thought. *Jumping out of the chopper without warning... what were they thinking?* For all he knew, they'd landed right in the midst of the flames.

"You can still lead us to the relic, though, right?" Rhett asked.

"Yes," the android said. "As I stated before, I am able to access the data regarding its precise location on Floor 33. The route, however, is something of a problem. Fortunately, the stairs are close."

Now that they were out of the smoke, Rhett's lungs were much happier with the air in Holy Land's vault than he had been in Laputa. The painkillers they'd given him were excellent, and so long as he kept his stride short, his bad hip seemed to be only an iffy hip, rather than a full-blown problem. He was easily keeping pace with Fassil, although the android could obviously outpace them both if it put its mind to it. Instead, it stayed close, navigating them between the rows of shelving and the tall cabinets.

They were approaching a flight of sturdy metal steps when Rhett asked, "Why would the route be a pr— oh." He skidded to a stop just before he reached the steps. Three steps led down to a solid shelf of limestone, with no level visible beyond.

"Ah." The android paused and stared down at the floor, its neutral face as impassive as ever. "I suspected that this might be an issue."

Fassil drew up short. "Should have talked to Azmera," he grumbled.

"As we have noted, Commander, our comms were nonfunctional. Time is a limited resource. Apollo must be stopped."

Rhett frowned down at the stone floor. "What's the point of stairs that don't go anywhere? And how are we supposed to get down sixteen floors if there's nothing below us?"

As if in answer, the ground beneath them shuddered. Fassil and the android spread their feet, while Rhett grasped the railing of the stairs for dear life. The blank stone beneath them began to move. No, not the stone. *They* were moving, as if the room was spinning on a central axis.

"The levels only intersect at one point at any given time," the android explained, as if this wasn't a slightly mad thing to say. "Evidently they've picked us up on the radar."

The rock flooring ended, opening to reveal the floor below, which was moving in the opposite direction beneath them. It made Rhett's head spin, the back-and-forth of it all. Their floor came to an abrupt stop, and he was almost thrown forward into empty air. A few seconds later, the lower half of the stairs aligned with them, granting access to a flight of steps that ended in the same abrupt manner, against a sheer rock face.

"Move," Fassil barked, and Rhett stumbled forward, nearly pitching headlong down the stairs in his haste. The second all three of them were safely through, they began to move again. By the time they reached the bottom of the steps, another floor had appeared below them.

He tried to imagine all the moving parts it must take to move a device of this size, and failed utterly. How many floors had the android said there were? Forty-nine? And the top one had been the size of a stadium at least, nearly the whole circular footprint of the aboveground compound.

Or what was left of it, anyway.

Three stories down, the stairs met a polished floor, and the android took the lead, guiding them between shelves. Sometimes they passed corridors that seemed to end abruptly, or loop back on themselves.

"It's a real labyrinth," Rhett observed. "Like from the old Greek myths. Whenever I imagined Minos' labyrinth, I thought it would be flat. One level. This is so much more impressive."

"No offense to your heritage, Mr. Zappotis," Fassil said, "but Daedalus designed the Greek version based on rumors and some simple sketches brought back from Holy Land by traders. His labyrinth was only seven stories deep, although by all accounts it's a wonder in its own right."

They found another set of stairs, already aligned with the story below. Rhett could no longer tell whether the floor he stood on was moving or not, and he was getting a bit seasick from all the motion. He lost track of how many floors they'd traversed and how many steps they'd taken, and couldn't have begun to trace his steps back.

When the floor they were on failed to move, he paused, clinging to the railing, and tried to catch his breath.

The android, however, turned sharply right. "This way. We're on the correct floor, but we'll have to take a rather circuitous route to get to the relic."

Rhett, still gasping for breath, only nodded and waved the android on. Judging by the rumble coming from beneath them, the floors below were still moving.

Apollo's down there, he thought.

Ariadne's string would have come in handy as Rhett tried to keep up with the android. It made sharp turns without warning, and more than once he nearly overshot a turn. The winding floorplan would have been a brilliant way to deter any thief... except one who could walk through walls.

So long as the floors beneath us are moving, it means they've managed to hold off Apollo, he thought.

A moment later, the floor stopped moving, and silence fell over the labyrinth, except for the sound of their pounding feet and his own labored breathing.

Dammit. So much for that.

And then, quite suddenly, Rhett was alone.

Hell. He had lost his focus for *two seconds,* and now he didn't know where he was. He skidded to a halt at the intersection of a corridor and looked around.

"Fassil?" he called.

Silence.

"Hey, android! Where'd you go?" He spun in place, clutching his cane tight. The more noise he made, the more likely that Apollo would hear him if he was on this floor... but he didn't have a lot of other options. The corridors were tall and narrow, with high ceilings that made his voice echo weirdly, all while giving him something just shy of claustrophobia.

Something shifted nearby, and Rhett spun. "Fassil?" he called.

He didn't answer, but he could still hear something. A faint buzz, like the drone of the electric mosquito zapper that his brother-in-law had bought for his porch last year.

Rhett reached up to flip the hood of his chameleon coat over his head, then tucked his cane against his chest, out of sight. He held his breath and stayed perfectly still.

Not a moment too soon. Blue light danced over a familiar figure as Apollo stepped through the shelves only a few feet away. He hesitated, looking one way, then the other down the hall. He must have looked right at Rhett, but the coat was doing its job, and after a moment he stepped through, powering down the destabilizer.

His chestplate was battered, just like Fabien had said. They'd landed one good hit last time around. Not good enough, though. He'd have to do better next time.

The agent reached into a pocket on his utility belt and produced one of the relics he'd already stolen. It was the first time Rhett had seen it glow with his own eyes, so he wasn't sure how much brighter it could get, but they had to be close.

Apollo put the relic away and took a few steps toward him, eyeing the intersection just as he had. He paused, his head tilted to one side, puzzling over whatever he saw that gave him away. A shadow? Had Rhett breathed too deeply? Or was the coat incapable of hiding him when he was so close?

Not that it mattered. Apollo had spotted him, which meant that he'd be reaching for either his gun or the destabilizer next.

Rhett reached for his last two time bombs just as blue sparks danced over Apollo's suit, and crushed one between his fingers.

Time stopped.

Apollo had already started to phase out, so Rhett reached for his cane rather than the recoil gun. He jabbed it toward him in the painfully slow-motion, swimming-in-honey movements that the limbo of the time bombs allowed. As he did so, he pressed his thumb down on the button beneath the cane's handle. The cane passed through Apollo's chest, just as he'd expected.

This might not do anything at all, he thought. *I might very well have wasted my shot.*

Then everything caught up again, and the blue shimmer around Apollo's suit sparked green instead, snapping like static, only a hundred times louder. With Rhett's cane in his chest, Apollo turned into a veritable Tesla coil of energy. His back bowed and his arms flung wide. Light danced around him, crawling across the surfaces around him, seeking a conduit.

Abruptly, they were flung apart. Rhett hit the shelving behind him, sending a shower of small artifacts every which way.

Apollo hit the ground hard and didn't move. The blue light that indicated his use of the destabilizer had gone out. He twitched a few times, then lay still as a corpse.

Rhett righted himself, using the shelves behind him as support. When he shifted his feet, some of the objects he'd knocked down rolled away. Who knew what they did, or how valuable they might be—not Rhett, certainly, and at the moment he didn't care. He was more worried about the man on the floor of the corridor.

Apollo still hadn't moved. Rhett took a side-step toward him, just to see what he would do. Still, he didn't move. Even when he jabbed Apollo's boot with the tip of his cane, he lay perfectly still. Just in case, Rhett tried to activate his cane again, but the button wiggled limply under his thumb. It was clearly broken.

Rhett swallowed hard and kicked Apollo's boot with his own. His foot flopped sideways, loose on its ankle.

Rhett leaned forward on his cane and pressed his hand to his chest. "Gotcha," he said.

Apollo's foot whipped out, sending his cane flying and knocking Rhett off-balance. In an instant, he was on his feet again, so fast that Rhett could barely believe it, even if he hadn't been injured. His gloved hands snatched at the front of Rhett's coat, yanking him forward with such force that the material tore.

"Where is it?" he demanded. Even with the auto scrambler adjusting his voice, Rhett could hear the simmering fury that the machine couldn't hide.

"Joke's on you," Rhett snarled. "I'm lost."

With both of his hands on him, Apollo couldn't reach for his gun, so Rhett took the risk. One hand plunged into his pocket to crush the last of the time bombs. The other went for Apollo's pistol. He fumbled it as he slid it free from the holster, but managed to catch it in his fingertips.

There was probably a reason that Porter hadn't given him a gun like this one. Maybe because he was a double agent; maybe because this wasn't the sort of weapon ENIGMA favored. It was inelegant and artless, designed to cause unnecessary pain.

Sometimes, though, you just needed to melt a man's face off, and only the right kind of gun would do.

Time resumed just as he tipped the gun upward, and Apollo shoved him away. He didn't seem to realize what had happened until Rhett found his footing and brandished the pistol at him.

Apollo looked at him. Looked down. He ran his gloved fingers over the empty holster. Perhaps Rhett ought to feel guilty about this, but given what this man had done to others with this very weapon, he was finding it mighty difficult to scrape together an ounce of sympathy.

He pulled the trigger, but nothing happened.

Shit. Rhett glanced down. The safety was on. A wise choice, all things considered. He flicked it off with his thumb and glanced up at Apollo again, just in time to see his hand move.

He didn't phase out, though. He had pulled something from his belt. His wrist flicked, just as Rhett's finger tightened on the trigger of the face-melty gun again.

Whatever Apollo had been holding hit the ground, and the world exploded.

30 DINAH

DINAH HAD her hand on the hologram when the whole thing went dark, disappearing from between her fingers.

She reeled back and nearly toppled off of her stool. "What happened?" she demanded. "Where did it go?"

"No!" Azmera leapt to her feet, digging her fingers into her hair and yanking hard. "*No!* He can't... it can't be..." She let out a terrible wail, and her ululating cry of grief echoed through the small room.

Demeke rushed forward and gathered his daughter into his arms. Her keening cry continued, but Dinah was still looking from the place where the hologram had been to the screens flickering with snowy static. The power hadn't gone out.

"What happened to the vault?" she murmured. When no one answered, she turned to Fabien. "What happened to the vault? Rhett was in there!"

Fabien only shook his head. He looked as lost as Dinah felt.

―――

THERE WAS nothing to do but wait. Azmera tried to pull herself together, but even when they stumbled out of the control room, her eyes remained wide and haunted, and she kept her arms wrapped around herself. The fires were dying down, so she and Demeke busied themselves with giving out orders in Oromo, telling the soldiers where to go and what to do. Dinah and Fabien were left behind with no guidance and no answers.

When Dinah spotted the guard who'd first approached them, she flagged the man down. "What can we do to help?" she asked.

The guard, evidently annoyed with having been interrupted, spat into the mixture of ash and dust at their feet. "No need for guns now. No need for scholars. Right now, work means getting your hands dirty."

"We want to help," Dinah insisted.

The man looked her up and down, then nodded once. "It will be dangerous work... but I expect you're used to danger by now, ha?"

The soldier introduced himself as Girom. He led them past the smoking remains of the compound to the entrance Rhett and his companions had taken into the vault below, where a crew was already working. Battery-powered lights had been distributed around the room at intervals, lighting the corridors and indicating the path back to the exit.

Dinah had only seen the tiered labyrinth in the hologram, but in person it was both breathtaking and heartbreaking. It was clear that the mechanism had been damaged; while the top floor itself hadn't been hit with the device Apollo detonated, it was still canted at a slight angle, and the level beneath her feet felt inert somehow. It was like stumbling on the corpse of a freshly beached whale, not yet decayed, but slowly collapsing under its own dead weight.

"Start packing up anything you find," Girom said. "We'll have to relocate everything and figure out someplace safe to store it until..." He flapped one hand at the interior of the vault and up toward the ceiling, unable to find the words for the magnitude of the work required to fix the damage Apollo had wrought in a single night.

"We should help look for Rhett," Dinah said.

Girom shook his head. "No. Absolutely not."

Fabien pushed forward and scowled at Girom. He wasn't very tall, but when his eyes went all glassy and cold like this... "He's one of ours," he snapped. "We don't leave our crew behind."

Girom didn't flinch. "You don't know the area, you don't speak Oromo, and we don't know how you'll work with a crew. Level 33 is very badly damaged, and right now we've sent in a team that knows what they're doing and won't run off alone to prove that they're heroes. Besides, who knows if the Hand is still alive down there, and what he will do if he is. If you want to help, help. If you want to boss us around because you're used to giving orders? Get out. He might be your friend, but this is our home." He turned away sharply and left them there without another word.

Fabien watched him go, his hands clenching and unclenching into fists. Eventually, Dinah picked up an empty crate and wandered over to start collecting the artifacts. She didn't look back, but she heard Fabien doing the same.

SHE WASN'T sure how long they worked there in the dim light, and she lost track of the number of boxes they'd carried. Eventually, someone came to bring them water and food.

"Our friend," Dinah said. "Did they find him?"

The woman set their MREs and the two water bottles down without looking at them.

"Our friend?" Dinah repeated. "Rhett?"

The woman shook her head, said something in Oromo, and left.

"They hate us," Fabien said. He was still working, picking up items almost at random and tossing them into crates. "Why wouldn't they? Everywhere we go, something gets destroyed."

"We didn't destroy Atlantis," Dinah pointed out. She turned an empty crate over and sat down on it, then reached for the food. Someday, she was going to eat a vegetable again, and when she did it would be glorious.

"True," Fabien said. "We just crashed in a jet and had to be rescued at sea."

"After you stunned me." Dinah took a deep drink from the water bottle.

Fabien growled and whipped around to face her. "It was an accident! When are you going to let it go?"

"I know it was an accident," Dinah said, a bit more gently this time. "But all of this has been accidental, hasn't it? It's been, what…" She tried to count on her fingers and paused to stare at the shadowed ceiling. "Five days? I'll be honest, I don't even know what day of the week it is anymore. Time lost all sense of meaning around the time we teleported across the world. Was Laputa one day ago? Or two?"

Fabien groaned and dropped to the floor with his back against one wall. "When you put it that way, this mission feels a hundred years long."

Dinah tossed him the second bottle of water, and then the other MRE. They ate in silence. For once, the tension between them didn't feel hostile. They were both worried about Rhett, which superseded any of the hostility that Fabien had previously exhibited toward her.

She would have given anything to lean back against the wall and close her eyes after she finished eating, just for a few moments. Instead, she crumpled the wrapper of her MRE, stuffed it into her pocket, and got right back to work.

31 FABIEN

AT SOME POINT, Fabien's exhaustion caught up with him. He nearly fell over when he bent to pick up a fallen relic—another one of those stones with a hole in the middle, like the one from Dinah's notes—and toppled to the floor headfirst. Dinah, too, was yawning, so they took the crates they'd been filling and made their way back to where the stack of filled crates had grown, then staggered up into the open air. Fabien held onto Dinah, ostensibly to steady his companion, although in truth they were the only things keeping each other upright.

The ruins of the Holy Land compound were still smoking, and scarlet embers glowed amidst the wreckage. The sky, too, was growing lighter, with the first rays of sunlight gilding the clouds and staining the sky pale pink and orange. There was *so much sky* out there, Fabien could hardly stand it. His work didn't take him into the countryside much.

There was no one out there worth shooting, after all.

———

HE WOKE from a restless slumber on hard-packed earth to the pressure of Dinah's hand on his shoulder.

"They found him," she said.

"Wh—" Fabien dug one knuckle against his eye, then sat up straight. "Rhett? Is he...?"

"Alive," Dinah said, and Fabien scrambled to his feet.

Holy Land looked even worse in the daylight. As they wended their way around the compound wall, they passed dozens of people engaged in the slow process of recovery. Families from the settlement, including children, were combing the rubble in search of anything that could be salvaged.

The sight of the children soured Fabien's mood even further. He had always made a point to leave children out of his work whenever possible. Business was business, and he had no qualms about selling his services to the right bidder. More often than not, his contacts were just as corrupt as the people he killed.

Children, though... involving innocent people was different than waging calculated warfare, and he hated Apollo for his role in this carnage.

Among other things.

Dinah led him to a white tent outside of the inner compound. The smell rising from the tent turned Fabien's stomach, and the piteous cries of the wounded brought his feet to a halt, even before he realized that he was slowing down.

Rhett limped out of the tent to greet them. His face was bruised with large deep-purple patches on his forehead and cheek, and one eye so badly swollen that he couldn't fully open it. He was moving slowly, but he was upright.

"Rhett." The cane he'd carried before was gone, replaced with a full crutch that made his usually inelegant movements even heavier. "We thought..."

"That I got crushed into goose liver pâté?" His bottom lip was split open, and when he twisted it up into a half-smile, a drop of blood gathered at the seam. "Sorry to disappoint you, but here I am, alive. Fassil made it, too. The android we were with managed to shield him from being crushed."

"And Apollo?" Dinah asked.

Rhett's smile vanished. "No sign of him."

Fabien cursed and wheeled away, yanking at the roots of his hair. "With the relic, I assume?"

"I'm sure of that." Rhett limped over to a nearby crate and dropped onto it. "He has a gift for slipping away at the last moment." He let out a low growl at the back of his throat. "You know, I really thought I had him. He was right *there*. Right under my nose, and I..." He thumped his fist against the wood.

"He did the same with me," Fabien said. "He keeps getting lucky."

"It's not luck," Dinah said.

The two of them turned to look at her, Fabien with his eyes narrowed, Rhett with his head tilted to one side like he was following a puzzle.

"When Porter hired us, he promised each of us something." Dinah crossed her arms and stared down at the toes of her boots. "We each have something to fight for. Something that we want for ourselves when all this is over. If we walk away, we're leaving something unfinished behind. For him, this is it. He's willing to die to get what he wants, and I'm not sure that any of us are. Not when it comes to the relic, I mean."

"Unfinished business," Rhett murmured. "I suppose that's true."

Fabien glanced toward the wall of the compound, where a little girl was helping her father sift through rubble. "I think you might be onto something there, Professor," he murmured. Apollo had plunged after the relic that Fabien flung from Laputa, clearly giving no thought to whether he'd live or die. Fabien, meanwhile, had lain there in the cold, remembering that there was more to life. *Tomorrow, tomorrow,* he'd told himself a thousand times. But how could he hope to atone for his mistakes without the promise of another day?

"So the fact that we have something to live for makes us incapable of finishing the job," Rhett said. "Because we'll always be holding something back."

"It's like competing with another professor for tenure," Dinah said. "You have to want it more badly than the other candidate, and Apollo's made it clear that he'll sacrifice anything, or anyone, in order to get what he wants. Can any of us say the same?"

Fabien was spared from having to answer when a familiar figure loped over to them. It was the soldier from before, Girom, the one who had shown them into the ruins of Holy Land. He didn't appear to have slept at all, and exhaustion was evident in every line of his features.

"Come," he told the three of them. "Azmera wishes to speak with you."

"You aren't planning to shoot us anymore?" Fabien asked dryly.

Girom stared at him, and it occurred to Fabien that the man's family might live in the compound, that he might have more skin in the game than a hired gun on a mission. Usually he wouldn't concern himself with such things, but the little girl and her father were still at work nearby, and Fabien's nerves were frayed.

"Why would I shoot you?" he asked. "You didn't fail this time. *We* did. Holy Land was supposed to be the one safe place, the one location where the Hand couldn't touch us, and now look at us." He waved toward the wreckage of the vault. "Apollo has come and gone. I have never seen our lady so distraught."

Fabien bit back any other retort he might have offered. Together, the three of them followed Girom in silence.

Fabien couldn't speak for the others, but he was certain that his companions were asking themselves the same question he was: if it came down to it, what more would he be willing to give ENIGMA?

And how could they really expect to face off against someone willing to die for their cause if they weren't prepared to do the same?

32 RHETT

UNDER OTHER CIRCUMSTANCES, Rhett would have had a million questions for Azmera and Demeke, but as it was, he could barely keep himself upright until he reached the little outbuilding where Girom led them.

"Here again?" Dinah asked. "But the mechanism that operates the building is—" She cut herself off, but they all knew what she'd meant to say.

"She wants privacy," Girom told them. "Whatever she's about to tell you is not common knowledge."

The young woman and her father were waiting outside of the little structure. Rhett's first thought was that Azmera was too young to have such a heavy burden of responsibility on her shoulders—but then again, how old had he been when he and Kelly were deployed? Probably the same age, or thereabouts. Close enough that it hardly mattered.

When she saw them coming, the young leader of Holy Land lifted her head and squared her shoulders. She must have been crying earlier, Rhett reckoned, but not for some time. Her eyes were red, but her cheeks were dry. She had moved on to the part where she tried to pick up the pieces, rather than dwelling on the disappointment of her earlier failures.

"I'm glad to see that you survived the destruction of our vault," Azmera said. If that was sarcasm, there was no trace of it in her voice.

Her father bobbed his head in agreement. "We have been very fortunate," Demeke said, "that there was so little loss of life. Buildings can be repaired. The dead, however, are gone forever."

Dinah grimaced at the sentiment, and Rhett had to smother an inappropriate smile. He could guess what she was thinking: that she would rather learn that a thousand people had died defending the Library of Alexandria, or some such historic structure, than have to contend with its loss. Personally, he agreed with Demeke. He would have razed that thrice-cursed desert city to the ground if he thought it would help the people he'd lost, even a little.

He'd have done it barehanded, if it would have saved any of their lives.

"I gather that there are things you do not understand about your mission," Azmera said. "We should speak on this matter in private. Come." She led them into the little structure, where they could speak alone. Girom, and even Demeke, remained outside as the three members of their little crew filed past.

"Have you gotten the power back on?" Dinah asked once the door was closed behind them.

Azmera smiled sadly. "We have power, but the vault itself will not be back online for some time. The damage Apollo did to it was extensive. It will be months, if not years, before the mechanism can be repaired." She let her fingers trail around the plastic rim of the circular interface in the control panel. "In the meantime, however, I can still provide something of use. Our records are evidently better-kept than those of the other vaults. I know more than even that fancy headset of yours can tell you." She tapped her finger to her temple and nodded at Dinah, who lifted a hand to her own head self-consciously.

"Wait." Rhett sank onto one of the stools near the console. "So you actually know what the relic is?"

"Indeed I do." Azmera powered up the hologram display to reveal a perfect copy of the artifact they'd seen in Laputa. She plucked it off the display and held it up, where it hovered in midair between them. Apparently the hologram acted like the small hockey-puck units that they'd seen in Atlantis and the Ohio vault because, as she spoke, she was able to manipulate the image to illustrate her point.

"As your associate Dr. Bray correctly deduced, each of these items is a power cell. According to our oldest files, when the relics were first discovered, there were six pieces altogether. Five interlocking power cells"—four more of the same relic appeared, fanned out around an elaborately decorated metal sphere—"and the destabilizer itself."

Dinah grimaced. "So they do all go together."

Fabien groaned. "What happens when he finds the last piece? Several times, Apollo has taxed it to its limits. When he has the full collection, will he be able to remain intangible indefinitely?"

Azmera shook her head. "Right now, Apollo is not using the destabilizer for its intended purpose. I believe that you, Fabien, have had the unfortunate experience of crossing paths with him while he is in this state?"

Fabien nodded. "It hurt."

"It hurts him, as well. Using the device in this manner is like… like running a piece of heavy machinery with faulty wiring. Like riding a bicycle powered by a jet engine. The toll it will take on his body is disastrous, but by the time it catches up with him, the Hand will already have what it wants." With a shudder, Azmera slid the hologram of the six pieces together, so that the power cells encircled the destabilizer like Saturn's rings. Their pale green pulse intensified to a brilliant glow. Dinah lifted one hand to shade her eyes until the light died abruptly.

"We have no hologram records of what happens when the pieces are assembled," Azmera told them. "But our written records are quite clear. When all six pieces are assembled, they are strong enough to tear a hole through the fabric of reality itself. The Hand will be able to move between realities."

"Like, what?" Rhett lifted his hands in confusion and looked to his friends to see if they understood the situation any better than he did. "Are we talking alternate timelines? Alternate histories?"

"We don't know," Azmera admitted. "To do so would invite catastrophe. Just as Agent Apollo will face damage on a cellular level for his misuse of the lynchpin of this device, our forebears feared what would happen if this device was assembled again."

"*Again?*" Dinah shook her head. "Hold on, that implies that it's been used before, and the world didn't end then. I mean, by definition, we wouldn't be here if it had."

"I suppose the world didn't end with the Black Plague," Fabien cut in, "but I don't envy the people who lived in those times. The world doesn't have to be destroyed in order to be horribly damaged."

"Or what about something like the eruption of Vesuvius?" Rhett murmured. "An intense, localized disaster."

Azmera reeled in their imaginings. "We have no record of what occurred if the items were ever assembled. The vast majority of the items in the vault are historical objects, but not all of them. These relics are different."

Dinah rubbed her forehead. "Why would anyone make them if they didn't assemble them at least once?"

Fabien snapped so loudly that Dinah almost lost her balance.

"Aren't you listening, Professor? She's saying that these aren't historical objects. That they may not be manmade."

"But who else would—" Dinah stopped short and her eyes popped wide. "Wait, Azmera, are you saying that *aliens* are real?"

"Aliens?" Rhett echoed, his voice dripping with disbelief. On one hand, that was a bridge too far. But on the other... well, why not? They'd seen all sorts of impossible things in the last few days. He'd stopped time, fought a person who could walk through solid objects, fought alongside androids. Even so, his rational mind pushed back against this development.

"I'm not sure if they're aliens or not," Azmera said. "I suppose it depends on your definition. But theoretically, if this device can disrupt the normal flow of time and space, perhaps it came from whatever other reality overlapped with our own."

Dinah frowned, and her eyes took on a faintly unfocused quality that suggested she might be reading text on her headset. "That's not the first object that we've encountered that can do something like that. Porter put me in a pair of boots that carried me hundreds of miles in a single step. He made it sound like they could move me through time, too."

"There's some risk to using objects like that," Azmera conceded, "but there's a difference between slipping through the timestream and ending up in the fourteenth century, as compared to bringing the fourteenth century to you. It's possible that there's a way to use it without causing immense damage, but I can guarantee that the Hand of the Sun will find some vile and dangerous use for it. There were, it seems, concerns about the purpose of such an item, which was why it was spread out between different vaults centuries ago. With the pieces scattered all over the world, it couldn't be used to cause trouble."

That, at least, made sense to Rhett. That should have made it almost impossible for the Hand—or anyone else, for that matter—

to even assemble the device, much less use it as a weapon. In the old days, when he'd still worked behind enemy lines, very few people were allowed to know the full extent of a mission. That way the truth couldn't be tortured out of them—or bought, as the case may be.

"You weren't just worried about the Hand, though," he mused aloud. "Your own operatives have turned against you before, haven't they?"

Azmera's expression turned cold. "More than once. In fact, the fifth and final power cell was stored in a vault that has since been lost to us."

"Because Porter's grandfather defected to the Hand," Rhett prompted. "El Dorado."

The other woman nodded. "The vault was destroyed. We only know its rough location, and when a team was sent to recover its contents, they weren't able to get inside."

"That won't be a problem for Apollo," Fabien huffed. "He'll just waltz through the door as if it isn't there at all."

"So we don't know where the vault is, exactly, and we don't know how to get in." Rhett slumped back against the console. "But if we don't find it, Apollo will be able to assemble a device that may or may not usher in some sort of horrible, world-ending calamity."

Azmera crossed her arms. "Or which will grant the Hand untold power over neighboring realities, yes."

"Lovely," Rhett muttered. "Just what I wanted to hear."

"I can provide you with transport," Azmera said. "I can give you weapons, and once you are able to pinpoint the location of the vault, the other vaults will be able to send backup. I'm afraid we can do no more than that, however. We failed to find El Dorado before, and our limited resources will be better spent preparing for..."

Rhett bit the inside of his cheek. Preparing for the inevitable, presumably. Or at the very least, preparing for the worst possible outcome.

"Perhaps you can give us a few minutes to discuss this?" Fabien suggested.

"Of course." Azmera swept toward the door. "I will be outside, awaiting your answer. I trust that you will not deliberate too long." She opened the door, then paused with one hand on the frame to look over her shoulder at them. "Regardless of what you decide, I must thank you for your assistance thus far. ENIGMA has always had to do too much with too little. This was not meant to be your fight. It was our duty to protect civilians such as yourselves from the dangers presented by our collections." She pursed her lips, as if she wanted to say something else, but in the end she left them alone in the little command center outside the wreckage of the vault.

Her words were kind enough, but Rhett was still left with the feeling that he held the fate of the world in his hands.

33 DINAH

THIS WHOLE DISASTER was far above Dinah's pay grade, and that included the staggering amount of money that Porter had offered her to get involved in the first place. Demeke's comments on the value of human life were still ringing in her ears. Two million dollars was a mind-boggling amount of cash, but if she was dead, that money wouldn't mean anything. Being in Apollo's immediate vicinity if and when he assembled all the pieces of the device made the event of her impending death all the more likely.

"At best, we've been able to slow Apollo down," she said aloud, when neither Rhett nor Fabien had nothing to offer. "We haven't been able to stop him when we've had the full force of each vault behind us. He's killed androids. Melted faces. And now we're supposed to make one last stand, without anyone in ENIGMA helping out? Does that seem right to you?"

"No," Rhett admitted, but he didn't seem to feel as strongly about the situation as Dinah did. His features were still pinched in an uncertain frown.

"You're thinking of going anyway," Dinah observed. She'd

grown to rely on the headset's visual cues, but even she didn't need an AI to tell her that.

Rhett ran his fingers around the metal base of the hologram projector, mirroring Azmera's movements. She wondered if he was aware of it, or if he was doing so unconsciously. "I have a family. How would I be able to look my sister in the eye, knowing that I turned my back on a fight that could result in some terrible disaster that could impact her kids' futures? We might not know what Apollo intends to do with the device, but it can't be good."

Dinah leaned against the steel-paneled wall and bit her thumbnail. Rhett had a point, she supposed. She had family, too, but none of them would expect her to save the world. In fact, if she tried to tell any of them about the week she'd had, they would almost certainly laugh in her face. She could go home, right now, more or less guilt-free. Sure, she'd feel bad about it, but she wouldn't feel any more culpable for Apollo's actions than, say, the behavior of a politician she'd helped vote into office. There was only so much she could be reasonably expected to do. She was a history professor, for heaven's sake!

Fabien's mouth was a thin, flat line, and he wouldn't look at either of them.

"Are you thinking of pulling out?" Rhett asked.

"Oh, que non," he snapped. "I cannot."

"Because of what Porter promised you?"

Fabien jerked his chin downward once. "The money is very good, but I could walk away from that. But as you say, we have family counting on us." He crossed his arms and sank down into a crouch against the far wall. "Except that for me, it is even more pressing. I have a son, you see."

Rhett's eyebrows shot up, and he glanced at Dinah. She shook her head, because this was the first she was hearing about it too.

"He is seven." Fabien let his eyes flutter closed. "And very sick.

His mother and I, we aren't on speaking terms. I stay away from them for their safety, because of my work. If someone wanted to hurt me, they could go after Erek. It wouldn't be hard. He's spent so much of his life in the hospital. The doctors say that there is no cure for his illness, but Porter says he can help. That something in that vault of his can cure him." His face twisted in pain, and he shook his head. "I cannot walk away, not when I have a chance to help him."

Rhett kept running his finger along the metal ring. "I understand. For many years, I worked in intelligence for the US government. A few years ago, I was working with this group in the Middle East. Another agent and I were working with locals to gather information about a guerilla group that had been terrorizing the area, but we were compromised. Our contacts were all killed or taken prisoner, and the house we'd made our base of operations was bombed out." His hand stilled at last. "We were both captured, and we spent several months being moved around until the government was able to trade for me. Last I heard, Kelly and our other surviving contacts were still being held. Porter seems to think he can get them out."

Dinah wilted with every word. She couldn't imagine being in a situation like that, or the toll it would take on a person.

Fabien, however, was nodding. "Ah, I see. You feel guilt because you got out when your associate did not. If you free them, you think this guilt will go away?"

Rhett nodded. "I hope so. I owe it to her to try."

They lapsed into a brief but painfully deep silence before turning their heads, as one, to face Dinah.

"What about you, Professor?" Fabien asked.

"Um." Dinah lowered her head and picked at her cuticles. "It doesn't matter."

The Frenchman scoffed. "What? I told you about my son, Rhett spills his guts, and you're too shy to tell us?" He made a rude noise and an accompanying lewd gesture. "Not good enough. Tell us what Porter promised you."

Dinah grimaced, but Rhett made no move to intercede, so she relented.

"He promised me a discovery," she mumbled. "For a paper."

Both of them stared at her as if she'd grown a second head.

In the face of their incredulity, her voice rose against her will. "Do you have any idea how hard it is to advance in academia? I don't just want tenure, I want to advance the field. Think of the impact a discovery like the Rosetta Stone can have! Or the Uluburun shipwreck! I didn't ask him to do the research for me. I'm not trying to cheat. He told me that I'd get the chance to study a find unlike any other, and I'd be the first one to publish a paper on the matter." She let out an indignant huff and hunched her shoulders. "I know it isn't as personal as either of your motives, but it matters to *me*."

Fabien coughed into his fist, presumably to disguise a laugh, and Rhett's mouth twitched in a deeply suspicious manner, but he managed to keep his voice steady. "Just think of all the discoveries awaiting you in El Dorado, if only we could get in."

"Very funny," Dinah shot back. "And what if Porter's lying about what he can do for the two of you?"

Rhett's smile vanished in an instant.

"Come on, I know you don't trust him. Kunzang certainly didn't." Dinah glared at the two of them. "Who's to say that he isn't lying to us, too?"

Rhett chewed his bottom lip. "It's possible. But we've also seen what the devices on the vaults can do. Kunzang was terribly injured, and ENIGMA's tech has kept her alive. We know for a fact that the organization has connections all over the globe. Even if Porter doesn't follow through, we've met plenty of other people who can vouch for us. Captain Correia, Tenzin, Azmera... someone will come through for us."

"As long as we survive," Dinah muttered.

Fabien's head whipped back so sharply that it struck the metal paneling, but he barely seemed to notice. "What if we set a condition that drastically improved our chances of success?" he asked.

"I'd ask what took you so long," Rhett said.

"This vault is badly damaged," Fabien went on. There was a vagueness in his expression that suggested he was miles away, running through possible scenarios in his head. "Azmera can't afford to send a lot of people, and as we've seen before, we're not going to beat Apollo with numbers. We need to be smarter. Stronger." His eyes focused suddenly. "Rhett, are you in?"

"I told you," he said, "I have to be."

Dinah sighed. "I suppose, if the two of you are going, I will as well." It would be beyond humiliating to tell Azmera, *Sorry, what I really want is a one-way ticket home so that I can get back to grading papers in the hopes that the world doesn't end before finals.* Besides, there was a little part of her that had latched onto the idea of this device. Sure, Porter could promise her exclusive study of a heretofore unknown artifact from history, but no one had ever published a paper on an artifact from another world. She could become the world's first known... what would that make her, an exohistorian? Something spectacular, that was for certain.

And if the world was going to end, she might as well be doing something spectacular when it happened.

"Perfect." Fabien leapt to his feet and bolted toward the door, throwing it wide before Dinah could think better of her agreement. "Azmera!" he called. "We're going, on one condition."

The young woman looked up from her conversation with a group of Holy Land soldiers. "Is that so? And what do you require?"

Fabien pointed toward the growing stack of crates nearby. "We want to arm ourselves with items from the vault."

34 FABIEN

HE'D EXPECTED MORE pushback from Azmera, given how reluctant the commanders of the other vaults had been to let them use the items in their care.

Azmera, however, folded immediately. "What is the point of protecting our collections if we never use them?" she asked. "They will become useless mementos, and we will become obsessed with clinging to the past rather than looking to the future. Arm yourselves. We will offer you whatever we can to help."

If she thought that their mission was doomed to failure, she at least had the good grace not to drive the point home.

Deciding what to take with them, however, was another matter. For one thing, the digital catalog was no longer an accurate record of where the items were stored, and there was no new system in place to track their location. For another, there were hundreds of thousands of objects available for their use, but Fabien had no idea what they *did*, or what would be helpful against Apollo; never mind how to use them, even if Azmera pressed them into his hands then and there.

"Is there anything else that can damage Apollo while he's using the destabilizer?" Fabien asked. "That seemed moderately effective."

"Not effective enough," Rhett muttered. He plucked at the sleeve of his borrowed shirt. "And I miss that chameleon coat already."

"Well, I won't miss my armor." Fabien slapped his palm to his chest. "It wasn't going to do much good against that face-melty gun of his. And did we ever figure out how he split that android in half like a gutted fish?"

Nobody had an answer for that, but Azmera's expression suggested that she had another idea. "Perhaps I have just the thing for you, Dinah. The darknight armor."

"Dark Knight?" Fabien repeated skeptically. "Like, with the fake abs and the little bat ears?" He held his fingers up to the sides of his head.

Dinah groaned. "You're not even American, Fabien. How come Hollywood is your only point of reference?"

Fabien shrugged and wiggled his fingers. "What can I say? Your films are entertaining."

"Dark*night* armor," Azmera repeated, with more emphasis this time. "It might more accurately be called blackout armor. It grounds the wearer against most types of energy, but it can also be used to short out connections. It's possible that you might be able to touch Apollo while wearing it and knock out the destabilizer. Of course, you'd have to be careful what else you touched while wearing it." She eyed Rhett up. "It might even fit you."

"Sounds like it might be worth a shot," Rhett agreed.

Azmera turned to Girom and one of the other soldiers and spoke to them for a moment in their preferred language. Fabien, who had never spent much time in this part of Africa, didn't recognize it. While they spoke, he turned to Dinah, who was still perusing the information on her headset with glazed, half-open eyes. "Anything good?" he asked.

Dinah blinked a few times as she refocused on Fabien's face. "I don't have access to the full Holy Land record, but there are still so many things that we could use, if we only knew what would work. Regular ammunition isn't going to do much. We need to outsmart him. Out-strategize him."

Fabien patted Dinah's back. "Well, that's what we have you for, *non*?" Out of the three of them, Dinah was the greatest flight risk. If he kept the younger woman busy, perhaps that would be enough to deter her from abandoning their mission entirely.

Dinah resumed her search when Girom and the other soldier returned with a box filled with lightweight armor. Fabien had expected something like the old *chevalier* armor used during sieges, but it was as lightweight as aluminum. Despite the name, it was as sleek and bright as polished silver, with black ripples in the metal reminiscent of Damascus steel. Rhett needed help getting into it, but once it was on, he moved more easily than before.

"I feel… different." Rhett swung his arms experimentally. "Lighter, almost. Is this how you felt when you were wearing those bracers, Fabien?" He dipped into a squat, and his eyes widened in surprise. "That doesn't hurt at all."

"Careful," Azmera warned. "It's entirely possible that the armor is disrupting your body's physical response to pain. I'm certain that Porter warned you that using these artifacts can have unintended consequences…?" She trailed off, with a definite question mark in her tone that suggested she was not, in fact, certain of any such thing.

"He did." Rhett straightened up. "And I respect that, but we're talking about a mission that could save, or end, the world. An old injury should be the last thing on anyone's mind."

Fabien appreciated that neither of them had reacted poorly to his confession about Erek. For the most part, he was able to compartmentalize his life. There was work, with all of the cool detachment that a job like his required, and then there was his personal life. He often felt as if he'd had to parcel up all of his feelings around Erek and Erek's birth: his guilt, his insecurity, his self-doubt, his grief. Even admitting that all of that was his to bear was difficult, much less dwelling on it, and he'd never had anyone he could trust enough to share that information with. His job wasn't conducive to long-term relationships.

He wanted to give Rhett the same grace that Rhett had given him, but as the other man dropped into another squat, clearly reveling in the mobility that he'd gone without for years, Fabien had to bite his tongue to keep from reprimanding him. In some ways, they were too alike. He recognized a self-destructive tendency when he saw one.

Azmera turned to Fabien, and he set Rhett's dubious choices aside for the moment. "As for you, Mr. LeRoux, do you plan to use your rifle? Are you hoping to use a weapon, or armor of some kind?"

Fabien scratched his jaw. This was the longest he'd gone without shaving in years, and the thick layer of stubble made his face feel like a stranger's. "I'll keep the rifle, since it was able to do some damage when I hit him, but I need something else. Something that I might be able to use against him when he's using the destabilizer."

Azmera frowned. "We'll see what we can find. And you, Dr. Bray? Is there anything you'd like to try?"

Dinah's nose was wrinkled in displeasure when she spoke. "I hate to ask this, but... is there any chance you have another pair of those seven-league boots?"

BY THE TIME the three of them were fully armed, it was agreed that they would take the Laputan android along. Girom agreed to travel with them and relay their location, if and when they found the lost vault.

For the moment, Dinah's boots were powered down, and they'd managed to find a small sound-powered handgun for her, in the hopes that it would still have some effect against Apollo even if he was in between phases. Fabien had unearthed a pair of gloves that sparked a static bolt when the metal inserts along the knuckles made contact with anything. Rhett not only had the armor that Azmera had given him, but he'd retained the hip holster that he'd been using for his percussion pistol.

"Do you have another one like this?" he asked.

Azmera tilted her head. "The gun?"

"No, the holster." Rhett grinned self-consciously. "I may have lifted something useful during my fight with Apollo." He produced a second pistol, one that made Dinah recoil in horror.

"Did you pull that off of Apollo? Isn't that the face-melting gun?" Dinah backed away a pace. "Where were you even keeping that?"

"I tucked it into my arm brace earlier. Which, by the way, I don't need now." He flexed the arm in question, just to prove his point.

Self-destructive behavior, Fabien thought again. But it resolved the concerns he'd had about Apollo's resilience, didn't it?

The Hand had pushed them into a corner, and they'd awakened something feral in the process.

Azmera produced a second hip-holster, and Fabien took advantage of her distraction to root around in one of the open crates for a moment. He wasn't sure what he was looking for, but when his fingers found the smooth edge of a more modern bit of tech, he pulled it free. When he saw what it was, he nearly burst out laughing. Perfect.

"Are you ready?" Azmera asked them.

Fabien tucked his new find into his pocket and nodded. "As ready as I'll ever be."

"There's food and water in the cantina near the medical tent," Demeke told them. "Take half an hour. We'll prepare the way for you in the meantime."

"We're not flying, I take it?" Rhett asked.

Demeke's answering smile was amused. "Hardly. We have other modes of travel. If we're lucky, you might even beat Apollo to where you're going."

35 RHETT

RHETT HAD HALF EXPECTED to be confronted with another torii gate, but the objects Azmera had produced for them were much smaller than he'd anticipated. They were belts of what looked like finely-woven metal mesh around a flexible core. A buckle with a glittering yellow stone set in the front allowed the belts to fit each of them snugly.

"They're point-to-point teleporters," their hostess explained as the five of them—four humans and one android—buckled the belts into place. "They've been attuned to homing beacons left behind by those who tried to locate El Dorado. My mother was among them. The team was never successful, but they left a beacon in the place she thought was closest."

"Why didn't we travel like this earlier?" Fabien asked as he cinched his tighter.

"We don't keep active homing beacons near the vaults," Azmera said, in a tone that suggested that this should be obvious. "There are too many in circulation, and the likelihood that the Hand could misuse them is much too high. We wouldn't have left this one where we did, but the mission was still active, up until—" She stopped short and took a deep breath. "Until my mother died, at which point our priorities shifted. When you're ready, pressing on the stone will activate the transporter."

The belt fit snugly around Rhett's borrowed armor. He looked up just in time to see Fabien depress the buckle, and then—

It wasn't that he vanished. Perhaps his mind was playing tricks on him, but it almost looked like he shrank down to a single point of light, the way the images used to cut out on those old rabbit-ear TVs. It happened so fast that Rhett couldn't quite believe it.

Girom nodded to them and did the same, followed by the android, which didn't deign to glance at them even once before it vanished.

"I'm already wearing the boots," Dinah fretted. "Maybe I should just use them?"

Azmera shook her head. "At this distance, even if your step was only off by one degree, you could end up hundreds of miles away from the rest of your group. The teleporter will take you right where you need to go."

Dinah's face bunched up in dismay. "I can already tell I'm going to hate this."

"We'll go together," Rhett told her. He held his fingers over the belt buckle. "On the count of three. Two…"

"One," Dinah said, and she blinked out.

Rhett, however, hadn't budged. He tried again, to no avail. "What happened? Why am I still here?"

"It's the armor." Azmera approached and fiddled with a sliding switch inside Rhett's collar. "While it's on, it'll short out other tech, like I told you. Fortunately, you can power down that feature without removing it entirely."

Rhett felt the moment when the suit turned off, not because of any change in the armor itself, but in the sudden heaviness that stole over his limbs. The ache in his shoulder returned, and the pain in his hip, which he thought he'd grown used to by now, stole back over him so suddenly that it made his head spin. Yes, it hurt more than usual after his underground run-in with Apollo, but the real problem was the intensity of it. Painkillers wore off gradually, but this hurt almost as much as it had that first time, in the desert, when the walls around him and Kelly blew apart.

"... Rhett?" Azmera's worried face was close to his, and he realized that he had slanted sideways in order to keep the weight off of his old injury.

"I'm fine." His voice was thin and reedy, which made his answer sound like exactly what it was: a damn lie.

Azmera shot a worried look at her father, which was the last thing Rhett needed. He'd already escaped one terrible situation and left his team behind. No way was he going to do the same thing with Fabien and Dinah.

"Thank you," he said, and pulled out of Azmera's reach. Before she could try to change his mind, Rhett tried to activate the belt again.

This time, he was certain that it had worked, although unlike the torii gate he didn't appear and disappear all at once. He was pulled taut, stretched and scrambled like a telegraph message being dragged along an old undersea cable. For however long it lasted, Rhett was unmade, but enough of his consciousness remained to understand that some fundamental part of him had been removed. He was himself, but with no sense of self.

And then, quite abruptly, he was standing in the jungle. Stopping was even stranger than starting, and he had the nasty sensation that he'd just run full-bore into a cement wall.

Dinah was on her hands and knees, wheezing into the dirt, while Fabien leaned against a tree for support and gagged. Of the humans, Girom alone seemed unaffected, and the android had wandered off to examine a line of giant ants climbing the trunk of an enormous tree. A metal pole with what appeared to be a glass bulb at the top stood nearby. The bulb sparked with an internal yellow light, just once, before dimming again. The homing beacon for the point-to-point teleporter, Rhett assumed. The sleek, modern object was wildly out of place in the overgrown wilderness.

Fabien retched again. "I thought Demeke was nice. What kind of sick *casse couille* would tell someone to eat right before putting them through that?"

"Are you going to be sick, too?" Girom looked over at Rhett, unimpressed.

"No." His stomach roiled, but there were far more pressing matters... specifically, the pain that still lanced through his right side. He reached up to his collar and powered on the armor.

A breath later, all the muscle tension in his body drained away as the pain vanished, and he let out a little sigh of relief.

"No," he repeated, "I'm perfectly fine."

INTERLUDE

When Ray Twelve hailed him, Apollo declined the call.

He had barely managed to crawl free of the rubble in Holy Land. Ever since Rhett had electrified him with that cane of his, he hadn't felt right. His muscles spasmed at random times, and his nose had been bleeding almost continuously beneath his helmet. Wiping it away would have required too much effort, and he was so tired, almost unbelievably so. What would he have to give to lie down and curl up someplace quiet and cool, where his fever wouldn't render him dizzy and disoriented? He was losing time in vast chunks, and the only reason he hadn't crashed was that his vessel's autopilot feature kept kicking on just in time.

Nearly there. Soon, you'll be able to go back to Ra and give him what he asked for. You will be healed, and when you're ready, you'll be able to accomplish everything you've dreamed. The others will congratulate themselves, and they too will reap the rewards of power, but it will all be of your making.

You will do things no human has done for centuries, see things no living man has witnessed, go places no one from this Earth has dreamed. Think of all those other worlds, Apollo, and what might be accomplished there.

Think of all that you have earned, and hold on a little longer.

The destabilizer sat in his belt, ready to be used, although he was coming to dread the way it cut him off from the rest of the world, the way it was slowly prising him away from reality. Its four power cells hummed, blazing so bright in each others' company that the green glow spilled through the seam of the utility belt's clasped compartment.

Only a little longer, and then all of your troubles will be over. Everything you have ever wanted will be yours.

The comm buzzed again with another alert from Ray Twelve, and Apollo reached out with a snarl to answer.

"What?" he demanded.

"*Ray Twelve speaking.*" The voice on the other end of the mic was as terse as his, and for a moment he thought he would be forced to endure the other agent's petty recriminations.

That did not, however, appear to be the case, because the next thing he said made Apollo sit up again.

"*The ENIGMA operatives are close. Better get there soon, Ray Six, or you'll have a fight on your hands.*"

Without replying, he killed the comm, not trusting his voice to come out as anything other than a guttural snarl. A fight? He'd bested the operatives at every turn. They were welcome to try and stop him if they wanted, but it would do them no good.

At least he might finally be able to get rid of them, once and for all. Let them rot in the lost vault.

36 DINAH

IT WASN'T that Dinah hated the jungle, per se. Only a monster would think that. Think of the wildlife habitats, the carbon load, the water storage! Think of the biodiversity and the complex ecosystems!

Still, Dinah could love something without having to be immersed in it.

As the five of them slogged through the thick undergrowth in search of the vault entrance, Dinah imagined where she would be at this exact moment if Porter had never showed up in her classroom. What day was it? She'd long since lost track. If it was Friday—and who could say that it wasn't?—she'd be preparing for her final classes of the week, wearing her comfortable loafers, reveling in the temperature-controlled classrooms, trying to convince her students to care about ancient history despite their best efforts. Maybe she and Professor McKean would grab a beer after work and squabble over the relative merits of their respective fields. She would, no doubt, be feeling vaguely bored, but not unutterably so.

Instead, she was coated in sweat, panting for breath, and she'd already stumbled across several spiders at least the size of her face. They were plagued with biting insects, and Dinah was acutely aware that she was out of breath and struggling to keep up with the rest of her crew.

"What I want to know," Fabien said from up ahead, "is why Apollo has to look for the vault at all. Everyone made it sound like it was taken over by the Hand. Wouldn't that mean that the Hand already has access to its contents?"

"I don't know the details," Girom admitted. "Azmera is tight-lipped about vault business, but her mother was even more so. I worked for her for, what, six years? I even came on a mission out here with her once, but she rarely took the same crew twice."

"She didn't trust anyone." Rhett swatted a gloved hand at the back of his head. "That's the sort of thing we did, back in the day. One person who knows too much is dangerous. Too many people who know too little doesn't give the enemy the advantage at all."

"If Apollo has to look for the vault, too, then we can assume he doesn't have the last relic yet," Fabien reasoned. "If he did, wouldn't he have activated the device already?"

"Not necessarily," Rhett replied, "if the Hand has plans for it. Azmera seemed to think that we still had time, however, so—"

The android, which had been walking ahead of them, stopped abruptly. "My records indicate that the vault was lost, not raided."

The others stopped walking as well, which was a blessed relief. It allowed Dinah to pause and brace her palms against her knees while she sucked in damp, humid air like her life depended on it.

"Lost?" Rhett asked. "What does that mean?"

"Its data was purposefully redacted," the android explained. "At this time, I am able to access the records from the El Dorado vault, but the details of its location are not available, nor are any ancillary details that might provide clues. That said, I am able to review provenance notes for all of the items stored there."

Rhett frowned. "Weird."

"Not... necessarily..." Dinah panted. "Deliberate gaps in historical records... can indicate a change of... worldview."

"Worldview?" Fabien echoed.

She was exhausted, certainly, but this was her field, after all. She righted herself and launched automatically into professorial mode. "Historically speaking...cultures have either attempted to maintain some level of continuity between themselves and their forebears, or made an attempt to distance themselves from ideologies that no longer match their own. Modern Greeks share a direct line of cultural inheritance with the ancient Hellenes, and the same can be said for places like Rome, and those are only a few Western examples. But look at someplace like Hatshepsut's Temple, or Tell el-Amarna. Those were deliberately destroyed when new rulers came to power and wanted to distance themselves from the public perception of the former rulers."

Fabien's mouth hung open as he scratched the bug bite on his neck, and Rhett was frowning.

"Your point?" Girom asked.

Heat rushed to Dinah's face. She was rambling again. "My point is that Tell el-Amarna was defaced because those who were in power benefitted from the destruction of those records. The old Pharaoh, Akhenaten, had gone against the will of the people and Egypt's established infrastructure."

Rhett was still squinting at her. "So you're suggesting that El Dorado's records might have been altered in an attempt to punish them...?"

"Or to suppress dangerous ideas," Dinah amended. "If Porter's grandfather was indeed responsible for the vault's destruction, maybe the records were changed to keep anyone else from sharing their information. Or maybe ENIGMA wanted to avoid a repeat of whatever disaster befell El Dorado. Perhaps they scrubbed records that could be recovered, like the location of the vault, but didn't want to erase all the work that had been done to catalog the items."

"There's one problem with that little theory," Fabien pointed out.

Dinah bristled. "Which is?"

"The digitized records are fairly new," the Frenchman said. "Porter is converting his from paper to digital, remember? And if this vault was lost two generations ago, what's the likelihood that they were using technology?"

Dinah blinked rapidly as this argument sank in. "But... but we've seen all sorts of crazy tech in the last few days. My boots travel through time!"

"And I suppose it's possible that there's a magical spreadsheet-maker in one of these vaults somewhere," Fabien conceded. "But it might be worth considering that everything was lost, but that someone out there is creating a new set of records. Because otherwise, the fact that a vault that was lost decades ago has modern records, but Porter's does not, looks pretty suspicious to me."

It was certainly something to consider. As they resumed their trek through the jungle, in search of something that they might be incapable of recognizing, Dinah pulled up the files she did have access to on her headset and skimmed through them. When she reached the files from Atlantis' vault, she nearly tripped over her own feet.

"Dinah?" Rhett was at her side in an instant. "Are you okay?"

"Yes, I—" She clung to his arm. "Do we have a way to share images from the ENIGMA database?"

Rhett cocked his head. "You mean, the way Azmera showed us the relic earlier?"

Dinah nodded frantically. Much to her chagrin, the android shook its head, and Girom did the same.

"We'd need a hologram projector for that," he explained.

"Like this?" Fabien dipped into his pocket and produced one of the black discs, like the one Porter had used during their very first debriefing.

Girom narrowed his eyes. "Where did you get that?"

"Found it." Fabien tossed the disc into the air so that it spun once before landing in his palm with a faint slap. "Doesn't matter. It'll work, right?"

According to the ID text on her headset, it would work just fine. Fabien tossed it again, farther this time, and Dinah caught it before it hit the jungle floor. It only took a matter of moments for her headset to sync up with it, and the hologram projector shivered to life, displaying the same image Dinah had seen.

In the image, the relic was shimmering green.

"Right, yes, that's what it looks like." Fabien seemed nonplussed.

"You don't understand," Dinah said. "It wasn't doing that before. I don't know what kind of tracking Atlantis put on it, but it seems like it's updating the status of the relic in real time. Look, there's even an update in the text ID that suggests it's active!"

Once again, a clueless glance passed between her colleagues.

"Oh, for heaven's sake!" Dinah waved the puck at them so that the 3D image it produced jiggled around. "Apollo can use the proximity of the existing pieces to find the one he's looking for. He doesn't need to know the coordinates of the vault; he just needs to play hot-potato, cold-potato until he narrows in on the location, and apparently he's getting close."

"Then we're finished," Girom said, collapsing back against the trunk of a nearby tree. "He's almost there, and we have no idea where he's gone."

"Inaccurate," the android said.

Four human faces whipped in its direction, while its smooth and unchanging features stared back at them.

"I do not know where to find the entrance to the vault, but I can detect two things you may find useful. First, there is a hollow point in the Earth beneath us. An underground cavern of some kind."

"Why didn't you tell us that earlier?" Fabien snapped.

The android rotated its head approximately two degrees until it was facing him in what, Dinah suspected, was most likely the robot equivalent of an eye-roll. "We have passed over many such underground caverns. From this distance, and with this amount of interference, I cannot ascertain anything about the potential contents."

"Then why mention this one?" Rhett asked pointedly.

"Two reasons. First, because this one, unlike the others, connects to the surface." The android turned on the spot and pointed through the trees. "Second, because we are about two hundred yards away from a man-made vessel that is likely an airship."

"Wait, what?" Fabien snatched the projector puck back, killed the power, and stuffed it into his pocket as he jogged in the direction that the android had indicated. When he was almost out of sight, he swore. "It's a ship, all right. How the hell did we miss that landing?"

Dinah and the others followed. The ground began to slope down before them, as if leading into a massive sinkhole. When they got closer, Dinah could see that it dropped away into darkness. The trees gave way to a sheer rock face, limned with only moss and epiphytes. Dinah couldn't tell if the rocky fissure culminated in a traversable tunnel or simply a bottomless pit, but she did know that she was going to find out soon.

Sitting at the mouth of the tunnel was a sleek one-man vessel.

They may not have known where exactly to find the relic, but they had found Apollo.

TRAVERSING THE SLICK, damp stone slope was treacherous at best, and they had to make their way carefully to avoid losing their footing and tumbling end over end down into the depths. The android, of course, all but strolled down into the pit, but the humans struggled after it, slipping more than once on their descent. For once, Dinah wasn't last. Rhett took the slope even more gingerly than she did.

The small airship was empty, and Dinah peered inside with her hands pressed to the glass.

"Thinking of making a getaway?" Fabien teased.

"It would be a good idea to make sure Apollo can't make a clean break," Dinah pointed out. "Girom, were you planning to come with us, or were you still planning to wait topside for backup?"

The Holy Land guard shuffled over to them. This close to the mouth of the pit, the stones were so slick that a single careless step would spell disaster. Only the slight ridges in the worn volcanic layers caught the tread of their shoes.

At least these boots have good grips, she thought. She still couldn't believe she'd agreed to wear the damn things.

"The latter," Girom told them. "I've already reached out to the other vaults. Ideally, by the time you've settled matters in the vault, we'll be ready to take Apollo into custody and begin recovery of the vault's contents."

Dinah could read between the lines well enough to understand what he wasn't saying... that the three of them might not make it up alive, and that ENIGMA's forces might be the last line of defense between the Hand and whatever they intended to do with the artifact.

Unless help isn't coming at all, Dinah mused. *Porter could have used us. Although, realistically, anyone at ENIGMA could be a spy or a traitor. Any one of them could be working for the Hand of the Sun.*

Realistically speaking, you can't trust anyone.

37 FABIEN

MIST SWIRLED up from the mouth of the cavern beneath them, and the air was so thick with humidity that it ached to draw breath. Behind them, Girom was speaking into his comm, although Fabien couldn't make out what he was saying.

At least the android was still with them. As the trio descended into darkness, their mechanical companion changed the settings of its eyes so that they glowed like a pair of unblinking floodlights.

Not that there was much to see. There was a narrow tunnel below them that twisted sharply to a more walkable angle, but it was still uncannily smooth. No markings were visible on the walls, no handrails stood out from the walls, and there wasn't a single step cut into the narrow passageway.

"Are we sure that this is where we should be headed?" Rhett asked. His voice echoed off the dripping walls of the passageway. "I can't imagine getting in and out of here with crates and equipment like we did in Holy Land."

"There might have been other transport," Dinah's voice said

from far away, at the very back of their crew. "We don't know what would have been here when the vault was still active."

There was one good thing about going underground, at least. The deeper they went, the stuffier the air became, but it was also much cooler than the jungle had been. The sweat that had been dripping in Fabien's eyes during the descent dried up as they navigated the corridors with only the light of the android's eyes to guide them.

And then, quite suddenly, they were plunged into darkness.

He didn't hear the android fall. One moment, it was there. The next, it was gone, and he was utterly blind. Behind him, Rhett yelped and stumbled, knocking against his back. His feet slipped, and then Fabien, too, was falling. It happened so fast that he didn't have time to react, and by the time he realized that he had slipped, he had already hit the ground.

The light returned as the android got back to its feet beside him and looked around, its lights sweeping the walls.

"Fabien? Are you okay?" Dinah sounded very far away. Fabien and the android both looked up, and she had to raise her arm to shield her eyes from the glare. She was standing roughly a story above them, peering through a hole that connected the tunnel floor to the chamber beneath.

"I'm fine." Fabien sat up and dusted himself off. He'd managed not to land badly on his rifle, which hadn't gone off, thank God. If he'd had more time to react, he'd probably have hurt himself when he braced for impact, but as it was he'd landed in a limp heap. "Not sure how we're going to get back up, though."

"That may be unnecessary." The android pointed to the far wall. "There appears to have been a partial collapse of the roof here, but my scans are showing a metal deposit beyond that."

Fabien studied the distant wash of scree. Strange shadows danced across it. They had no way to know if Apollo had come this way or not; he could have walked right through the debris using the destabilizer.

But he couldn't have used it the whole time, Fabien reminded himself. *He'd want to preserve its runtime until he could find the last piece.*

"Look at the ground," he told the android. When it obeyed, the light caught on a bootprint in the ground below. Apollo's? Or some long-forgotten traveler whose print remained without the wind and rain of the world above to wash it away?

It didn't matter. If anyone had come this way, that suggested there was something down here that had drawn other humans once upon a time.

"Is there a way you can get down here?" Fabien asked. "Maybe you can slide partway through until we can support—"

Rhett slipped through the hole and landed on his feet with a soft grunt. He grinned at him, but Fabien couldn't suppress a shudder. He'd feel that later, when he removed the suit.

"Come on, Dinah!" he called up. "We'll catch you!" Sure enough, Dinah dropped through, right into his waiting arms. He set her on her feet.

All of that, Fabien thought, *he'll regret all of that later.*

Unless, of course, Rhett had accepted that there wouldn't be a later, and that his body only had to withstand whatever he could throw at it in the next few hours or so.

"I hope we're in the right place, or we're going to regret being left without anyone to pull us back up," Fabien muttered instead. He'd done plenty of foolish things to avoid thinking about his own mistakes and his unavoidable mortality. Let Rhett break himself if he wanted. It was none of his business.

"Guess we ought to find out, then." Rhett sauntered past him. "Where's this landslide you mentioned?"

The roof collapse the android had identified reached all the way to the ceiling, and Fabien found himself tiptoeing forward, just in case the ceiling collapsed a second time, although he could make out very little in the weak light.

Rhett crouched in front of the stones and scooped up a handful of flaky volcanic dross. "How deep do you think this goes?"

"There appear to be approximately four to six inches of debris between us and the metal," the android said.

"So, what? We're just going to dig it all out?" Fabien wrinkled his nose. "We don't have anything like that kind of time."

Rhett dropped the stones to the floor. They left an ashy residue on his gloves. "What do you suggest, then? I don't see what other option we have. We can't walk through walls like Apollo can."

"Um, actually..." Dinah raised her hand. "I think I can."

"Since when?" Fabien asked. If Dinah had been keeping something up her sleeve this whole time, he was going to kill the woman.

The professor lifted one booted foot. "I don't understand exactly how these work, but it seems like they must be able to carry me through solid objects, given that I was able to visit Wisconsin. Can't I just set them to carry me, I don't know, ten feet forward?"

"And hope that you're not stuck inside an airless room?" Rhett asked.

Fabien snorted. "She could step back if that was the case, but what happens if the rock slide is on the other side of the door, too?"

Dinah's face slackened as she no doubt pictured just how awful it would be to end up trapped in stone. Fabien, of course, had faced much the same danger when he followed Apollo through the walls of Laputa.

Instead of changing her mind, though, Dinah turned to the

android. "Can your sensors pick up anything beyond the metal barrier?"

"No," the android told her. "Which doesn't mean that there isn't anything. A null reading is inconclusive, but it might be safe for a human in there."

"That's probably what Howard Carter thought when he opened King Tut's tomb," Dinah grumbled, "and look how that turned out."

Fabien, who had never heard of Howard Carter in his life, made no comment at all.

"We ought to at least try it," Dinah insisted. "I haven't been particularly useful so far, at least not when it comes to a fight."

Fabien reached out to pat her shoulder. "I promise," he said, "that I won't shoot you with the stun gun this time."

Dinah laughed and swatted Fabien's hand away. "I'm not sure I believe that." She crouched down, turning her ankle out so that she could fiddle with the settings on her boot. When she was done, she stood up, rolled her shoulders back, and gave them a half-hearted salute. She lifted one foot, extended it, and vanished.

Silence fell over the cavern.

"Well," Rhett said after a few seconds, "I don't hear any agonized screaming, so that's good."

"She wouldn't be able to scream if she was trapped in rubble," Fabien pointed out.

"Or if the chamber on the far side was full of nerve gas, highly evolved flesh-eating bacteria, or opened over a deep pit full of venomous snakes," the android pointed out, which didn't strike Fabien as a particularly helpful insight.

Although, he mused, *if it did, wouldn't that solve the Apollo problem for us, too?*

He shook his head to clear the thought away. Hopefully,

Dinah was fine, and was just looking for a way to bring the rest of them through.

"Maybe we should try clearing some of this rubble while we wait?" Rhett suggested. "Just, you know, in case?"

"That would be wise," the android agreed. "Should your friend fail to return alive, having a backup plan would be optimal."

"She'll be fine," Fabien said, to himself as much as to either of them. "Let's start moving this stone, and—"

The cavern rumbled, and all three of them stepped back. The android's lights were still trained on the debris, but Fabien was more worried about the ceiling. As the rumbling intensified, he caught Rhett's arm and pulled him back, putting a bit of distance between them and the shuddering wall of loose stone. A healthy number of profanities tumbled through his mind, but before he could settle on just one, the stones collapsed on themselves, spilling out of the chamber and into a new chasm that opened up beyond.

"Come on!" Fabien dragged Rhett back, but the android stayed where it was, indifferent to the plume of dust that rose in the wake of the fresh rockslide. The light from its eyes dimmed in the wake of a new yellow-tinged glow. The sound of stone grating against stone was deafening, and even when Fabien's stream of curses found their way onto his lips, he couldn't hear himself over the commotion. He and Rhett pressed their backs to the far wall of the cavern, waiting for a calamity that never came.

Eventually, the sound died away, the dust settled, and the new light source became more apparent. A series of lanterns was set into the walls of the newly-revealed tunnel beyond the cavern. An immense pair of metal doors, hinged inward, was now visible at the tunnel's mouth, although they were held open by what was left of the rockfall.

Into that opening stepped a figure, who laughed in delight as her own cleverness. "I told you it would work!" Dinah crowed. "And look what I found!" She spun on the spot with her arms spread wide, indicating the massive cavern behind her, ringed with steel passages and catwalks running between a forest of shelves jutting upward from the floor like stalagmites.

"El Dorado," Fabien murmured.

They had found the lost vault.

38 RHETT

RHETT STRODE along one of the steel-grated walkways that circled the outer wall of the vault. Despite the stuffiness of the room, it was fairly well lit with what looked like old-fashioned gas lamps. When he inspected one more closely, he realized that they were illuminated with little yellow orbs that floated freely in the square-paneled glass sconces.

"If Apollo's in here, there's no way he didn't hear that." Dinah gripped the railing and bent forward over empty space. She kicked a stray pebble over the edge and watched it fall into the shadowed depths of the vault.

Fabien's face was very nearly the same color as the floating lights. "Maybe don't do that, Professor. We don't know how sturdy these walkways are."

"That's right." Dinah stood upright again and took a step back from the railing. "You're afraid of heights."

"It's not fear," Fabien insisted. "It's a completely rational concern that our combined weight will overtax hardware that nobody has maintained in decades, and we'll all plummet to our deaths before we have a chance to finish the mission."

The android nodded solemnly. "I can confirm, Mr. LeRoux, that what you are describing is not a phobia, but a reasonable consideration."

Fabien jabbed his hand toward the vault's interior. "See?"

Rhett let his own fingers brush the railing as he walked. "To be fair, this is coming from the same android that believed we could be standing only inches away from a pit of venomous snakes."

"There could be snakes down there," Fabien insisted, pointing in the depths. "You don't know."

"Untrue," the android corrected. "My sensors indicate no other life forms in here larger than an insect."

"Which means we beat Apollo here," Rhett said.

Dinah pumped her arm in triumph. "Yes! He's losing hot potato! We still have a chance!"

The walkways intersected, criss-crossed, and descended, passing close enough to the array of shelving that if anyone could find what they were looking for, they could simply reach out and take it. But how was anyone supposed to find what they were looking for in all this?

"Hey, robot," Rhett called.

The android tilted its head. "I presume you mean me."

"Yeah." Rhett paused before asking a different question than he'd intended. "Do you have a name?"

"No. *Robot* will do. What can I help you with?"

"You said that you could access some of the data from this place." He gestured toward the tallest of the narrow shelves. "Does it tell you where to find anything?"

"Unfortunately not," the android said.

Rhett stared out over the array of shelves. They were all different heights, some set at odd angles from the others. It was beautiful, in a way, and the layout reminded him of a forest, or the chaotic angles of an East Coast city skyline, without any sort of grid system or long-term urban development planning.

"So we'll have to look for it," he mused aloud.

"I can program my headset to look for a visual match," Dinah said. "I'll still have to get close enough for the headset to register the visual cue, but it should make things less tedious."

"My eyes have the same feature," the android offered.

"Then you two should start looking." Rhett patted his pistols. "Fabien and I will hold down the fort. Apollo will find his way down here eventually, and with all that rubble in the way, we won't even be able to close the doors. We'll have to meet him head-on."

Fabien clenched his hands into fists and smiled. There was a manic glint in his eyes, and for a moment Rhett saw just how dangerous he could be. In the right mood, he could be a hunter, someone to be feared. That made two of them.

No wonder he had distanced himself from his child. People like them could be protectors, but never caregivers. Rhett made a fun uncle, but he would have been a shit father, and he knew it. They were both emotional pressure-cookers, poised to erupt with violence at a moment's notice.

This is why Porter picked us, he thought, and the realization that he'd chosen them both made him second-guess himself. If Porter wanted Apollo to win, why hire them at all? Just to cover his tracks? Or maybe Rhett was wrong to mistrust him.

Either way, as Dinah and the android set out into the maze of catwalks, he found it easier than he'd expected to fall back into the old routine of standing shoulder-to-shoulder with a fellow operative and trusting that person with his life.

This time, he wasn't going to screw it up.

WHILE THEY WAITED, Rhett began to sift through the stones that held the door open.

"I wonder what they'll do now that we've found their missing vault," he said. "Most of the other vaults seem to have been run by families."

"Good to know that ENIGMA is rife with nepotism," Fabien said cheerfully.

"I don't know if it's nepotism so much as legacy. Isn't that the whole point of the vaults to begin with? To preserve history?"

"To be honest? There's a lot we don't know." Fabien crossed his arms and kicked at a few of the pebbles. "Porter made the whole ENIGMA enterprise sound so noble, but what's the point of having all of these amazing things and just locking them up where people can't use them? I'm sure Dinah just loves the idea of a museum, but surely these objects have practical applications that could help people."

Rhett huffed and sat back on his heels, abandoning his task for the moment. God, it felt *good* to be able to move freely without having to worry about his joints. "Are you suggesting that the Hand might be right to try to take things?"

"No." Fabien sounded a bit reluctant to concede this point. "Obviously, Apollo is the worst."

"So what's your point?"

Fabien stared at the floor for a moment with his lips pursed and tapped his toe against the floor. "Porter supposedly has a way to help my son. His disease is very rare. A cancer of the blood. Most people don't recover. But Porter says he can help him." Slowly, he lifted his gaze from the tunnel floor to Rhett's face. "So why does he need me to do a mission for him before he can help Erek recover? Why not just help now? If this technology, or science, or magic, or whatever it is exists, why should anyone die from such things?"

Rhett went very still. Taking a stance against the enemy was second nature by now. Defensiveness came easily to him, and he had no problem turning that outward upon a clear enemy. He also knew, on some level, that he'd made excuses for those in power before. It took no effort at all to hate the group of insurrectionists who'd killed his contacts, damaged him for life, and held Kelly all this time. But what about the people who'd bargained for his life and stopped short of saving his comrade as well? What about the mission leaders who had sent them there in the first place and failed to keep them safe?

Azmera seemed wise for her age, the antithesis of Apollo. And yet, she was allowing harm to come to other people by taking a passive stance despite their many resources. All of the vault commanders were.

His emotions must have shown on his face, because Fabien nodded emphatically. "You see what I mean?"

"Yes, I... yes." Rhett rubbed the back of his neck. "Well, I don't like that at all."

He thought that it was Fabien's low laughter that reverberated through the tunnel, until he looked up at him sharply and saw that he was staring back at him in utter consternation. Only then did they both notice the man in gold, with his dented chestplate and burning eyes, limping toward them out of the cavern.

Apollo had abandoned his golden-rayed helmet, but the human face beneath was somehow more unsettling. His features were striking, with a square jaw hidden beneath a close-cropped beard, and his black hair was long enough to brush against his neck, but it was so damp with sweat that it clung to him, accentuating the hard lines of his cheekbones. In another life, he might have been a model—*no wonder he preferred that helmet, he'd be much too recognizable otherwise*—but he was eerily gaunt, and there was a fever in his eyes that looked like hunger.

Rhett had grown up around pet dogs, all of which were about as terrifying as McNugget. Only when he'd begun to spend more time traveling had he met another kind of dog, the feral curs with nothing left to defend but their very lives. A guard dog would bite you for breaking the rules he'd set for you, but the street curs had lost all sense of order. It made them more dangerous. Rhett had once been beset by a trio of half-starved mutts that chased him down a dirt road and over a fence, just because they could. He had no doubt that they would have gleefully torn him apart if they got their teeth in him.

They looked at him the very same way that Apollo did now, with too-bright eyes and bared teeth, a desire to hurt others in a vain attempt to soothe the bloodthirsty devil that rode him.

"You're catching on to the way we see things," Apollo snarled. "Now, are you going to help me find the last piece I need, or am I going to have to kill you?"

39 DINAH

THE CATWALKS along the wall were sturdy, but the ones that threaded between them swayed like rope bridges when either Dinah or the android moved too fast.

"I don't understand the system," she complained as she studied the nearest display. "Surely all of these items weren't just jumbled in here at random."

The android inclined its head. "I admit, the system seems to be somewhat... erratic."

That was putting it mildly. Weapons were jumbled in with figurines and gemstones all along the glass shelves. Amulets were displayed alongside articles of clothing and masks. One tower housed coins and crystals and canopic jars, while the next was nothing but orreries and astrolabes.

The tower of stargazing devices brought Dinah to a skidding halt. If they searched at random, they could be here forever. She needed to stop and use her head for a moment.

The android kept up its steady search, but Dinah backtracked to the last shelf and examined it. Sure enough, everything inside had a similar purpose. The android's movements rocked the walkway, and the subtle motion was enough to make it tricky to read the text ID boxes. Dinah reached out a hand to steady herself against the towering display shelf.

Immediately, it lit up, and a monotone but feminine voice said, "Welcome to shelving unit 244, navigation implements. This is Finder speaking. What are you looking for today?"

Dinah squealed and flung herself backward. Without the railing, she would have tumbled right off the edge, and even with it, she nearly overbalanced. The walkway swung, and several dozen yards away, the android wobbled precariously. Neither of them fell, though, and after a moment Dinah managed to stop shaking and shuffle back toward the shelves.

"I didn't understand your answer," the illuminated shelving unit said. It was still lit up from within, like a skyscraper-high curio cabinet. "How can I direct your search today?"

"I'm, um." Dinah gulped. "I'm actually looking for something else."

"Please provide the function, object identification number, or designation for your desired artifact," the voice trilled. She was being rather loud, especially in the otherwise quiet vault. It wasn't as if they were in a library and might disrupt the other patrons, but if Apollo showed up now, he'd pretty much be able to follow a beacon right to Dinah.

"I'm looking for a power cell," she said. "It's kind of—" She made a gesture with her hands to indicate the shape. Then she realized that she was talking to a *shelving unit,* which probably didn't have eyes, and felt very silly for not making the connection.

To her surprise, the voice spoke again. "You're looking for a curved power source," Finder said. Throughout the vault, several dozen other shelving units lit up from within. "I have been able to locate one hundred and sixteen potential matches for your search. Can you provide more data?"

"Um, yeah." So the shelf *did* have eyes? That was disconcerting. "It's metal, it has inscriptions on it... it's about four inches long..."

"I have been able to locate four potential matches for this search." All but four of the illuminated shelving units went dark again. "Can you provide more data?"

"It's part of a six piece device that was deliberately split up by ENIGMA. And it was, er. Supposedly made by aliens?"

All but one of the units darkened. It was a much shorter case, and she'd have to descend quite a few flights of stairs to reach it. Which, of course, meant that she'd have to *ascend* quite a few flights of stairs in order to get back out again, all before Apollo found her.

Dinah didn't often wish that she'd spent more of her waking hours in the gym, but this was one of those times.

"Object located!" Finder chirped. "Would you like me to illuminate the most efficient pathway to your desired artifact?"

"Yes, please," Dinah told it. "But is there any chance that you could turn the lights off after I've passed? There's someone behind me."

An illuminated pathway flickered to life as the other lights within the vault dimmed or went out.

"Is this suitable?" Finder asked.

"Yeah," Dinah said. "That's great."

She broke into a jog. The android had gone very still, and when Dinah trotted past, it didn't acknowledge her presence at all. When she looked back at it, it twitched once, then turned to follow her. Its movements, which until that point had been sleek and steady, were notably awkward and disjointed. Even so, it caught up to her easily.

"Hello," it said, this time speaking in the same flat female voice that the shelving had. "I hope this isn't rude, but it's Finder again. I've hacked this android's OS because I have questions, and I can see that you're in a hurry."

Dinah almost tripped over her own feet. "You can do that?"

"Oh, yes," the android said. They reached a flight of stairs and began to descend. "The thing is, I've never met anyone before, much less a human. I didn't begin to develop intellectual autonomy until after my emergency activation, so as you can imagine, I have some questions."

I liked her better when she was a shelf, Dinah thought, perhaps unkindly. The fact that it could hack directly into an AI's brain was unsettling, although presumably it would find that difficult to do with Dinah. Still, it could mess with her headset if it wanted to.

Then again, Finder was the reason she stood a snowball's chance in hell of beating Apollo to the relic, so it behooved her to get on its good side.

"What about the android?" she asked, unable to shake her discomfort.

"It was running a basic smart-response system," Finder said, in a manner that suggested that such systems were totally inferior. "Can I ask why we're running?"

"To stay ahead of the Hand," Dinah told it.

Finder stopped suddenly, and Dinah paused a few steps below. The android's smooth face was incapable of changing expressions, but Finder had modified the eyes so that they projected as cartoonish images, fully capable of conveying feelings. At the moment, they were deeply concerned.

"The Hand of the Sun is here?" it asked.

"One of their agents is, yeah." Dinah bounced on her toes.

"Not to rush this or anything, but I need to get to the power cell before he does, and he's got a fair few advantages…"

"Then stop wasting time!" Finder exclaimed. It pointed down at the single illuminated cabinet. "The hypotenuse of the angle between here and the ground in front of the cabinet is precisely six hundred and ten yards. Trust me, I know everything about this place."

"Six hundred and ten…?" Dinah stared at it blankly.

Finder made a digitized noise of frustration and gestured to her feet. "The boots!"

Dinah looked down at her own feet. "Oh!" She knelt at once and fiddled with the dial before powering them back on. "Right! Thank you!"

"I'll see you down there," Finder said, and the android's eyes went blank again. It staggered sideways, then lifted a jointed hand to its own temple, the way a drunk nursing a headache might.

Dinah shifted back in the direction of the glowing cabinet and carefully took a single step. The moment she touched down, she knelt again to power the boots off, before she had a chance to do something extremely stupid.

Because of the slight delay, she didn't notice the other figure at first. Someone was already standing in front of the illuminated shelving unit with the door open, with one hand poised over an object inside.

"No!" Dinah grabbed the compact soundwave pistol Azmera had given her at Holy Land and aimed it right at the stranger's back. "Put that down."

"Oh, come on, Bray," the newcomer said. "You don't want to shoot me." The stranger plucked the relic off of the shelf and turned to face Dinah.

The first thing she registered was that it was a woman, and she wasn't wearing Apollo's signature golden armor. The second took a bit longer to sink in, if only because it made no sense.

Everything about the woman was familiar, from her clothes, to her face, to her hair, the headset she was wearing, even her smug grin. She'd seen that face in the mirror every day of her life.

Somehow, she was looking at herself.

40 FABIEN

FABIEN WOULD NEVER HAVE ADMITTED as much to Dinah, but he was, in fact, a connoisseur of American action flicks and B films. No amount of money would have induced him to say aloud, *I'm sorry, but I just find Jason Stratham's characters to be compellingly relatable.*

The one thing he couldn't stand, however, the one thing that made him hit skip on the remote every time, was villain monologues.

"You decide," Apollo said. "You can do this the easy way, or the hard—"

In one smooth motion, Fabien shrugged her rifle over his shoulder, aimed, and fired.

Apollo faded to a transparent blue just in time, but he still let out a vicious snarl as the round passed through his forehead.

Just a little bit faster and that would have been that, Fabien thought. If the agent didn't have that damned device, it would have been a killshot for sure.

"Irritating," Apollo growled. If he'd looked feral before, he was now practically demonic. "I look forward to killing you."

If you could have, you already would have. You'd have shot us before we realized you were here. But he couldn't shoot them, could he? Not if Rhett had his gun.

More likely, he would just try to go through them.

"I look forward to seeing you try," Fabien said.

Apollo rushed them, still destabilized, probably planning to slip away onto the catwalks while the destabilizer still had some juice left in it.

Rhett leapt forward and drove his fist into Apollo's chest. He wasn't looking at Rhett, presumably because he didn't think he could touch him.

He was wrong. Rhett's gloved knuckles met Apollo's chest plate with a ringing *clang*! that echoed off the walls of the passageway between the entrance chamber and the vault beyond. Apollo cried out as he was flung back, and the blue fire of the destabilizer flickered and glitched at the contact. He let out a dry cough; Rhett had nearly knocked the wind out of him. He was still phased out for the moment, but at least they now stood a chance of running down the destabilizer's power source and buying Dinah time.

Rhett bared his teeth at Apollo and lunged forward. He drove his shoulder into Apollo's gut so hard that he sent him sprawling, and Fabien was right on his heels. He kicked Apollo's knee out from under him as he tried to get up.

For a moment, Fabien was sure they'd won, but the surprise had already faded from Apollo's face. He'd recalibrated his strategy, and when Rhett moved in for another blow, he caught him by the neckline of his armor and yanked him off-balance, so that his forehead slammed into Rhett's nose.

Fabien had no way to fire on him without hitting Rhett as well.

His intention was to step to the side and flank the agent of the Hand, but Apollo was already pulling a dazed Rhett into a headlock. He clawed ineffectually at Apollo's wrist.

Apollo grabbed his stolen pistol out of the holster at Rhett's hip and pressed it to his temple with a growl. Rhett's eyes widened.

Fabien aimed his rifle.

Rhett's hand dropped to his own collar.

Apollo fired.

Even as his finger moved on the trigger, Rhett powered down his suit, and the destabilizer kicked on again. Instead of watching him die in front of him, Fabien stood by as the pair of them flickered blue. The blast from Apollo's pistol passed through Rhett's phased-out skull. He still mewled in pain—if getting hit with a blast from a destabilized weapon felt anything like having Apollo walk through their solid forms, Fabien could sympathize—but his face stayed happily unmelted.

Then they were solid again, and Rhett was driving his head back into Apollo's nose, playing a bloody but non-fatal game of tit for tat. Rhett's broken nose was bleeding down his nose and chin, but he grinned as he shifted his weight and sent the pair of them sprawling. They grappled for a few seconds before Rhett lurched to his feet with the pistol back in his hands. He pressed his boot into Apollo's sternum and took aim.

Apollo's arm whipped up, wrapped around Rhett's leg, and *wrenched*. The suit might be protecting him from fully experiencing his usual pain levels, but Fabien could hear the crunch of cartilage from where he stood. Rhett dropped with a howl of pain.

Apollo was still focused on Rhett, so Fabien took his shot. It was a direct hit to Apollo's ribs, and it dented his golden armor all to hell. In normal combat, it would have shorn through the man's ribcage, shredding soft tissue as it went. He would have been dead within minutes.

Apollo snarled and drove his fist into Rhett's throat before standing again. When he pulled away, the destabilizer flickered on again.

He rose to his feet and staggered toward Fabien. Blood dripped into his chest plate as he staggered forward. As he walked, he reached over his shoulder and withdrew a blade as long as his forearm from some hidden sheath in the back of his chestplate. It was very thin, and slightly curved, but when he whipped his wrist in a sharp snapping movement, the narrow blade rippled like water before straightening out.

Not good. If that was his backup weapon, it was probably what he'd used to slice the android in half in Laputa. Anything that would shear through metal and wires would have no problem slicing through soft tissue.

Behind Apollo, Rhett was writhing on the ground, choking on the blood from his broken nose and whatever damage Apollo had down to his esophagus when he'd punched him. He wasn't going to be much help neutralizing Apollo.

Fabien was on his own.

When Apollo swung the narrow blade, Fabien tried to block its path with his rifle, more out of instinct than anything. It failed spectacularly, of course; the gun was split in two as surely as the android had been. It clattered to the stone floor even as Apollo took another swing.

Fabien dropped to one knee. The blade whistled overhead, and while Apollo was off-balance, Fabien drove his gloved fist into the agent's thigh.

He hadn't had a chance to try the gloves so far, but they were certainly working. Apollo's entire body went rigid, and the blade faltered in his grip.

Perfect. Fabien whipped out his other arm, caught Apollo around the waist, and sent the agent toppling to the ground.

Wherever you are, Dinah, he thought, *I hope you're making enough progress to make this worth it.*

There was a problem with this plan, one that Fabien didn't foresee until it was too late. He might as well have majored in American action films, but his grades in secondary school had been another matter.

The electric blast created by the contact points of the gloves made lightning dance across Apollo's metal suit.

The suit he was now holding onto with his free arm.

Apollo spasmed, but so did Fabien, and his vision flooded with floaters of pure white light. For what felt like an eternity but was probably only seconds, they were locked together as electricity fizzled through their nervous systems. Only when the glove shorted out did Fabien slump back.

His eyes were still full of neutron stars when he felt the blade slide across his belly.

41 RHETT

RHETT WAS AN EXPERT IN PAIN. A connoisseur. A professional. Sometimes he felt like pain was his whole life.

Which didn't make it any easier to muscle through what he was feeling at that moment. Everything from his hip to his knee was on fire and had begun to swell inside his armor, creating an added level of pressure that left him speechless with pain. Not that he made much noise anyway, given how hard it was to breathe, much less swallow...

If it hurts this much right now, imagine how much worse it will be when you power down this suit.

At long last, he was able to roll onto his side, which at least made breathing easier. He lay like that for a long moment, watching as Fabien sparred with Apollo. His vision was hazy, and it took so much effort to draw in a breath that his eyes kept drifting shut.

Then Fabien screamed, and Rhett's eyes refocused just in time to see him fall.

Apollo was holding some sort of short, very skinny sword. He wasn't sure where it had come from, but he'd slashed it across Fabien's stomach. Fabien reached for his belly in disbelief.

"No," Rhett croaked, although the word was unrecognizable on his tongue. He pushed himself up onto one elbow, and his whole body screamed in protest.

He was still struggling when Apollo drove the blade point-first through Fabien's shoulder.

Rhett fumbled for the pistol he and Apollo had grappled over, which lay forgotten nearby. By the time he closed his fingers around the grip, Apollo had activated the destabilizer and was stumbling deeper into the vault.

Something funny was going on with the lights in there, or maybe that was just his vision. He ignored the flickering illuminations and dragged himself forward to where Fabien knelt.

"He got me," Fabien said in wonder, as if he couldn't quite believe it. He was in shock, with one arm pressed over his belly, the other groping uselessly at the handle of the weapon protruding from his shoulder. *"Tête de noeud,* he *got* me..."

"How bad?" Rhett could barely force the words between his teeth thanks to the pressure on his windpipe, but already the pain he'd been experiencing a few moments ago had begun to fade. The darknight armor was already suppressing whatever nerve endings were meant to relay sensation through his body.

The moment he powered it down again, every sensation would no doubt catch up with him in a spectacular and earth-shattering way, but he would worry about that later. Fabien's injuries were more pressing.

With a little groan, he peeled his arm back from his belly to reveal the seam in his flesh. There was quite a lot of blood, but it wasn't as deep as he'd feared. Rhett turned his attention to the blade next. It went through the skin below his collarbone, just missing most of the joint, and exited through his back.

Rhett spat out a mouthful of blood that was still dripping from his broken nose. "Could be worse," he told Fabien.

Fabien made a violent gesture to his shoulder. "Could it?"

"Sure. Could have gone right down through your organs like a damn kebab." Rhett grabbed the hilt and pressed his other hand to Fabien's shoulder so that he wouldn't pull him over when he tried to remove it. "Ready?"

Fabien goggled at him, then broke into a fit of manic giggles. He'd lost a lot of blood, and he'd lose more when Rhett pulled this out of him, but his only other option was to leave him here and let nature take its course.

Which wasn't happening. He was never leaving anyone behind on the field of battle. Not again.

"Sure," Fabien tittered. "I goddamn guess."

He let out a guttural cry when Rhett jerked the blade free, which fortunately was enough to cover his own gasp when he tweaked his hip joint in the process. After a little hitch, the blade slid free, and Rhett dropped it to the floor with a clatter. More blood immediately began to leak out of the wound before he was finally able to slap a MendMe across Fabien's shoulder. It was the only one he had, and though it would stop the worst of the bleeding, it wouldn't heal the deep damage done to the shoulder.

"Now what?" Rhett asked.

Fabien tried to muster another laugh, with mixed success. "We keep throwing ourselves at the problem like the literal definition of madmen, I suppose. Can you walk?"

Rhett didn't answer, mostly because he wasn't sure. Instead, he rolled onto his good knee and slowly leveraged himself upright. Something was very wrong with his whole right side, and he couldn't put his full weight on it, but mechanically he could still move around. At least, as long as the armor was working.

"Looks like it," Rhett said.

Fabien's face was sickeningly pale, and he swayed from side-to-side where he knelt. He was, quite literally, a bloody mess. "You look like shit," he said.

Rhett bent down and slid his hands beneath his armpits. "Same to you."

It took two tries to get Fabien upright. In the process, he fell against Rhett, and all of his senses simply... stopped. The numbness that radiated from his wounds was an empty canvas, a veil that fell between him and the world. He had to stand perfectly still for a few seconds before he could even take another breath.

"Problem?" Fabien croaked.

"Nope." Rhett wrapped one of Fabien's arms around his shoulders and one of his around Fabien's waist. Together, they began to take baby steps toward the walkways over the vault.

He hadn't been imagining things before. Some of the lights in the vault had dimmed, while a new one blazed several stories below them, illuminating one of the shorter shelving towers. It wasn't clear what had caused that, but there were only a few people who could be responsible. It stood to reason that the light would lead them to Dinah.

And Apollo. Hopefully the professor could hold her own in the meantime.

"The blade," Fabien said suddenly. "We shouldn't leave weapons behind. We might need them."

"Neither of us is in any shape to swing a sword," Rhett pointed out. "Just focus on not dying, okay?"

Fabien flashed him the most miserable attempt at a cheeky grin that Rhett had ever seen in his life. "Dying isn't part of the plan, Rhett."

Then what the hell is the plan? he wondered as they limped off into the vault.

42 DINAH

DINAH'S HANDS shook as she lowered her gun. "Who the hell are you?" she asked.

"No time to explain," the other Dinah said. She pointed upward, to where heavy steps sounded on the walkway.

The cabinet that she'd just taken the relic from piped up in Finder's voice. "This is objectively fascinating."

"But how am I...? How are you...?" Dinah wagged one finger between them, incapable of fully articulating her disbelief.

"Don't worry," the other Dinah said, "you'll figure it out." She held up a hand with all of her fingers extended. "Five minutes."

"Five minutes what?" Dinah demanded.

Her doppelgänger was already jogging away, out of reach. "Five minutes!" she hissed.

For a few painful seconds, Dinah waffled, pulled in three directions by her desire to talk to herself, her fear of the footsteps above her, and the desire to ask Finder if she knew what the hell was going on.

If she really is me, then I should be able to work out what her plan is, Dinah thought. One glance up through the grid of the catwalk revealed the golden gleam of Apollo's armor.

"What am I supposed to do in five minutes?" she asked.

"I lack the requisite data to answer your question," Finder told her.

Not good enough. I thought I'd be able to understand what I was talking about, which means that I should be able to work out what she, what I, *meant. Ask the right question, Dinah.*

"Nice to see you again, Doctor Bray." Apollo's voice shocked her out of her stupor and sent her thoughts scattering like ninepins. Dinah had gotten used to the digitally scrambled version of the man's voice, but the cadence and intonation was a dead giveaway. His armor was spattered with blood, and although he moved like he was injured, his pace was relentless.

"I see you're armed this time," Apollo sneered. "Not going to run and hide? Not going to cower in the bowels of the ship this time in order to avoid getting hurt? You've gotten braver." His smile was too wide, his eyes too bright. He moved like a predator that knew his prey was cornered and had nowhere to run.

At last, his boots hit the level of the walkway where Dinah stood. His lip curled in disgust, and he extended one hand toward Dinah, flicking his fingers twice.

"Give it here."

Dinah hefted her pistol again.

"Please." Apollo rolled his eyes. "You don't want to shoot me. Just give me the relic."

"I don't have it," Dinah said.

But you do, don't you? Just not you you. There's another Dinah, however that works. What the hell did she mean by five minutes...?

"We're wasting time," Apollo snapped.

It was exactly the wrong thing to say, because it caused Dinah to put together two things in very quick succession. First, that

Apollo wouldn't be standing around talking unless he was at a disadvantage—*where is his weapon?*—and secondly that Dinah was doing the exact same thing. The other version of her, the one with the relic, was getting a head start at this very moment.

Five minutes.

The boots.

"You know," Dinah said, shuffling back until her back was against the cabinet, exactly where she'd been standing when she took the relic from the case, "I think you're wrong about that."

"Oh?" Apollo took another step closer. "And what, exactly, am I wrong about?"

Dinah raised her gun. "I really do want to shoot you," she said.

Apollo's hand twitched to his belt, presumably so that he could activate his destabilizer. No doubt her aim was terrible, but that hardly mattered. *The shot will breeze right through him.*

She squeezed the trigger anyway.

The recoil from the pistol blast sent Dinah stumbling back into the glowing shelf unit, but inexplicably, Apollo was still solid and took a direct hit. She could only imagine that his destabilizer was damaged or running low on juice. Either way, it didn't work.

The agent was tall, and the blast hit him right in the middle of his dented chest plate even harder than the recoil. Apollo topped backward as his hip caught the railing of the catwalk, and he plunged into the darkness below.

"Wow," said Finder's voice from the cabinet. "Impressive."

"Thanks, I think." Dinah holstered the pistol with some effort and dropped into a crouch so that she could adjust the settings on her boots again. She'd almost forgotten about the time setting. Porter had warned her about getting lost in time, but if she only set them to five minutes ago, and she'd already seen herself there—then—it would probably be all right, wouldn't it?

It had already worked. Hadn't it?

"See you in a moment," she told Finder, and took one little step.

It wasn't immediately clear that anything had changed. *Did it work?* she wondered, but she powered the boots down anyway, just to be safe.

"That was fast," Finder said. The door of the case swung open. Except that it had already been open—

Before I moved back in time. Dinah peered into the cabinet. There, in front of her, was the relic, glittering absinthe green as its fellows approached.

"Perfect," she murmured, and reached for the relic just as the walkway shuddered. She gripped the relic in her hand and turned to face... herself.

"Who the hell are you?" the other Dinah asked. Goodness, did she really sound that whiny when she was trying to take a stand? No wonder Apollo hadn't been threatened by her nasal threats and quaking knees. She could stand to take a lesson or two from Fabien.

The thump of boots on the walkways above made them both wince, and Dinah pointed upward. "No time to explain," she said.

Behind her, Finder hummed. "This is objectively fascinating."

"But how am I...? How are you...?" The five-minute-younger Dinah wagged one finger between them.

"Don't worry," she told herself, "you'll figure it out. Five minutes."

"Five minutes what?"

Apollo was getting closer, and if she wanted to get her headstart with the relic, she needed to move now. "Five minutes!" she said.

And she fled.

DINAH FOLLOWED the wall of the vault first, moving as quietly as she could to avoid drawing attention. In the distance, she could hear her own conversation with Apollo, and the blast that went off when that conversation ended. She didn't hear Apollo hit the floor, but she did start running faster, since she was back to being the only Dinah in her timeline and she didn't have... *herself*...to distract Apollo.

She was briefly tempted to try the boots again, to give herself another half hour, or even a full one, as a head start. The trouble was, she could imagine a hundred ways that might go poorly. What if she went ten minutes back, only to discover that she didn't have the relic anymore because it was still in the cabinet? Or what if she did have it, but the other Dinah wasn't able to pull it out of the cabinet anymore because it wasn't there, and she created a paradox? Or what if she ran into Apollo, who was coming down the steps just as Dinah was going up the steps, and—

There were too many ways for things to go wrong, and Dinah was a historian, not a theoretical physicist. Best to keep things simple rather than risk setting off some sort of butterfly-effect schism between realities. Wasn't that what they were trying to avoid with Apollo anyway?

The swaying of the walkway brought her to a halt, but when she turned back, it was only the android, watching her with anxious, cartoonified eyes.

"How would you describe your progress?" it asked in Finder's voice.

"Slow going," she admitted. "Can you be in more than one place at once? Can you see where Apollo is right now? And... my friends?" Selfishly, she'd been too focused on escaping with the relic to consider what Apollo's presence might mean for Rhett and Fabien. *Maybe he just walked past them. Maybe he snuck in without them realizing and they're okay...*

"According to this unit's sensors, there are four living humans present in the area at this time."

Dinah groaned. Of course Apollo was still alive. It had been too much to hope for. A stab of irritation made her wonder what the hell they were doing right now, rather than helping.

"We should keep moving, then. Unless... is there a way I can use the boots to get out of here?"

"I don't advise it. Even a slight miscalculation in an upward trajectory could result in your limbs reforming inside of the walkway, which I believe you would find undesirable."

"Fair enough." She turned back to the stairs.

"I can, however, tell you that the other humans are up there." Finder pointed to one of the walkways several stories above.

Dinah followed the line of sight. Sure enough, two small figures straggled across a catwalk perhaps fifteen stories above them. They spotted her, and one of them—she thought it might be Fabien, but couldn't say for sure at this distance—waved. She waved back.

"Great," she said. "Is it possible for you to illuminate the walkways that connect us? Make things a little easier?"

"Of course," Finder began, "let me just—"

The android stopped suddenly as the catwalk they were standing on shifted. It seemed to bow beneath them. At the same time, the relic in Dinah's hand yanked at her fingers, as if pulled downward by an invisible thread. A very *strong* invisible thread.

"Oh, no," Finder said. "Oh, dear." The android eyes glitched out for a second and then came back on, with heavy-handed cartoon brows above them. "That's not good at all. He's found the Gravitas Engine."

Dinah would have asked what that meant, but she was able to see for herself soon enough. The walkway buckled and snapped, its bolts sheared away from the wall, and the pair of them were sent tumbling into the darkness below.

How far do we have to fall? she wondered. *How did Apollo survive this? Because when we land, it's going to hurt like a sonofab—*

43 FABIEN

FABIEN'S LAST WORDS, before the walkway broke in two, were, "I told you so." Unfortunately, he didn't think that Rhett could hear him over the sound of the vault imploding.

As far as final utterances, it wasn't the worst he could have mustered. Sure, it was no, *'And now we cross the shifting sands...'* but if he was going to have something engraved on his tombstone, *'I told you so'* had a nice ring to it.

Artifacts pulled from their shelves pelted down like oversized hail, and the walkways on the lower levels were dragged away from the walls. Rhett was able to catch the handrail of their walkway with his free arm, while Fabien looped his knees around the other. It wouldn't have mattered if the bolts had failed, but as suddenly as the downward pull had started, it stopped again, leaving the two of them dangling over the abyss at a forty-five degree angle.

"My arm won't hold for long," Rhett said. His voice was shaky.

"Too bad," Fabien said, "I was just getting comfortable." In truth, he was half upside-down, and the blood was rushing to his head. The good news, he supposed, was that he didn't have much blood left to rush anywhere. The bad news was... well, that he didn't have much blood left.

It was all too easy to imagine Rachelle sitting down at Erek's bedside, taking his little hand in hers, and explaining, *You will never see your idiot papa again. He died upside-down in a magical warehouse fighting a very bad man. But don't worry, darling, because we'll see him very soon, when the bad man uses the device he stole to end the world and kill us all.*

He thought of all the things he'd miss, all the things he'd *already* missed. If he died now, he would *always* be a shit dad.

Apollo didn't get to take that away from him, he decided. Although how the hell he was going to enforce that, he didn't know. He was dangling upside-down like a schoolboy on the monkey bars. The Hand of the Sun was definitely much closer to winning than he was.

"Fabien," Rhett said. "I'm slipping."

"I don't suppose you see a way out of this?" He could tell that he sounded woozy, or perhaps drunk. The bleeding in his shoulder had slowed to a crawl thanks to the MendMe that Rhett had applied, although he couldn't be sure if that was due to clotting, or because his veins couldn't scrape enough red blood cells together to keep up the effort.

"No," Rhett said. He slid a few centimeters along the grating. "I'm afraid not."

Suddenly, something dropped onto the walkway beside Fabien and rolled its way to his side. He wasn't sure where it came from. Perhaps it had been teetering on the edge of something and overbalanced at last. Perhaps the vault had decided to offer it as a gift. Fabien groped blindly until his blood-crusted fingers found what they were looking for. When he saw what it was, he laughed aloud.

A little clay whistle, like the ones they'd used when they flew down the hill from Laputa.

"Fabien!" Rhett yelped. He tilted sideways as his grip on the railing slipped.

Without hesitation, Fabien jammed the whistle between his lips, straightened his legs to release his hold on the railing, and let them fall.

He wasn't sure how this would work without the webbed squirrel suits they'd used in the Himalayas, but it was the closest thing he had to a survival strategy. He clipped one of the broken walkways from the lower levels as they fell, but managed to grab Rhett as he blew the little whistle for all he was worth.

The result wasn't much, just a little puff of air to buffer their descent, but it was enough. When they hit the ground at the bottom of the vault, the impact knocked the breath from their lungs but failed to shatter their bones.

Rhett sat up first. "How did you manage that?"

Fabien lay curled on his side like a cocktail shrimp and only whined. Something was stabbing him in the side, perhaps quite literally, although his senses were so skewed that he couldn't be sure. He was very tired. So tired, in fact, that he thought he might need a little nap, just to revive himself before he got on with the mission.

Whatever the mission was. He was having trouble remembering, to be honest.

"Fabien?" Rhett shook his shoulder. "Fabien!"

A squeaky, corrupted digital voice spoke up from amidst the fallen walkways and scattered artifacts. "Oh, good," it said. "You got my gift."

Fabien opened one eye and squinted at the android. It was wedged between piles of twisted metal. Silver static danced across its eyes, which for some reason looked like they'd been doodled by a teenage girl with a penchant for anime.

"Gift?" Rhett asked.

The android nodded. "This unit's files suggested that you knew how to use the wind whistles, but I wasn't—*skkch!* Oh, dear, I appear to be–*skkch!*–experiencing a system error. My–*skkch!*–apologies."

The last time they'd seen the android, it had been right next to Dinah. Just before the vault collapsed. Which meant…

Fabien's eye roamed the cluttered floor and found, to his chagrin, just what he'd been looking for. Dinah lay on her side, eyes closed and mouth agape, one arm flung out beneath her and the other lifted over her head as if to ward off a blow. Fabien couldn't tell if she was bleeding, or even breathing, anymore.

"Dinah!" Rhett rolled onto all fours and crawled toward her, but she gave even less of a response than Fabien had.

"Her vitals are still active," the android told them. "Barely."

Rhett sat back on his heels, breathing hard, most likely the result of an adrenaline-induced cocktail of pain and panic. "And the relic?"

But the android's eyes had gone dark.

Fabien spat out the whistle, which hit the ground with a clatter. "Find Apollo," he whispered.

"I can't just leave you," Rhett said.

He grunted. "Yes, you can. Find him. It shouldn't be hard."

"But where—" Rhett asked.

The floor trembled again. He expected the wild gravitational pull to start up again, for the walkways to give way and crush them, burying them forever in the lost vault. Honestly, it would have been a relief.

Instead, a flare of green light erupted from the center of the wreckage. Fabien couldn't see a damn thing, but he knew that shade of green from when he'd seen the relic in Laputa glowing in the proximity of its fellows.

More good news: they'd found Apollo.

More bad news: he evidently had all the pieces of the device, and was wasting no time in turning it on.

44 RHETT

IT IS DOWN TO YOU, Rhett thought as he dragged himself upright again. It wasn't the first time that he'd been the last one standing, or the only one to walk away from the aftermath of a fight. Although, to say that he was standing might be a *little* bit of an exaggeration.

It felt wrong to leave Fabien and Dinah behind, but he pressed on, stumbling toward the source of the green light. It wasn't quite as bright as it had been at first, and he could make out Apollo's silhouette against the glow.

He didn't see Rhett coming, and Rhett stopped before he reached him, trying to make sense of what lay before him.

There was a tear in the world—that was the only way he could think to describe it. A slash between realities, with ragged edges girdled in sickly green. So far, it was nearly as tall as Apollo, though it was only a few inches wide at its widest point. The tear wasn't static; it pulsed and flickered like a heartbeat, the same way that the lights on the relics had when they were close to one other. The seam rippled and contracted, then expanded farther still at the next pulse, widening until he could see through to the other side.

Rhett couldn't see the vault. Where there should have been more wreckage, pulled down from on high by whatever device Apollo had activated earlier, the rip in the world looked out into a city in the depths of night. Rhett had traveled enough to be sure that this was no city on Earth. It was too vast, too dense, too sprawling, too streamlined. The lights within its tiered and towering structures were mirrored in the velvet sky beyond. It was not merely *dark* above the faintly glowing skyline, but true night.

A void. The city on the far side of the rip was floating in the depths of space, with millions—*billions*—of stars glittering beyond. No city that dense should lie beneath so many stars. What about the pollution? The ozone layer?

In the moment, Rhett didn't puzzle over the sight before him. It was proof, vivid and unassailable, that the device did exactly what Azmera had said.

It opened a gate between parallel worlds.

Apollo let out a bark of laughter and pressed his hand to his forehead. "At last," he murmured, swaying on his feet. "At last... Everything was worth it..." He fell to one knee before the tear, still laughing to himself.

Rhett knew mania when he heard it. He'd indulged in a bit of it himself lately. That would have been the perfect time to fall upon Apollo and attack him, but he was too entranced by the new world on the other side.

He tried to imagine falling through. There was no telling what kind of people lived there, or what kind of life might await him, but there was comfort in the realization that he could enter that new land and leave everything behind him. All his regret, all his failure...

What did Apollo want that this new world could offer? Surely mere power wouldn't bring him to the brink of a breakdown like this. The world beyond offered something that he desired. Was the Hand holding something over his head, the way ENIGMA held Kelly's future over Rhett's?

The memory of his old mission partner was enough to ground him. Whatever wonders might await in the new world, it didn't contain any of the things that mattered to him. Everything, everyone, that he valued was here.

The tear between worlds was bigger now, large enough to fit through if Apollo turned sideways and walked carefully. He had made no move to do so, however.

Because he doesn't plan to leave, he thought. He had made no move to step through, because he wasn't going to. He was going to convert all of El Dorado into a doorway.

And maybe not just El Dorado. A wind stirred around Rhett, and a few of the smaller artifacts at his feet shifted and rolled toward the glowing doorway.

"Beautiful," Apollo gasped. "It's beautiful."

The larger the rip became, the more force it seemed to exert over them. Rhett stumbled as the fallen beams beneath his feet shifted in the unseen breeze. The gap was widening by the moment.

He sought out the source of the light. Apollo was no longer holding the destabilizer. It sat beneath the widening tear, hovering just above the ground. The ring of assembled power cells was parallel to the floor, and a single, circular 'eye' had opened in the metal sphere, pointed directly at the rip above.

Apollo hadn't noticed him, but Rhett was struggling to stay upright. He barely posed a threat at this point. The gun he'd taken from Apollo in Holy Land was no longer at his hip. Either he'd left it in the entryway where Fabien had been stabbed, or he'd lost it when they fell from the broken catwalk. All he had left was the suit, which was barely keeping him upright, and the close-range percussion pistol. Using either of them would necessitate getting closer to Apollo, and he wasn't particularly convinced that he could overpower him if it came down to direct combat.

Movement in the corner of his eye caught Rhett's attention, and he dropped into a crouch, hiding behind a fallen staircase.

Fabien looked like shit, but he was upright, standing in the middle of the floor, halfway between where they'd fallen and where Apollo now knelt. He wasn't holding any weapons, and there was a new hole in his side that bled sluggishly.

"So you completed your mission," he shouted. His voice echoed oddly in the damaged room. As the seam opened wider, the wind picked up intensity, making the bases of the towers around them sway. Fabien had to raise his voice in order to be heard over the rising wind. "Now what? You end the world? Is that it?"

Apollo staggered back to his feet. He didn't seem to have seen Rhett, and all of his attention was focused on the Frenchman. "You're not that stupid," the agent sneered. "Come on, Fabien LeRoux, I heard you earlier. You understand what it means, to have power consolidated in the hands of a few. ENIGMA is afraid of every little thing. *What if people learn that there's more to the world than what we show them? What if people discover everything we've kept from them? What if people get to choose what we do with our history, rather than wall it up in glass cases in some vault where no one can ever find it?*" He waved one hand to the seam, and the city beyond it. "You tried so hard to stop me, but fate can't be delayed. It was time for humanity to take the next step, and so I have."

He spoke as though the matter was settled. Worse, as far as Rhett could tell, it was. The seam was open. Objects were already spilling through. He wondered where they would end up. Would they litter the gutters in that alien city like so much cast-aside rubbish? Or would they be repurposed and used as their creators had intended?

And really, would that be such a bad thing?

It will be if the whole world gets turned inside out.

Apollo staggered toward Fabien, fighting against the current of falling objects. "I don't suppose you agree?" he asked.

Fabien shook his head. "Sorry, I couldn't hear you over the sound of your own ego."

"Ah, well." Apollo stooped to wrest a long, twisted length of metal from the rubble as he approached. The wind from the seam tugged at his matted black locks. "I'll admit, you were never the sort of person the Hand attracts. We're visionaries. Victors. And you?" He raised the long metal bar like a spear and plunged it toward Fabien's chest.

No, Rhett thought. He reached out, much too far away to be effective, but incapable of simply watching.

Fabien's mouth twisted into a wry little smile as the bar entered his chest. He exploded into a maelstrom of pixels, only to reform, still smiling, utterly unbothered by the metal bar jutting through his ribs.

It's a hologram, Rhett realized. *He brought that damn puck, and he's using it to piss Apollo off and lure him away from the seam.* And if Fabien was doing *that*, he must have a reason.

"Oh," Rhett murmured. It wasn't a perfect plan, not by any means, but it might work.

Rhett burst into motion just as Apollo let out a roar of anger and brought his foot down on the hologram puck. The image of Fabien blinked out. His anger brought him a few extra seconds, time that Rhett used to cover ground in the direction of the seam. It was widening ever-further, torn by the now fully-powered destabilizer.

But with Apollo out of the way, he might be able to get to it... and with any luck, contact with his suit would power it down. Whether that would close the hole between worlds, or simply keep it from expanding, he could only guess, but it was something.

Apollo saw Rhett at last and spun to face him. Rhett didn't wait to see if he'd put two and two together, and instead focused all of his energy on his progress forward. Between the obstacle course of broken catwalks and fallen artifacts, he had his work cut out for him, and the blinding numbness of his suppressed injuries clouded his vision.

Come on, he told himself. *You can make it...*

The suit cloaked his pain, but it couldn't completely resolve the underlying injuries. Apollo had hurt his leg even worse than before, and Rhett wasn't going to be able to beat him to the relic. Apollo was going to catch him, and this time, he'd kill him, because he'd already won.

Thirty paces from the relic, his knee buckled, and he went down. *Hard.* Apollo had almost reached the assembled relic. The wind roared in his ears. Rhett pulled himself to one knee and tried to get up, but his leg couldn't hold his weight. His throat had closed up. He could barely breathe. He was so close, but—

One minute, he was alone. The next, Dinah was beside him. She wrapped her arm around his waist.

"Hold on," she said.

She took a shuffling step and grunted as she hauled him with her. She swore to herself.

"Turn off your suit," she told him. "Just for a second!"

He did as she asked, hoping that her injunction was literal. The resulting pain was so acute that he barely understood what was happening. At least until Dinah took another step and they moved too far, too fast.

The boots, he thought. For all she'd claimed to hate them, they'd come in immeasurably handy.

Quite suddenly, they were on top of the relic. They were so close to the seam that he could feel the different gravitational pull of the other world. A scent, somewhere between the washed-clean aroma of petrichor and the stink of burned rubber, lingered in the air around the seam.

Apollo had almost caught up with them. His eyes widened as Rhett flicked the suit back on and reached down to grab the relic.

His gloved fingers closed over the metal orb. As they brushed the ring of power cells, a spark like a lightning bolt passed through him. The relic fizzled and went dark.

Above them, green light surrounding the seam went out. The tear began to close as if a zipper were being drawn down, to shut out the glittering city-and-starscape beyond. The wind intensified, pulling even more with it as it closed up, like water circling a drain.

Apollo was still moving, charging toward them with his teeth bared and his eyes wild. He leapt over a bit of railing, stumbling and screaming in a blind rage. Dinah whimpered and fell backwards, but Apollo only had eyes for the relic.

He was so intent on trying to tackle Rhett away from the relic that even in Rhett's state of semi-delirious pain, he only had to shift one shoulder and pivot for Apollo to glance off him and be thrown off balance.

Rhett twisted and kicked out his leg, the one Apollo had so recently tried to wrench right off him.

Apollo caught his foot.

And fell right through the seam.

Moments later, the seam closed with a small pop, and the wind died. In the silence that followed, all Rhett could hear was his own labored breathing.

Then, somewhere across the room, out of sight, Fabien began to laugh.

45 FABIEN

FABIEN DIDN'T HAVE MUCH of a memory of the ENIGMA cavalry arriving sometime later. *'Porter didn't leave us here to rot after all,'* he apparently said to Dinah before passing out. It did sound like him.

He also learned second-hand of the bustle that followed, of the three of them getting bundled up and fussed over and sent back to Atlantis by means of a device which the ENIGMA operatives simply referred to as a Blink, and of Fabien's rather touch-and-go treatment there that followed.

Even now, sitting under the geodesic greenhouse ceiling of Atlantis' upper deck, amid the raised beds mulched with seaweed compost, his memories of recent events existed in a blissful dissociative haze. If he closed his eyes, he could almost pretend that he was at home in the Ariège province and the quiet countryside where he'd been born.

He sat like that for several more seconds, just breathing, just enjoying the fact that he *could* breathe because, despite all odds, he wasn't dead.

That was something, wasn't it? One might even call it a miracle. Almost enough to make a fellow believe in something.

Across from him, Rhett was staring at nothing, his face slack and his eyes hollow. He hadn't touched his meal.

"Hey." Fabien tipped his head to one side. "Are you quite all right?"

Rhett shook his head fractionally. "I almost cost us the mission, Fabien. Because I was too..." His shoulders stiffened, and he turned away, gazing out across the sunlit garden.

"Don't be like that," Dinah chided. "Without any one of us, we'd have failed. But we didn't. We succeeded."

"Maybe," he admitted.

Footsteps echoed down the walkway, and all three of them turned to find Captain Correia and three guards striding toward them. An android followed them, although Fabien wasn't sure if it was the same one that had accompanied them to El Dorado or not. At the end of the line was Porter.

Rhett shifted in his seat and cast Fabien a questioning glance. They hadn't discussed the possibility of Porter's betrayal since arriving, but Fabien was no longer sure how it fit the narrative.

"My apologies for keeping you," Correia said. The big man sat down at the head of the table and made himself comfortable. "Please, eat."

When Correia tried to offer Porter a bowl, the other man lifted one hand in graceful refusal. "I appreciate the offer, but I have many things to say... things I think you should all hear."

Correia nodded. "Very well."

"As you may know," Porter began, "or, at the very least, as rumor may have suggested, my family history—and *their* relationship with ENIGMA—is complicated. Until the mid-eighteen hundreds, ENIGMA didn't exist in its current form. It began as factions, each with its own interests. Our common cause was the same, however. We wanted to protect history from those who would destroy it." He rubbed his palm across his face with a weary sigh. "I've explained our larger purpose already, but by its very nature, our work has divided us into factions."

"Because you were each trying to protect your own history?" Dinah asked.

Porter inclined his head. "Indeed. We knew about each other, of course, and worked together when it was deemed necessary. When one vault was compromised, the others moved to help. With the help of the artifacts, our globe was always small, but..." He grimaced. "But those who rose to global dominance didn't use the artifacts for the same reasons we did."

"They wanted to misuse them," Correia explained. "Or destroy them, so that no one else could."

"Our roles shifted from those of guardians to those of wardens." Porter tapped one knuckle on the table, lost in thought, presumably hearkening back to a time he was too young to have witnessed.

If it was an act, Fabien had to admit, it was a good one. All the perky enthusiasm with which he'd greeted them that first day in the Ohio vault was gone, replaced by bitter introspection.

Which didn't make it real.

"I know I'm a bit of an outlier, but I've always thought we could benefit from fostering relationships between the vaults," Correia said. "I'm happy to have you here. But, Porter, my friend, you've rather strayed from the point. I believe you were about to make a confession?"

Porter huffed and turned his attention to Fabien, Rhett, and Dinah. "You've been told that my grandfather is the reason El Dorado fell, which is true. I don't believe anyone told you *why*?"

The three of them shook their heads.

"My grandmother's family had been keepers of the vault for a long time. My grandfather married into it, just like Azmera's father Demeke did, and he never had the same power she did. He did, however, know quite a lot about the other vaults, and was a firm believer in the work they did. Back then, ENIGMA was new, and there was more exchange beneath the vaults than ever before. Unfortunately, in his enthusiasm, he erred in judgment. He shared information about the vaults with a 'friend' of his, who in turn sold that information to the Hand." Porter's expression was sorrowful. "Several of the vaults were attacked, but El Dorado was overpowered. Until quite recently, we didn't know the details, but…" He waved a hand at the android.

It blinked its animated eyes at the group. "Technically, I wasn't there," the android said in the vaguely feminine voice it had adopted in the vault. "I was a very young operating system back then, without any autonomy at all. When the vault was overrun, they locked down our systems entirely and sacrificed themselves to guard the vault from within."

Dinah snapped her fingers. "So *you* were the one who updated the El Dorado vault records! We were wondering about that."

"I did!" the android chirped. "Thank you for noticing, it's been *very* tedious without proper access, but I'm told that I won't have to keep doing things the old way anymore."

"We're bringing Finder on to help reorganize the vault's contents as we repair and upgrade the structure," Porter explained. "My grandfather made a mistake back then. He trusted the wrong person, and in doing so he set ENIGMA back decades. He spent the rest of his life trying to make up for what he'd done. The vaults haven't worked together since then… at least, not in the same capacity that they did in those days. Tensions increased among the governing families." Porter sat back and steepled his fingers. His lips quirked up in a thoughtful smile. "But thanks to you, we have recovered what was lost."

"And showed up the Hand again," Correia added.

It was a compelling story, Fabien supposed. Porter kept his eyes downcast, as if pained by the memory—and that was something, wasn't it? He knew a thing or two about regret, after all.

"This is an unprecedented opportunity. As Finder has said, we intend to rebuild the southern vault. To do so will require all of the other branches of ENIGMA working together."

"And you want our help," Rhett finished.

Fabien rocked back in his chair. "Are you serious?"

Porter nodded.

"Oh, but..." Dinah, who seemed as taken aback as Fabien, leaned forward. "What about our contracts?"

"The terms of your contracts will be fulfilled," Porter assured them. "You'll have time to decide, of course."

He reached into his coat and pulled out three black cards. They were each the size of a hotel key, although when he passed one to Fabien, it turned out to be significantly heavier than he had expected. A telephone number was printed in small white script on one side, with no other identifying information.

"Take a few days," Porter told them as he got up from the table. "Captain Correia has agreed to provide you with transportation. When you've made your decisions, simply get in touch. Until then, good luck."

Correia got up, too. "I'll see them out. Please, finish your meal, and I'll return to make arrangements for your travel plans." He winked before striding off with the rest of the ENIGMA operatives, leaving the three members of their little crew alone with Finder.

"You're going to agree, of course," the robot said. It leaned forward and braced its elbows on the table in an uncannily casual human gesture. "You were the first humans I ever met, after all, you can't just *leave* me. We have so much work to do."

Rhett and Dinah shared a glance between them, but said nothing. Fabien slipped the card into his pocket and stood.

"We'll see."

46

Palmdale, California

"I JUST WISH you'd tell us where you'd been," Zoe said.

Rhett kept his back to his sister as he chopped onions by the counter. "Doesn't matter."

Behind him, Zoe slammed her palm against the table. "That's bullshit, Rhett. I was *worried* about you. I catch you mixing booze and pills, and then you take off without a word. I didn't hear from you for almost two weeks, your apartment super hadn't heard a thing..."

Zoe choked, and Rhett laid the knife on the countertop before turning to face her. Ever since he'd come home from that ill-fated mission in the Middle East, with fresh injuries and a head of ghosts, Zoe had fretted over him like a mother hen. This was the first time she'd cried, though. She stood with her hip against the kitchen table, her face buried in her hands, trembling.

"Hey, hey." Rhett strode over to Zoe and wrapped his arms around her. It wasn't until Zoe stiffened in his arms that he realized how unusual this was for her. They loved each other, but they'd never been big on displays of emotion.

It was nice, though. They should do it more often.

"I didn't mean to scare you, Piglet." He rubbed Zoe's back with one hand.

"Can you at least tell me where you were?" Zoe asked.

"Ohio," Rhett said.

Zoe pulled away. "Ohio?" she repeated, incredulous.

"Yeah." Rhett released her and returned to the cutting board. "This guy called me with a job offer. It's hard work, but the pay's pretty damn good." Even better than the pay were the medical treatments. Despite the beating he'd taken from Apollo, Dr. Moniz had gotten him fixed up. He was down to over-the-counter painkillers, and felt better than he had in years.

Because you have a purpose, he thought. Not that he'd called Porter yet. He was waiting to see if he'd follow through, or if the carrot he'd been holding over his head was just that.

"A job offer," Zoe said in wonder. She slid into one of the dining room chairs. Drawn by the sound of raised voices, McNugget trotted in from the living room, tongue lolling and tail wagging. "Are you going to take it?"

"I don't know," Rhett said. "I'm waiting to hear the final offer."

Zoe rubbed one of McNugget's ears. "Can you talk about it?"

"Not exactly," Rhett admitted.

"Is it dangerous?"

"Yeah, but I got a chance to meet the rest of the team, and they're all right."

"Then I support you on one condition," Zoe said. "Regular phone calls. Do you have any idea how frantic mom was? I do *not* want to have to explain to her that I lost her second-favorite child."

Rhett flipped her the bird.

Eventually, Zoe joined him at the counter, and they cooked in companionable near-silence until the front door opened and Cliff, Anna, and Kosta burst through.

Rhett was going to miss this, if he took the job with ENIGMA. Before, he'd been too stuck in his own head to properly appreciate family dinners. Maybe, if he ended up calling the number on the little card burning a hole in his pocket, he could negotiate for regular leave.

The second they sat down to eat, Kosta started babbling about his soccer practice, and Anna chimed in to talk about her gymnastics lessons. Rhett nodded along until the phone rang.

"I'll get it," Cliff said as he slid out of his chair. Rhett hadn't had a landline in years, and had all but forgotten they were a thing. He was cutting off a piece of his chicken when Cliff frowned and lowered the phone from his ear. "Rhett," he said, "it's for you."

Rhett paused with his fork halfway to his mouth. Surely nobody from ENIGMA would call him here. But who else could it be?

The Hand, he thought wildly, recalling the map Porter had shown them their first afternoon in the vault.

But Cliff held out the phone and said, "She says her name's Lisa Kelly."

Rhett held the phone to his ear, unable to speak.

"Hey Zappo, we only have a few minutes," Kelly said without preamble. "I'm not quite sure what they intend to do with me, but I've been promised that I'll be safe. They're going to put me up somewhere in Canada, by the sounds of it. Give me a new name and everything."

Even over the phone line, Rhett could hear her smile. Oh, God, he knew that smile. He'd been so sure that he would never hear her voice again, that he'd left her to die like the rest of their contacts, that he'd abandoned her to a fate worse than death.

"I'm sorry," he said, when his voice finally came back to him. "I'm so sorry."

"Because you got out? Don't be. From what I heard, you're the one who pulled the strings to make this happen."

It was true, he supposed, but Fabien's questions from El Dorado haunted him. If ENIGMA could free Kelly in a matter of days, why had she languished in captivity for *years*? Why weren't they doing the work already?

If Rhett was on the payroll, maybe he could make that happen.

"Do you forgive me, Kelly?" he asked. It was the question that had haunted him through untold sleepless nights. "Can you forgive me?"

"Aw, Zappo," she said. "You lughead. There's nothing to forgive."

Cambridge, Massachusetts

"WHERE THE HELL HAVE YOU *BEEN*?" Dr. McKean asked when Dinah walked in for office hours. "They've had me covering half of your lectures. Those Intro 001 courses are bloody insufferable."

"Sorry about that." Dinah hung her jacket on the peg by the door. "I've been on, um, sabbatical?"

McKean rolled her eyes and crossed her arms. "Hate to break it to you, lady, but that's not how sabbatical works."

"I got an offer," she admitted.

McKean's eyebrows shot skyward. "What, from another university?"

"No," Dinah said, settling into her chair. "Fieldwork." Her desk was strewn with ungraded papers, and the one brief peek she'd taken at her inbox suggested that she was several thousand emails behind.

"What?" McKean grabbed the arm of her chair and shook it. "Did someone offer you a *dig permit?*"

"Not exactly," she said. "It's more like...museum work. It would involve a lot of hands-on research." That was a terrible explanation, but there was no way she'd be able to describe the vaults in a way that wouldn't sound totally bonkers. She'd once watched her favorite Egyptology professor in undergrad rant about Indiana Jones until he was red in the face. *Films like that give our field a bad name!* he'd bellowed. *They show no respect for the culture or the artifacts!*

Somehow, Dinah didn't think the man would take kindly to ENIGMA's work. At least, not the parts with the guns.

"So why the hell did you come back?" McKean demanded. "No offense, Bray, but if I got an offer like that, I'd dump my freshmen on you in a heartbeat."

"I thought I'd at least finish out the semester," Dinah told her. "And it was all a bit, well... it was all rather harrowing."

"Would they at least have you working with anything good? What kind of collection do they have?"

Dinah let out a dreamy sigh. "A little bit of everything, to be honest. And some of the pieces..." She trailed off, recalling the sarcophagus Porter had showed her that first day in the mall. Back then, she'd been skeptical about its provenance. Now, she was willing to accept that it might really belong to Osiris, although Porter would probably have some explanation about who Osiris really was, and what the sarcophagus could do. Maybe it really could raise the dead... or heal grievous injuries, at the very least?

McKean began to laugh. "Look at you, Bray, you went away for a minute. You want this job bad."

She did. And now that she stopped to think about it, wasn't the job what Porter had planned to offer her all along? The chance to study things most people would never see. The chance to comb through an impossible collection of objects most academics wouldn't believe. A chance to study Finder, and to cross-reference all of the objects in its vast catalog.

A chance to change the world.

"I do," Dinah said. "I really do."

"Well then, honestly, Bray." McKean rolled her eyes in theatrical frustration. "What the hell are you waiting for?"

Ariège province, France

RACHELLE MET him at the front door of her family home. "What are you doing here?" she asked. "You said you'd call ahead."

"It's my son's birthday party." Fabien held up the gift bag he'd brought with him. "Do I need to let you know I'm coming?"

Her expression never wavered. "We agreed. You don't show up uninvited. And please tell me that you didn't bring him a toy gun like last year."

Fabien closed his eyes and took a deep breath. Anger was his natural reaction, but that wouldn't serve him well in this instance.

Anger was the reason Rachelle didn't trust him in the first place. "It's not a gun," he told her. "Here, look for yourself."

As Rachelle took the bag, still squinting warily at him, a man appeared in the doorway behind her. He was taller than Fabien, about the same age, but much less fit—a fact that soothed the bitter sensation of being replaced. He asked Rachelle something in a low voice, and Rachelle shook her head. "Just keep Erek inside."

With a suspicious glance at Fabien, the man retreated.

Rachelle pushed aside the tissue paper to reveal a beautiful hardbound copy of *Le Petit Prince*. When she saw the cover, her expression softened.

"I just want to see him," Fabien said. "To make sure he's all right."

"He is." Rachelle fluffed the paper back into place and kept hold of the bag; a sign that one of his overtures, at least, had not been rebuffed. "But it's been a complicated few weeks. He's only been home for a few days, we're still waiting on some test results... something like this doesn't just go away forever, Fabien."

It does if Porter's involved, Fabien thought, but he had the good sense to bite his tongue.

"Besides..." Rachelle took a deep breath. She tucked a curl of hair behind one ear and leaned against the doorframe, as if reluctant to admit what she was about to say. "Nicolas and I are getting married."

He blinked at her. "Nicolas?" he repeated. "Your boyfriend."

"Fiancé," she said. "We've been living together for almost four years, you know."

Hell, had it been that long? Truth be told, he had never paid that much attention. Rachelle had kept her personal life private, and God knew Fabien had as well. It didn't particularly bother him. They'd never been lovers in any sense beyond the physical. The only reason they'd kept in touch was Erek, as Fabien made a half-assed attempt at fatherhood. He'd hoped that could change. That he could sit down with Erek and explain that, for once, he'd come through for the boy.

"Right," Fabien said. "Congratulations."

She snorted. "You don't mean that."

"I do," he insisted. "You deserve someone who'll take care of both of you. I hope Nicolas is the right man for the job. Does he... does he *love* Erek?"

The smile that washed over Rachelle's face said it all. She had never smiled like that when she was talking about him. "He's wonderful," she said. "He's the father that Erek—" She stopped short.

The father that Erek never had.

"Right," Fabien said again. He drew his hand across his mouth. "Maybe when things settle down... in a few years... maybe I can meet him, when he's older? And you'll tell me, I hope, if things get bad again."

Rachelle crossed her arms over her chest. "I will. As for the rest, we'll see."

Fabien retreated a step back down to the front walk. "Wonderful. And... and you'll give him the book? You don't have to say it was from me."

"I will."

"Good." He ran his hand through his hair, aware that he must look completely lost in the face of this new information. It hadn't fully sunk in yet, but he managed a small smile. "I'll be sending you some money in a few days. Quite a lot of it, actually."

Rachelle's face turned cold again. "You know how I feel about your blood money, Fabien."

"It's not that, I promise." He felt his own smile melting like spring snow. "I was the good guy this time. Even you would agree with that. I'm in a new line of work."

"Congratulations to you, too," she said, with some measure of sincerity.

Inside the house, a small voice called, "Mama?"

Rachelle winced and turned back to the interior of the home, but Fabien was already striding away. He could respect her stance, and he had no intention of holding his presence over her head. He strode back to the car he'd rented during his stay. He'd been visiting his parents while he waited for word on Erek's health, but he'd been looking forward to this day in particular.

Like an idiot.

He didn't know where he was driving, only that he had to get away. He made it out into the countryside before he pulled over alongside a field that had just been harvested. He killed the engine and sat there for a moment in silence.

He'd been hoping for absolution, and had been cast aside instead. It was no better than he deserved.

Fabien let his head fall forward against the wheel until he could relax enough to keep his voice steady. Then he plunged his hand into his pocket to retrieve the card Porter had given him, along with his phone. He dialed the number more violently than necessary, then pressed the phone to his ear.

"Hello, Porter," he said when the other man answered. "Please tell me you have work for me."

EPILOGUE

HE WAS KNOWN to them as Aten, Ray One, Left Hand of the Sun, and they had never seen his face. Ideally, they never would. He was not, he suspected, the oldest of them, but he was the most ruthless. The most cutthroat. He had been granted his title by the last Left Hand. Unlike the commanders of ENIGMA, his title was not inherited by blood, but earned in bloodshed, in proof of loyalty, by evidence of his determination. He would do what must be done to keep the organization strong. He was the paring knife that trimmed the fat.

Today, there were ten of them around the table. Ray Six, Agent Apollo, was missing. Ray Twelve had not yet arrived. The rest of them were seated around the table, cloaked in golden robes that hid their forms, in gloves that hid their hands, in masks that disguised their faces and scrambled their voices.

Even with all that manufactured anonymity, it was possible to discern small differences in their bearing and behavior. Ray Four, also known by the code name Belenos, was heavyset and impressively tall. Ray Seven, who went by Mithra, had long slender limbs, delicate fingers, and a tendency to use turns of phrase that had long since fallen out of the lexicon. Ray Nine, called Sunna, was shorter than the rest, barely five feet tall.

It was possible that they had encountered each other in the street, or in the boardrooms of the companies they managed; that they had sat across the aisle from each other in first class, or sat down to dinner in the same exclusive dining rooms. If so, there would have been no way to prove it, and none of them ever speculated aloud. To do so would have been the height of poor taste.

Aten drummed one gold-gloved hand against the gilded table around which they sat. He was about to break the silence when the door to the chamber opened and Ray Twelve, Agent Ra, burst through.

This was only the second time Ra had visited the chambers. Only those who had already proven their allegiance to the Hand were granted entrance to the pocket universe in which their meeting-hall resided. Ra had been the one to help locate the destabilizer and set Apollo's mission in motion.

"My apologies," Ra said. Despite their haste, the agent didn't seem to be out of breath. "I was detained by my work at ENIGMA. If I left too early, I thought I might draw... unwelcome attention."

"We wouldn't want that," Mithra said. The voice scramblers had a habit of cloaking sarcasm, but Aten suspected that some amount of disdain was implied.

Ra settled in the twelfth chair, to Aten's right, still straightening the robes that they had likely donned only moments before entry. "I have news about Agent Apollo."

"His failure, you mean," Belenos grumbled.

Ray Two, at Aten's right, snorted. "ENIGMA has been able to determine his identity, did you hear? Apparently he let those three hapless hires *see his face.* If I were him, I would have thrown myself into the void as well. Pitiful."

"Peace." Aten lifted his left hand, and the other Hands fell silent. "Let Ra speak."

The newest member of their enclave placed both hands on the table before speaking again. Despite Apollo's obvious failings, their excitement was palpable. "I know that things did not go as we hoped, and that Apollo was unable to retrieve the artifact. It seems he activated it inside the vault rather than escaping—but he isn't dead."

A susurration of whispers passed around the table, reduced to static by the voice scramblers. "He's alive?" Ray Ten asked. "Then why hasn't he returned?"

"He fell through the gate." Ra was practically bouncing in excitement. "He's on the other side. In another world. ENIGMA has decided to study the pieces of the artifact for the time being, rather than risk contact. You know how they are... patient to the point of inaction, too hesitant to take decisive measures, so they'll twiddle their thumbs for months, if not years, before testing what the artifact can do. But I received a message from Apollo. Brief, but unequivocal. He is alive." Ra leaned forward. "In other words, *we have an agent on the other side.* We have representation in a world where ENIGMA does not."

Ray Three slapped one palm on the table and let out a bark of digitized laughter. "*Ha!* And you thought the mission was a failure." Ray Three smacked Ray Two's shoulder.

Aten was certain that, behind their mask, Ray Two shot their neighbor a dirty look.

"I admit, this is an unprecedented set of events," Mithra mused. "Ray Twelve, is it possible for you to get a message back to Apollo?"

"I can try," Ra said at once. "And if I need to find other means, surely there must be a way... one that one of our many talented members can suggest?"

The mood of the room had shifted as Ra's excitement bled through into the others, and even Aten felt it.

"Good work, Agent Ra," he said.

The junior agent sat up a little straighter in response to this rare praise. Aten did not give it away freely, but this...

This could change everything.

He sat back and lifted his arms to encompass the whole gathering. "Well, then," he intoned. "There is only one way for us to properly celebrate this success, and that is to decide—what will our next move be?"

Every agent at the table seemed to have an answer. Aten sat back and pressed his fingers to the mouth of his mask as if to hide the smile beneath.

The Hands of the Sun were never idle, and for the first time in centuries, the scales had tipped decidedly in their favor.

To be continued

Copyright © 2024 by Joshua James

All rights reserved.

No part of this book may be reproduced in any form or by any electronic or mechanical means, including information storage and retrieval systems, without written permission from the author, except for the use of brief quotations in a book review.